"We've seen several really nice houses today. Have you seen anything you like?"

He heaved a loud sigh. "What do you think of this last one?" His attitude was far from interested and anything but enthusiastic—two surefire signs this wasn't the house for him.

"Oh, no," Gwen chuckled, shaking her head. "I don't offer that kind of advice to a client."

"Don't think of me as a client, think of me as the man who wants to rock your world."

The look he cast her made everything inside her turn to liquid heat. "All the more reason to keep my opinions to myself," she told him with a sly, sideward glance.

Joel barked a laugh. "Do you have any idea how hard it's been walking into all these bedrooms and knowing there's nothing I can do to you in any of them?"

"No," she said with a playful pout as she slid a hand up his thigh. "Tell me how *hard* it's been?" She kneaded the tense muscle beneath her fingers.

"You're not helping," he growled. "And stop that," he added. Lifting her hand from his leg, he moved it to the steering wheel.

"Stop what," she questioned as she licked her upper lip with a languid swipe of her tongue.

"If you don't stop looking at me like that I'm going to bite the buttons off your blouse," Joel told her through clenched teeth.

She could see he was fighting for self-control as she shifted the car into gear. Changing the subject might be the best course of action for both of them. She was ready to bite a few buttons herself.

Reviews

"There isn't one emotion left to experience in this warm, heartfelt love story. The characters are charming and larger than life, and you can't help but fall in love with each and every one of them in this sequel to DAMN THE MAN. Be prepared to read this one without stopping."

~Virginia D., Author and former editor and reviewer for ***Rendezvous Reviews***

Other books by Michelle L. Witvliet
from The Wild Rose Press:

Damn the Man
Available in both digital and print format.

"Nothing disappointed me in this book. Awesome job...I can't wait for more from this promising author."

~Lena C., ***Fallen Angel Reviews****—5 Angels and Recommended Read*

Damn Good Man

by

Michelle L. Witvliet

This is a work of fiction. Names, characters, places, and incidents are either the product of the author's imagination or are used fictitiously, and any resemblance to actual persons, living or dead, business establishments, events, or locales, is entirely coincidental.

Damn Good Man

Contact Information: info@thewildrosepress.com

Cover Art: *Angela Anderson*

The Wild Rose Press
PO Box 708
Adams Basin, NY 14410-708
Visit us at www.thewildrosepress.com

Publishing History
First Champagne Rose Edition, 2009
Print ISBN 1-60154-430-8

Published in the United States of America

Dedication

For Madeline,
who bravely faced the beast and won,
and in heartfelt memory of those
who lost their courageous battles.

Chapter One

Twice divorced Gwen Marconi was in the market for hubby number three.

It wasn't like she was desperate or anything. She was an attractive, self-sufficient, financially independent businesswoman who didn't need a man to make her life complete. She just wanted another one because she loved the concept of a man and a woman legally joined together until death, or divorce, departed them.

What she hated was the whole selection process. She sucked at it, which might explain the two exes and countless wannabes who, for innumerable reasons, had been scratched from the running. But she never gave up hope of finding one good man out of a sea of losers. Was that asking too much? She was beginning to think it was.

She'd been giving it a great deal of thought lately and, being a realtor, decided that finding a husband should be more like buying a house. Punch the required qualifications into a select data base, and voila, out pops a carefully culled list of potential mates. She'd like that. There were too many variables left to chance doing it the old-fashioned way.

Case in point: The big jerk standing in front of her.

As she flexed her jaw and touched the stinging place on her cheek, she silently congratulated herself for not only managing to attract another loser, but a hitter this time, as well.

She couldn't remember how many doubles he'd

tossed down during dinner, but it had been enough to make her take his keys, drive them to her house, and invite him in for a cup or two of strong, black coffee before calling a taxi to take him home.

The second she informed him that coffee and conversation were the only things he'd be getting from her that night, he'd backhanded her across the face with the speed and accuracy of a prize fighter. The force of the blow had sent her reeling against the counter as stars exploded behind her eyes.

Her insides quivered with opposing elements of fury and fear, which translated into her waffling between wanting to scratch his eyes out or running for her life. A third option reigned supreme.

"Get out," she sputtered as she rubbed the place where her wrist bone had met hard rock maple cabinet.

"Gwen, baby," said *Jack the Hitter* with a husky drawl. "You know I didn't mean to do that." The predatory rattle in his whiskey-soaked voice made her skin crawl. She cringed and backed away.

Never taking her eyes off him, her blue gaze narrowed warily as she inched along the counter. "I said get out." Her stomach churned and bitter bile rose in her throat. The very thought of him coming anywhere near her made her struggle against the overwhelming desire to retch. For a split second she though she was actually going to be sick. She pressed her fist against her stomach in an obvious effort to calm her momentary reaction.

Then again, maybe she shouldn't fight the feeling. Giving back the dinner he'd bought was one way to communicate her complete and utter revulsion for the man. She resisted the urge to smile from the image that popped into her head of him covered in partially digested pasta primavera, and decided not to press her luck. The last thing she wanted to do was give him cause to smack her again.

As he reached for her, she screeched, “Don’t touch me!” She forced herself to settle down and repeated more calmly, and with a great deal more conviction, “Don’t ever come near me again.”

“Come on, honey, don’t be like that,” he crooned.

“You’ve got five seconds to leave before I report you for assault.”

He threw back his head and laughed. “I’ve got too many buddies on the force for that to scare me.”

“Four.” She had a few friends on the force, too, including tho chief.

“You don’t know who you’re dealing with.” With a menacing glint in his eyes, he took an intimidating step closer. “Just who do you think they’re going to believe, me or the town tramp?”

In spite of the personal affront, Gwen held her ground. “Three.”

He crossed his arms and assumed a defiant stance. “I’m not leaving.” There was a deadly evenness in his tone and for the first time that night Gwen felt real fear for her safety.

From out of the corner of her eye she acknowledged the woodblock knife holder to her right and it crossed her mind to grab the biggest and sharpest and fillet the son-of-a-bitch where he stood.

The thought shriveled and died as swiftly as it formed because in all likelihood she’d wind up being the one getting deboned. She snatched up the phone instead and held it in a manner that suggested she was about to dial.

“Two.” Her heart thumped against her ribcage, feeling like it was about to tear loose from its connections and explode, as she stared him down. “What’s it going to be, Jack?”

“I don’t need this shit!” He ripped the keys from her fingers and stormed out.

Only after she heard his car squeal out of the driveway did she realize she’d been holding her breath. It exploded from her chest in a shrill whoosh as she dialed the police.

“I want to report a drunk driver,” she said, still weak in the knees and shaking. After hanging up, she gave in to the wave of relief and collapsed against the kitchen cabinet. She clasped her hand across her mouth and sobbed.

Catching her reflection in the window over the sink, she saw a face that looked like a dreary, monochromatic watercolor left in the rain. A muddy mess of eyeliner and mascara streaked down her cheeks.

She grabbed a paper towel and moistened it under a tepid trickle to wash the remaining remnants of that man off her face and out of her life, which, when she thought about it, was all the consideration that hot-tempered bastard deserved.

In spite of her dreadful track record in the men department, it never ceased to amaze her that she always managed to land on her feet, high heels and all. She was what the daytime talk show hosts commonly called a serial survivor. Sad but true, that was her in a nutshell.

She was grateful that her daughter hadn’t been home to witness her mother getting slapped around by Jack the Jerk. Then again, if Samantha had been home she wouldn’t have even considered bringing him there in the first place.

Although Samantha was only fifteen, she was light years ahead of her mother in the boyfriend department. The boy she was presently dating was already more of a gentleman than Jack could ever hope to be.

Not about to give Jack a chance to double back and catch her unaware, she checked all the doors and windows, the whole time wondering when she’d let her life get so messed up and out of control.

This was not the first time she’d asked herself

that question. It was one she'd asked herself time and time again. Yet regardless of how many times she'd asked it, she wasn't any closer to an answer then she was the first time she asked it when her first marriage failed, and her second, and when every other relationship followed the same destructive path. Maybe she tried too hard. Maybe she didn't try hard enough. The reasons for failure were endless. The answers, unfortunately, were not nearly as prolific.

The jangle of the phone jarred her. Gwen cleared her throat and answered.

"Hi, Mom!" The upbeat sound of her daughter's voice was just what she needed to lift her sagging spirits.

"Hi, sweetie. How'd it go tonight?" Samantha played on a sixteen-and-under softball team with girls from all over Northwest Indiana. Since she was twelve, her summers were spent traveling from one tournament to another.

"We won both games tonight. I hit two doubles and a triple in the second game."

"That's great. How'd you do in the first game?" Gwen could almost guarantee her child's answer about the game in question would not be nearly as enthusiastic as the second. Samantha had a keen knack for avoiding less than great news.

"Coach didn't put me in until the fifth inning to pinch hit for Jasmine. I sacrificed bunted and flied out. But I pitched the whole second game and only gave up three hits and no earned runs."

"Terrific! It sounds like your bat is finally coming around, too."

"Yeah. Uh, did anyone call for me, Mom?"

"I just got home a little while ago and I haven't checked for messages yet. Anyone in particular I should be checking for?" As if she didn't know. For the last couple of months Davey Chapparelle had become a frequent caller and guest around their house. Not that Gwen minded her daughter's choice in a boyfriend. Every bit as handsome as his famous NASCAR father and already as tall, Davey was a nice young man who came from a good family. Without question, Samantha had better sense in choosing men than her mother. Thank God that genetics didn't seem to play a part in matters of the heart.

"You know if you'd get me my own cell phone I wouldn't have to bother you with checking for my calls."

Gwen laughed. "Oh, so you need a cell for my sake? What a considerate child I have."

"You know what I mean. How'd your date go tonight?"

"Catastrophically."

"In other words, same old stuff, huh?"

"Yeah, but as of tonight he's history. I kicked him to the curb."

"Good for you, Mom. I never liked Jack anyway. He always gave me the creeps."

"How come I'm just hearing about this now? I need you to be my voice of reason, Samantha. From now on I'm not going out with anyone you don't approve of."

"Are you sure that's really what you want, Mom?"

"Yes. Absolutely."

"All right, but you may never have another date again."

Gwen touched her tender cheek and hoped any bruising could be covered with makeup. Her daughter didn't need to know every detail. "I'm beginning to realize there are worse things than never having another date."

"You okay, Mom?" Concern came through the phone as easily as her words. Samantha was not only smart and talented, she was perceptive.

"I'm fine," Gwen answered.

"Look mom, I've got to go. Coach just called a team meeting before lights out. Love you. Bye."

Still smiling, Gwen hung up the phone. Her daughter always made her smile. Samantha was the best thing that ever happened to her and the one brilliant accomplishment in her otherwise less than spectacular life. She regretted a lot of things in her life, her impetuous elopement at seventeen to Terry Hudson being at the top of her list. The daughter they created during their rocky, short-lived marriage was not another.

Chapter Two

Gwen parked her dark green Lincoln Town Car in the graveled municipal town lot and hurried past the still unmanned attendant's booth. She paid an annual parking fee for the privilege of slipping past the shack without grabbing a time-stamped ticket from the automatic dispenser. Dressed casually in pale linen slacks, pastel floral print blouse and low heeled sandals that showed off neatly polished blushing peach toes, she walked the half block to the Starbucks for her usual straight up grande before heading to her storefront office three doors down. One of the stores situated between her office and the coffee cafe was a vintage poster, print and framing shop that currently featured military memorabilia in honor of the upcoming Fourth of July holiday.

"Hello, handsome," Gwen greeted the stoic-faced marine staring out from under his shiny brimmed dress cap from the circa Viet Nam recruiting poster displayed in the window. Unable to smile or return her greeting, he continued to look long and hard into the hearts and souls of every aging draft dodger and anti-war protester who passed. Gwen waved and smiled at the shop owner as she continued to her office.

Just as Gwen unlocked the storefront entrance, she heard her name called.

"Gwen!" A plump, pleasant-faced woman dressed in a daisy-appliquéd, denim jumper, flower-embellished flip-flops, and a bright yellow, floppy sun hat scurried toward her from the park across the street.

"Hi. Peg," Gwen greeted the directress of the daycare facility on the south side of the square as she sipped at her daily dose of caffeine.

"I was hoping I'd catch you this morning," Peggy gushed. "I wanted you to be the first to know the new playground equipment was installed yesterday afternoon."

Gwen smiled. "That's wonderful. I'm so glad to hear your fundraiser was successful. I'll try to stop by to see it later."

Peggy Holloway's eyebrows rose dramatically as she cast Gwen a look that let her know she wasn't fooled for a second. "It was you who sent the certified check for the balance of what we needed, wasn't it?" Her question was posed rhetorically.

Gwen cast the woman a benign smile. "You're mistaken, Peg. I can't take credit for the contribution." And she never would. That was the beauty of anonymity. She enjoyed doing good deeds. She wasn't looking for a pat on the head or a wall full of "in appreciation" plaques. All the thanks she needed came in knowing she was making a difference. Regardless of how it came about, her growing success was due to the people of the community. It was only fair that she give some of it back to their children.

"Well," Peggy drawled doubtfully. "I still think it was you, but since I can't prove it, I won't press the matter."

"Sounds like an excellent idea to me," Gwen agreed with a wink as she let herself into her office.

Saturday was ordinarily a busy time for Gwen and her staff. It was a day so many folks started their house-hunting. This Saturday, however, was inordinately quiet. By ten o'clock she'd had numerous phone inquiries but only six scheduled showings for that afternoon, all of which she assigned to associates. The rest of her five member staff were working from their homes that morning or already in the field. Even the young woman hired to answer the phones on the weekend was currently out of the office running errands.

Gwen preferred to stay in the office on Saturdays and took advantage of the rare lull to play catch up and clear away everything that somehow managed to accumulate on her desk throughout the week. She was in the process of shredding confidential information from past clients when she heard the door chime.

"I'll be right with you," she called from the other side of the office partition separating her desk from the rest of the staff. A little privacy was the only luxury she afforded herself in the cramped office space. If the place wasn't so ideal otherwise she would have relocated a long time ago, but as they say in the trade: Location, location, location.

"Take your time," a deep, male voice responded. Then a child's giggle bounced through the air and around the partition. So, from those little auditory clues, Gwen concluded it was a man with a child—a family man.

Gwen took a moment to smooth her honey-blonde, shoulder-length pageboy as she stepped out from around the partition and approached the man who was currently crouched on one knee to the toddler's level wiping her face with a moist baby towelette. A twisted string of connected wipes trailed out of the blue and yellow quilted bag sitting on the floor beside him.

She couldn't help notice how gentle and patient he was with the squirming, uncooperative little girl. There was only one other man she could think of that was this good with kids. Good thing, too. The house she'd sold him a few years back had five bedrooms and it seemed that he and his wife were hell-bent on filling every one.

"It's a little like trying to wash a moving car, isn't it?" Gwen observed. When he turned to the sound of her voice, she couldn't help thinking how familiar he looked. But she met so many people in her profession. It wasn't easy remembering every face.

"Hello," he said, smiling as he stood, and stood, and stood. It seemed to take forever for him to reach his full, impressive height. Gwen's eyes traveled upward and she found herself pleasantly surprised. No petite flower herself at five-nine, she judged this guy to be at least six four and built like a basketball player with broad shoulders and long, muscular legs. If it weren't for the steel-framed glasses, he looked like a mature version of her recruiting poster marine, right down to the short-cropped haircut, strong chiseled features, and steely blue-gray eyes.

Back away from the handsome stranger, Gwen told herself. The man had a small child with him, which almost always meant a significant other somewhere is this beautiful family picture.

What can I help you with today, Mr...."

He extended his hand. "Joel Hubbard."

His handshake was warm and firm, and she noticed that he held it a tad longer than necessary.

The name was more familiar than his face. Hubbard? Joel Hubbard? Of course!

"You're the principal at the junior high," Gwen exclaimed in a manner that sounded like she was more frightened at the realization than surprised. It was like that for her whenever meeting anyone in an authoritarian role. Gwen always felt like people could take one look at her and know she was a high school dropout with nothing more than a GED and a real estate license to show for her impetuous youth.

"I was until the end of this term. I'm going into private practice and need a bigger place so I can set up a home office."

"Practice?" she questioned. "You're a doctor now?"

"PhD. I'm a psychologist."

Good lord, she was way out of her league with this client. Maybe when she was through finding him a house she could arrange to be one of his first patients. She often thought she'd benefit from therapy. "I'm Gwen Marconi and I'd be happy to help you find a suitable home for you and your family, Doctor Hubbard."

"Please, call me Joel," he said with a warm, friendly smile. "The title is just a required formality."

So what brings you to Marconi Realty, Joel?" She ushered him and his daughter into her office.

"A friend of mine recommended you."

"Really? Who might that be, if you don't mind my asking?"

"Nick Chapparelle."

Ah, the happily married man who was single-handedly trying to repopulate the neighborhood. She might have known they knew each other. Those types of family men always traveled in the same circles. *Like finds like*, her mother never failed to remind her whenever she tried to elevate her social standing back home. *Stick to your own kind,* was another of her mother's favorite sayings.

Of course, if she'd listened to her mother she'd still be living in Sweetwater, Arkansas, barefoot and pregnant with kid number eight just like her momma. In spite of the roundabout way she took to get there, her present life was a damn sight better than what she left behind.

The toddler tugged impatiently on her father's hand. "Emme, stop. We'll leave in a few minutes." He smiled apologetically. "We were on our way to the park when I noticed your office was open."

"So tell me Mister, uh, Doctor, I mean Joel."

This man had her completely rattled. Taking a deep breath in an effort to restore her equilibrium, she cleared her throat and said, "Tell me what you're looking for and I'll start searching for you. I can have a list of likely prospects for you by early next week. How does that sound?"

"Sounds great. I'm really anxious to get moved and settled by fall." He reached into his pants pocket and withdrew a small black leather case. Opening it, he produced an embossed business card. "Here are my numbers, both home and cell, and present address."

Gwen reached for a new folder and stapled the card to the outside. She would enter the information into the client database later.

"What exactly are you looking for?" Gwen questioned, as she reached for a yellow legal pad to take notes.

"I'm not really sure," he answered honestly. "My wife did all the hunting and legwork the last time we bought a house."

"Then maybe I should get together with your wife."

"My wife is deceased," Joel responded.

"I'm so sorry for your loss," Gwen replied.

"It's just me and Em now."

"She must miss her mother very much."

He touched the child's red curls. "She never knew her mother." He picked up the little girl and the child threw her arms around his neck. Pressing her lips to his cheek, she gave him a loud smack.

Gwen's heart went out to the both of them. It was obvious that the father doted on his only child and the little girl adored her father. It was time to redirect the conversation to a less serious subject. "Is Em short for Emily?"

"Actually, her name is Mary Elizabeth, which was soon shortened to initials, or Emme, then just

Em." Emme squirmed from her father's arms and toddled curiously around the desk. She gazed at Gwen with huge blue eyes fringed with long dark lashes. Emme was a beautiful child and Gwen smiled, remembering her own daughter at this wide-eyed, inquisitive stage.

"Would it be easier if we did this another time?"

"I'd really like to get this started. Basically what I want is a house large enough for the two of us and a live-in housekeeper slash nanny. I also need extra space to set up my practice. If I find the rest of the house suitable and there's adequate property, I'm willing to consider building an addition for an office suite. My current home is too small and doesn't have enough land to expand."

"Then you also have a house to sell?" Gwen questioned.

"Gosh, I guess I do." He sounded surprised.

Gosh. The man actually said gosh in such a manner that suggested it was a word he frequently used in his everyday vocabulary. It must be from his dealing with impressionable youngsters for so many years, she reasoned. He kept his language clean and appropriate. She liked that. It showed a great deal of character and respect.

"Have you considered building from the ground up?" Gwen suggested. "You'd get exactly what you wanted that way. I have some fabulous wooded lots available on the edge of town."

"I don't think so." Joel shook his head against the idea. "An addition is one thing. A whole house is quite another. I really don't want to deal with all that."

"I understand. Building a house can be a daunting experience." Gwen stroked Em's shiny curls. "Give me a few days to see what I can find. I'll run the specs through multiple listings and get back to you early next week."

Joel extended his hand across the desk. “Thanks, Ms. Marconi. I appreciate your patience.”

“It’s Gwen, and that’s my job. I won’t give up until I find the perfect home for you and your daughter. I guarantee it.”

He smiled gently. “I trust you to do just that.” From behind the steel-rimmed glasses, his gaze settled on her face. “Nick was right about you.”

“About what precisely?”

“He said you really knew your business and I wouldn’t be disappointed with you.”

“I was totally against selling him that house, you know, and told him so in no uncertain terms. It needed so much work. But I’ve heard he’s done some wonderful things with it. I understand it’s quite a showplace now.”

“The house really is gorgeous. Nick put his heart and soul into the renovations, and of course Maggie’s creativity finished the interior decorating. They’ve created a very warm, comfortable, welcoming environment for their family and friends.”

She gave a quick chuckle. “Ever growing family from what I hear.”

She never meant for her statement to sound like anything more than what it was—a simple declaration of indisputable fact. Gwen never intended on sounding so catty and critical, but she immediately realized that’s precisely how her comment was interpreted the second she saw his reaction.

Joel’s stature visibly stiffened. “Nick and Maggie Chapparelle are close friends of mine and two very special individuals.” His tone was defensive and she detected a distinct chill in his voice that wasn’t there a second ago.

“Please, don’t misunderstand,” Gwen stammered. “I really didn’t mean anything by that.” Shut up, she told herself.

Joel shrugged off her apology and came around the desk to collect his daughter who now sat contentedly on Gwen's lap scribbling on the yellow tablet. "Let's go, Em."

The child went with her father without argument and glanced over her shoulder with a shy smile and a little wave as they left. Gwen waggled her fingers in return and forced a smile.

Way to go, Gwen, she thought. There goes one client she didn't expect to hear from again. She tapped her fingers on the desk and realized the manila folder with his business card was beneath her agitated hand. Before she could change her mind, she picked up the phone and dialed his home number. At the moment she preferred to leave a message than speak to him directly.

The number picked up on the fourth ring.

"You've reached the Hubbard residence. Leave your message at the tone." Now there was a straightforward, no nonsense message. If there was one thing she found annoying it was voice mail messages meant to be cute or cleaver.

"Joel, this is Gwen Marconi. I want to apologize if I spoke out of place and said anything to offend you this morning. I'll refer your file to one of my associates if you'd prefer to work with someone else. You have my numbers. Please don't hesitate to call if there's anything else Marconi Realty can do for you." Yeah, like she'd be the first person he'd call, she thought with a sarcastic roll of her eyes and a derisive shake of her head.

She felt a little better after leaving the message. Not great, but better. It was the right thing to do. No reason for the business to suffer simply because she didn't know when to keep her big mouth shut. She hoped she could salvage something out of it.

Chapter Three

Gwen always left the office in the capable hands of her associates on Sundays. It was the one day of the week she designated for spending with her daughter. When Samantha was home, that is, which wasn't very often lately. Now that she was older and getting more involved with developing her own relationships and activities, Gwen found herself spending more and more Sundays alone and had already decided a few years ago that it was time to find a few new interests and activities of her own.

By mid-morning she was dressed in black spandex shorts and hot pink tank top, determined to complete her run through the designated neighborhood course in record time. She'd already completed her usual five-mile circuit through the park, around Pine Arbor Cemetery and past the Presbyterian Church's rear parking lot. Now she was on her way to the track behind the hospital for a lap around the mile long course before heading home. Training for her first turnaround 10K charity run scheduled in early August, she was following an 8-week regime developed by a personal trainer to prepare her for the event.

She usually ran in the evening after work, often with her daughter, but she knew Sam wouldn't feel like running when she got home that afternoon considering the simple fact that she'd gotten plenty of exercise running around a softball field all weekend. Samantha undoubtedly had a more social type activity planned for the evening, one that would not include her mother. If she wanted to spend any time at all with Samantha, Gwen figured she'd better get her run in early. As much as it killed her to admit it—Samantha was growing up and didn't need her mother the way she once had. She seriously wondered how much longer it would be before their occasional duo turned into a permanent run for one.

When Samantha had first suggested they start running together, Gwen had refused to even entertain the idea. Not only was she already in her early thirties, she was not built like an athlete. How could she comfortably run without looking like she was smuggling two overfilled water balloons under her shirt? She was no Dolly Parton, but she was by no means built for any activity that required bouncing up and down, either. The fact of the matter was that she was fortunate enough to have a small waist, which made her look bigger north of the equator by comparison. Regrettably, her hips were judged by the same comparative value. She had what some would call an enviable hourglass figure. She begged to disagree. All it ever did was get her into trouble from the moment she blossomed more than twenty years earlier.

After presenting these legitimate concerns to her daughter, Samantha dragged her to the nearest sporting goods establishment and introduced her to industrial strength sports bras specially designed for women with larger than average dimensions. Gwen had eyed the restraining garment with appropriate reservation but reluctantly agreed to give the engineering marvel a fair trial before passing final judgment. The bra combined with a tight fitting spandex top for additional support worked surprisingly well and the rest, as they say, was history. From the first day she placed one foot in front of the other and finished gasping for oxygen, Gwen was hooked.

She found running amazingly freeing and

exhilarating, and the runner's high she experienced was indescribable. It was a sight better than bad sex but a tad worse than good—an inspiring discovery she prudently refrained from divulging to her teenage daughter.

Before long she was running as often as possible and felt positively sluggish when she missed a day because of schedule conflicts. She even joined a gym with an indoor track so she could run during cold or inclement weather. It was the one thing in her life she did just for herself. She was in better shape physically than she was in her twenties, and more importantly, she was mentally stronger and better able to cope with whatever surprises life had up its sleeve.

Feeling the beginnings of a cramp in her calf, she stopped to catch her breath and stretch it out. With her palms pressed against a utility pole, she extended one leg behind her and flexed the Achilles until she felt a good stretch. In spite of the fact that she'd been running for almost three years, she'd never run more than four or five miles at a time. A 10K run was a little more than six miles; a turnaround doubled the distance, which added up to approximately half a marathon. She needed the additional training to get in shape.

Realizing she had pushed herself further than ever before, she seriously considered walking the remainder of the distance to her modest thirtysomething-year-old tri-level located more than two miles away in an older part of town.

In spite of being able to afford something bigger and more impressive like so many of her colleagues, she elected to continue living in the house she'd bought when her second marriage ended. There had been a brief time a few years earlier when she was going through a particularly insecure period in her life and she believed a bigger house in Cartwright

Corners was what she needed to turn her life around. It didn't take long for her to come to the conclusion that a bigger house came with an equally bigger mortgage. Sinking herself deeper into debt was hardly something to put her insecurities to rest. There was that, and the simple fact that she didn't want the hassle of moving from the level of comfort and security she currently had. She quickly realized that money in the bank was a much warmer, reassuring security blanket.

The final insight came about six months ago when she realized she didn't need a big house to prove her success. Her record as a realtor spoke for itself. Her car was big and impressive because she used it for business, same for the designer clothes she wore for work. It was all for show because if there was only one thing she'd learned from her older and wiser second husband, Vic Marconi, it was that people preferred doing business with someone who looked and acted the part. Her money was safely invested where it would do the most good—securing her daughter's future.

In reality, she was financially comfortable. In comparison to her past, she was wealthy beyond her wildest dreams. Having been raised in a household barely able to rub two nickels together to make change for a dime, she appreciated and respected the money she earned through years of long hours and hard work.

Little hands were suddenly patting her outstretched leg. Looking over her shoulder, she found Emme Hubbard dressed in an adorable pink sundress embroidered with scattered rosebuds. With a sweet little smile, she said, "Hi."

Huge, blue eyes and glossy dark red hair pulled into two curly ponytails tied with pink ribbons made her look like a porcelain doll come to life with the wave of a fairy godmother's magic wand. The child's good-looking dad stood a few feet away looking equally handsome in dark gray slacks, pale blue dress shirt and tie. Oh boy, his fairy godmother didn't do too badly on him either. Gwen felt desperately underdressed in her sweaty running clothes.

He smiled. "The second Em recognized you she broke from my grasp and ran to see you."

"Hello, Emme. You look so pretty this morning." She gave the child's hair a playful flip as she turned her attention to the father. "You look pretty spiffy yourself."

"Thanks," he said with an almost shy, 'aw shucks' demeanor. "We were on our way home from church and decided to head to the Parkside Café for lunch."

"You live close enough to town to walk?" She hadn't connected his address to the location. Gwen pressed her palms against her forehead and cheeks to blot the sheen of perspiration accumulated on her face. Wispy strands of hair clung to her moist temples, escapees from the tightly twisted blonde locks held against the back of her head with a springy clip.

"Just a few blocks down that way." He pointed over her shoulder.

"That's a good selling point." Gwen watched Em crouch and start picking dandelions from the parkway. A butterfly fluttered past and momentarily captured her attention before she returned to her flower-picking task. Three-year olds were so easily distracted. The innocent scene took Gwen back to a time when her own daughter was that age. Only due to financial circumstances Samantha was never dressed nearly that nice at three. She was always clean and neat but secondhand shop hand-me-downs were the only way she could keep her quickly growing child adequately clothed. That her daughter's closet was now stuffed beyond capacity was more from Gwen's over compensating for the lean years than Samantha's take-it or leave-it attitude about staying fashionably trendy.

"You must live in the general vicinity too," Joel commented.

Gwen nodded. "About two miles off Main." She gestured in the opposite direction from his house. An uncomfortable silence settled between them.

"I got your message," Joel finally said. "I didn't mean for you to think I wanted a different agent."

"You left so abruptly I kind of got the impression you'd rather not deal with me."

"I'm sorry about that. It's just that I tend to overreact whenever it sounds like my friends are being criticized. Maggie was my wife's dearest friend. I don't think I could have gotten through the whole ordeal of her death without Maggie's support."

"I honestly didn't mean to sound critical of the Chapparelles. In truth, I'm a little envious of the charmed life they lead."

Joel thoughtfully nodded. "How about joining us for lunch?" he suggested.

"Thank you, but no." She pushed back the damp strands from her face. "I couldn't possibly go into the café looking like this."

"You look fine." He waved his hand in such a way to dismiss her misgivings. "I see people looking a lot worse in there all the time."

Gwen startled at his abrupt honesty, yet immediately realized he didn't mean anything deprecating by what he said. "I would have never guessed you to be such a sweet talker, Doctor Hubbard. Compliments like that could easily turn my head."

"Oh, gosh, I didn't mean you looked bad, I just meant you don't look any worse than the other...." He stumbled over his words, which came out no better than his original comment. Shifting his weight from one impeccably polished wing-tipped foot to the other, he hung his head and rubbed his fingers across his tightly knit brow, as if the action would clear his mind and un-muddle his thought process. "I don't know what's come over me. I can't remember the last time I had this much trouble talking to a girl."

"And I can't remember the last time I was called a girl." Gwen laughed, utterly charmed by this middle-aged schoolboy. Most of the men she met acted more like school bullies than schoolboys. Somehow she inexplicably knew this man wasn't acting—his behavior was genuine and very captivating.

Emme tugged on Gwen's hand and offered her the dandelions she'd collected. "Thank you so much, Emme." Touched by the child's sweet generosity, Gwen took the weedy yellow bouquet from Em's chubby fingers.

"I can't believe she's taken to you like this," Joel commented in amazement.

"I'm as surprised as you are since I usually send small children screaming into the street when they see me coming," Gwen remarked.

"That's not what I meant. It's just that Em can be kind of shy around strange people... I mean strangers. Please don't think for a moment—" he flustered as he cut himself off in mid sentence and hung his head. "I've done it again, haven't I?"

"Joel, stop. I was joking." She couldn't help laughing.

Emme tugged on her father's trouser leg. "Daddy, I'm hungry."

"Go, feed your daughter." Gwen encouraged. "I'll call you in the morning and arrange a time for us to get together so I can appraise your house and get it on the market."

"Why don't you come by this afternoon?"

His eagerness to start the tedious process of selling his house took her by surprise. Most people hated having their homes invaded by even one realtor let alone a multitude of critical-eyed strangers.

"I would but I already have other plans."

"Of course, tomorrow then."

"Bye!" Gwen took off down the street at an easy jogging pace, waving at the pair as they stood hand-in-hand waving in return. Her calf muscle had relaxed during the time she spoke to Joel and she felt reinvigorated from her longer than normal rest period. In no time at all she was running at full speed. The image of a tall, handsome man and a little redheaded girl kept popping into her head as her arms and legs pumped in rhythm with her steady breathing.

Whoa, halt, back off and stop right there, she told herself as she slowed her pace to a power walk. He's a client—nothing more. Not only did he have a small child, he was a widower to boot—a double discouraging factor if there ever was one and two things Gwen always tried to avoid. Too bad, too, because Gwen found Joel Hubbard a charming change from the men she usually attracted.

Yeah, like she ever had a chance with a man like that, an annoying little voice inside her head taunted. Where in the hell was that discouraging voice when the losers beat a path to her door?

Chapter Four

"I'm home!"

From the spare third bedroom turned home office, Gwen heard her daughter come banging through the front door. Next there came the sound of her heavy canvas sport bag hitting the slate entry with a resounding thud.

"Mom? Hello? Anybody home?"

"I'm upstairs. I'll be right down." Gwen closed her internet connection and pushed away from the sleek, black modular desk. Barefoot and dressed in a comfortable pair of black capris and pink V-neck tee, she hurried down the stairs to welcome her daughter home. One week, one day, or anything in between, she always greeted Samantha with open arms and the heart of a mother who missed her child.

Samantha still wore her dirty uniform. Her long, heavy auburn hair was pulled back in a single thick French braid and her face and neck were smudged and streaked with a mixture of sweat and dirt.

Gwen plucked at the grimy jersey. "Took off right after the game, huh?" It never ceased to amaze Gwen that as fastidious as her daughter was about her appearance any other time, it didn't bother her one bit how she looked when she played ball. Sam's philosophy was if a player was still clean at the end of a game she didn't play hard enough.

"Straight from the field," Samantha confirmed as she enthusiastically greeted her mother with a hug and a kiss on the cheek. "Ummm...you smell good."

"New shower gel," Gwen explained.

"I'll have to give it a try. Did Davey call?"

Gwen grinned. "Only five or six times in the last two hours."

Sam dug into the side pocket of the canvas bag and produced a trophy. "We won the tournament."

Gwen eyed her daughter. "Have you gotten so blasé about winning that it's not such big news anymore? There used to be a time you would have come in waving that thing high over your head and screaming."

"The winning part is still fun, it's these darn trophies I can't stand any more. I'm running out of room. They seem like such a waste and serve no useful purpose other than collecting dust. Do you think it would be rude to refuse?"

"Yes," Gwen answered. Her one word reply was issued in a tone that brooked no rebuttal. As much as she might agree with her daughter on principle, she couldn't very well condone this act of ungrateful defiance. "Learn to appreciate your successes in every form."

Samantha perched the trophy on the fireplace mantel in the living room, successfully ending the discussion on that subject. "What's for dinner?"

"Barbeque ribs and baked sweet potatoes."

"Yum. How long before we eat? I'm starved."

About an hour." She eyed her daughter and grinned. Samantha was built like a fashion model, pitched like a major leaguer, and ate like an offensive lineman.

"Great! Plenty of time to shower and call Davey before dinner." She started up the stairs with long-legged strides.

"Bag," was all Gwen had to say to make her daughter stop in mid stride, reverse gears, and return to the foyer.

Samantha frowned as she picked up the bag. "Are you that good or am I that conditioned?"

"Combination of both, I think." Gwen said. "We've been together for almost sixteen years. We understand each other, that's all."

"Yeah, that must be it." Samantha agreed with a grin. She shouldered the hefty bag and headed up the stairs with an easy lope.

Watching her tall, athletic, practically grown daughter, it suddenly dawned on Gwen that the days of just the two of them were numbered and her daughter would soon be gone.

It was much sooner than she ever imagined. Davey showed up just as Samantha was loading the dinner plates into the dishwasher.

"So what are your plans for tonight?" Gwen asked as she forked the leftover ribs and placed them on a sheet of foil.

"Just a movie at my house," Davey answered as he dropped his tall, lanky frame into the nearest kitchen chair. He eyed the ribs as she began to fold the foil. "Those sure smell good."

"Here you go, Dave." Gwen placed them on the table in front of him. "Be my guest."

"Well, sure, okay. Don't mind if I do."

"You're saving me the trouble of finding them hiding at the back of the fridge two weeks from now and wondering what they used to be." She watched him peel back the foil. "Let me get you a fork and plate."

"Don't bother. This is fine." He picked up the four-rib slab with his fingers and sank his teeth into the tender barbequed meat.

"At least let me get you a napkin." Gwen reached for a napkin from the ceramic holder on the counter and decided at the last second to grab the whole thing. He looked like he would need more than one.

Samantha shared a smiling sideward glance with her mother. "Disposal Man strikes again."

Without missing a finger-licking beat, Davey laughed. “Yeah, that’s me. Dad says he bought stock in two major supermarket chains out of desperation just to help defray his losses at the grocery store.”

“I’ve seen your mother at the store. Her cart is always so loaded she can barely push it to the checkout.” What she didn’t mention was that Maggie barely acknowledged her when they happened to cross paths. In all fairness, she had to admit that since their children had started dating Maggie’s nod and cool half-smile had evolved into a somewhat friendlier greeting but it was still far from congenial.

Gwen had developed a thick skin over the years. Not that she was completely immune to the slights and outright snubs, but she’d learned not to let them bother her anymore. Fortunately Samantha never experienced any residual backlash from her mother’s past mistakes—for that Gwen was truly grateful.

“Who’s picking the movie?” Sam questioned with obvious concern. It had become a running joke with them about his family’s choice in movies, more specifically the male Chapparelles.

“I thought I’d let you pick tonight. We’ll stop by the video store on our way back to my house.”

Samantha wiped her hands on a dishtowel and said, “Your mom will be happy to hear that.”

“Mom’s not home.” Davey said matter-of-factly as he crumpled the empty foil between his fingers and tossed it into the nearby trash can. “She dragged the babies to some quilt expo in Milwaukee this weekend. She won’t be home until late tonight.”

Gwen’s highly developed maternal antennae beamed in on Davey’s innocent slip of the tongue. “Your dad raced today, didn’t he?” she questioned.

“Yeah.” Davey answered in a manner that led her to believe he didn’t have the slightest idea to where her questions were leading. “At Michigan International Speedway. He came in third.”

"So what you're telling me is there's no adult home at the present time?" Gwen queried, ready to quash their plans. If there was one thing she learned about reputations it was that once they were tarnished it was all but impossible to put back the original shine. She wasn't about to let her daughter make the same stupid mistakes she had. She was admittedly over protective about where Samantha went and with whom. Her activities were carefully monitored and on occasion vetoed, which was where this evening's plans were headed if she didn't get some appropriate answers.

"Mom!" Samantha exclaimed. "I can't believe you're making such a big deal out of this."

"I understand your concern, Mrs. Marconi." Davey interjected. "But my dad's home."

"How is that possible?" Gwen asked.

"The race was only two-hundred miles away. We were home a few hours after it finished."

"We? You were at the race?"

"Uh huh. Danny too."

What did you drive home in, his racecar?"

"No, ma'am. His Cessna. He flies his own plane now. He says it's quicker and less of a hassle than commercial flights these days."

Oh," was all Gwen managed to utter after hearing this latest development. What more was there to say except, "Have a nice time." She turned to Samantha. "Do you need me to pick you up later?"

"I'll see that she gets home," Davey assured Gwen.

"Not on the scooter." She didn't want either of them zipping around town on that thing late at night.

"I'll use my dad's truck."

"You don't have a license," Gwen was quick to point out.

"No, Mom, but he does have his permit, and his

dad will be with us." Samantha was obviously perturbed.

"Midnight."

"Yes, ma'am," Davey answered obediently as Samantha grabbed his hand and pulled him toward the door. They stopped only long enough to snatch their helmets from the entry bench before heading out.

The house was suddenly filled with an uncomfortable, eerie silence as she watched her daughter climb onto the back of Davey's apple red Vespa. Gwen couldn't help feeling a little sorry for herself. Alone again, she thought. The ticking of the hall clock thundered through the quiet rooms and the annoying kitchen faucet drip pinged against the stainless sink like spring rain on a tin roof.

All cruel reminders of how soon it would be before Samantha packed her bags and headed off to college, leaving Gwen to suffer the silence on a long-term basis. Although the cord had been severed a long time ago their ties were stronger than ever. They might be closer than most mothers and daughters but never were they so dependent on one another they couldn't exist independently. Gwen had made sure that Sam was raised self-sufficient and independent. They shared a normal healthy relationship and Samantha was moving away from the nest at a normal, healthy pace, a tad too quickly to suit Gwen perhaps, but normal nevertheless. Just the same, it made Gwen wonder what exactly she was going to do with the rest of her life when she wasn't a full-time mother hen anymore.

The phone jangled and startled her out of her maternal reverie. "Hello," she said, sounding distant and hoarse. She cleared her throat and said again, "Hello?"

"Gwen?"

"Yes." She was always hesitant when hearing a

man's voice she didn't immediately recognize on her unlisted land line. "Who is this?" Just as she spoke the doorbell chimed insistently. Why did these things always happen at once?

"It's Joel."

"Hubbard?" she questioned as she moved from the kitchen toward the front door.

"Uh huh. I was wondering if you'd like to go out for a cup of coffee or something."

"Now?" she asked.

"That was the idea, but if this is a bad time..."

"No, no, now is fine, I guess," she answered with mild reluctance. "Shall I meet you somewhere?" The doorbell chimed again. "Will you hold on a sec, Joel? There's someone at the door." Pressing the cordless receiver against her chest, she walked to the door and pulled it open. Her eyes widened with pleasant surprise at who she found on the other side.

Chapter Five

"Hi." Joel smiled as he snapped shut the shiny silver flip phone between his palm and fingers, then stuffed the compact cell into the pocket of his khaki walking shorts. "I would have felt very foolish standing here if you had told me no."

Gwen gazed at him with the phone still cradled in the palm of her hand. This was not the kind of man who beat a path to her door. If that was what he was doing? Was that what he was doing, she wondered. Although strangely panicked at the very idea, she managed to keep her suspicions in check. Jumping to a wrong conclusion this early in the game could lead to an irreparable situation.

"My wife's parents drove down from Michigan this afternoon," he said as he shifted from one foot to the other. "And took Emme back with them for the week," he finished in a way of explaining his sudden appearance at her door. "I found myself suddenly very alone in a much too quiet house and had to get out of there for a while."

"That's funny because I was just thinking the same thing myself when my daughter left with her boyfriend."

"That was your daughter on the scooter with Davey Chapparelle?"

Gwen nodded.

"I've met Samantha a couple times at their house. I never made the connection."

"Different last names will do that. Hudson was her father's name."

Joel looked like he was processing the

information as he silently nodded with a thoughtful expression. "Now I see the resemblance."

"You really think so? I've always thought she looked more like her father." If he was nothing else, Terry Hudson was a handsome devil. He just didn't have anything else going for him to help the good-looking part develop into a complete human being.

"You don't look old enough to have a daughter that age."

"Is that a polite segue into finding out how old I am?"

"Of course not," he stammered. "I would never be so presumptuous." He pursed his lips to stop himself and dropped his head with a sheepish grin. "You're teasing me again, aren't you?"

"Uh huh," she replied as she glanced past him. "Where's your car?" The only vehicles she found were the ones she recognized as belonging to the neighbors and there was nothing in her driveway either because her car was in the garage. "How did you get here?"

He pointed to his pair of impressive feet covered in pristine white sneakers. She resisted the urge to ask if those canoes came with paddles. But that would have been rude considering she hadn't been blessed with the daintiest feet in the world either. Her healthy size tens managed to counterbalance her 36 Ds quite nicely, thank you very much, and kept her from looking like she was always walking into the wind. On the heels of that thought came the one about a man's feet and another part of his anatomy, and she caught herself from glancing at his crotch with a quick turn of her head and a sharp cough.

"It's only fifteen blocks, and four of those are short ones. That's the beauty of this town." The smile that lit his face might have started with his full expressive mouth but it worked its way quickly to his bespectacled blue-gray eyes. Beautiful laugh lines formed at the corners, telling Gwen they had developed over the course of a lifetime. "Nothing's too far away."

Gwen found herself smiling back. "It's one of the things I like about it, too."

"I hope you don't mind my taking the liberty of looking up your address." He sounded shy and apologetic.

She couldn't quite understand this man standing in front of her. He was bold enough to show up at her door uninvited but apologized for doing so in the very next breath. Gwen was intrigued to say the very least.

"No, of course not. I don't mind at all," she stammered. "Except I'm not listed in the phone book."

With a sly grin, he said, "You are online."

"I just hope some of my lesser-satisfied clients aren't as smart as you are. There are a few I'd rather never find out where I live."

"I don't believe it." He clutched his chest in mock surprise. "You have dissatisfied clients?"

"Show me a realtor who doesn't," she retorted as she stepped aside and gestured for him to come in.

"It's such a nice evening. I think I'll wait for you out here." He backed down the stairs as she closed the door.

In her bedroom, she pocketed a house key and a folded twenty and slipped into a pair of black leather sandals. When she stepped outside she found Joel sitting in the freestanding swing she had situated beneath the silvery-green boughs of a aging Russian olive. He immediately stood upon her exit and gestured for her to lead the way down the curved marigold and coleus lined walkway.

"How about ice cream?" They said in almost perfect unison. Their surprised laughter came together harmoniously.

"Great minds but with a single thought," Joel murmured as he fell into a comfortable pace beside her. Their shoulders occasionally touched as the sometimes uneven sidewalk caused one of them to shift one way or another in an effort to avoid tripping on the unleveled surface. "Beth and I used to do that all the time."

"Beth was your wife?" She said it as more of a statement than a question.

He nodded but didn't answer aloud. He crammed his hands into his pockets and his posture slumped considerably, looking like a man who had just had a concrete yoke hoisted onto his shoulders.

"I'm sorry. I didn't mean to pry. I know it must be difficult."

"Sometimes," he answered straightforwardly. "Em's been such a blessing. I'm not sure what I would have done without her."

"How long have you lived in Sherwood?"

The weight appeared to lighten somewhat as he straightened and flexed his shoulders. "Gosh, let me think...we moved here when I accepted the position at the junior high. So around eight years, I guess."

"What prompted a move to Indiana?"

"My wife grew up here. I knew how badly she wanted to come back to the region so I applied to positions in the area."

"You initiated a career move because of your wife?" She couldn't believe what she was hearing. Terry wouldn't have gone across the street for her unless she was standing there naked, holding a case of beer in one hand, and a bag of pretzels in the other.

"It seemed like the right thing to do." He shrugged. "Her folks lived here at the time and a lot of her friends. The only time she left the state was to go away to school. That's where we met. I, on the other hand, was a born and bred military brat and never had a hometown per se. Moving wasn't such a big deal for me."

"I'm sure she appreciated what you did." Gwen was a little astonished by how freely he offered these pieces of personal information.

"I know she did, and I'm glad I was able to do it for her. She followed me when I was in the service without complaint. I figured it was only fair to consider her needs when I made the transition into civilian life."

"Marines, right?" she queried.

"No, Army. Why'd you think Marines?"

"I don't know…" She shrugged casually. "Maybe it's the crew cut."

He laughed and rubbed a hand across his bristly brown hair. "Yeah, that's probably it. My wife used to tell me the same thing." Then he fell silent, and for a few lengthy minutes the only sound that passed between them was the slap of her sandals against her bare feet and the change jingling in his pocket with his cell phone.

"So, how about you?" Joel finally spoke up. "How long have you lived here?"

"I moved to the area shortly after my divorce seven years ago."

"Samantha's father?" He asked in a manner that suggested he was trying to fill in a few blanks.

"No. Samantha's father was my first husband. I didn't move here until my second husband and I split up."

"Second husband?" He sounded surprised. Or was it appalled? She couldn't tell for certain, but she could make a wild guess. "How many husbands have you had?" he blurted, than quickly added, "No, don't answer that."

"What?" she asked, startled. "Why not?"

"Because it's none of my business, that's why. I

don't know what made me ask you such a personal thing. I'm sorry."

"I don't mind. It's no secret that I've been married twice."

Gwen cast a sideward glance at Joel and studied his thoughtful profile. It looked like her past marital status had given him pause to rethink his reasons for being there. She wasn't surprised by his reaction, and he wasn't the first. After all, everyone knew there had to be something wrong with a woman sporting a pair of divorce decrees.

"You know, every so often, I detect a slight twang in some of your words. What is it? Texas, Oklahoma?"

She breathed a little laugh. "West Arkansas, actually. You're good. I haven't had anyone ask me about it for several years now."

"I collect accents like some people collect coins or stamps. It's a hobby I acquired from living in so many parts of the country over the years."

"I really thought I'd finally lost it. Looks like I've still got some work cut out for me."

"Don't try too hard. It's nice. I like it."

She tipped her head and cast him a thoughtful grin. "I'll try to keep that in mind."

"What remarkable circumstances brought you all the way to Indiana from Arkansas?"

"Nothing remarkable about it. When I was seventeen I wanted out of Sweetwater so badly that I hopped into Terry Hudson's pickup and never looked back. Two husbands, one kid and a dozen towns later here I am."

"When did you give up your job with Reader's Digest?"

"Huh? My job with what?"

He began to chuckle. "You just managed to reduce your entire adult life into two succinct sentences. I just figured you got your training from the best condensing folks in the business."

"I've never been comfortable talking about my past. Believe me, Joel, you got all the highlights without the boring details."

"Maybe someday you'll be comfortable enough to give me the unabridged version of Gwen Marconi, the adult years."

"Maybe," she said softly, all the while thinking there were things she didn't want to remember let alone reveal.

They came to a stop in front of the old-fashioned ice cream parlor that looked like it had been there since the 50s, when in fact it had only been there for just a few years, built when the town's leaders decided to try bringing businesses back to the downtown area by creating a Capraesque Main Street that looked like it was right out of a *It's A Wonderful Life*. So far their ambitious plan was working. Gwen looked around and was pleased to see the number of people walking around the town square.

The scalloped pink and white striped awning that ordinarily stretched across the storefront was currently rolled back. The sun had long since set and the need to protect the curly cue wrought iron tables and chairs supplied for those who wished to enjoy their frozen treats alfresco was no longer required. Gwen chuckled at the recently added whimsically painted plate glass window depicting a herd of charming dairy cows in assorted flavors grazing in a field scattered with candy sprinkles and nonpareils. In the distance, a rock candy volcano spewed a river of chocolate lava. The shop was a delight for the eye as well as the palate.

Joel opened the door and stepped aside to allow Gwen to enter. She was, to say the least, secretly pleased by his gentlemanly treatment. How odd that she found the simple gesture so engaging. She stepped inside the crowded shop with Joel close behind. For a brief moment he moved so close his breath raised the hairs on the nape of her neck. His nearness combined with the open ice cream freezers and air-conditioning made her shiver and she rubbed her arms to generate a little warmth. It also caused her nipples to stand at attention and salute from the drastic drop in temperature. She plucked at the front of her shirt to adjust the fabric from clinging to the hardening peaks and hoped nobody noticed.

Many of the adults sitting at the tables greeted Joel as did their children. He acknowledged them all with a congenial smile, a friendly wave, or a pleasant nod but never left her side to prolong the greeting. His fingers rested ever so lightly on the small of her back as he ushered her to the counter to place their order. Just another simple gesture Gwen found utterly charming. She could tell this subtle attentiveness was without forced effort or even conscious thought. Joel Hubbard was a gentleman.

"What'll you have?" Joel questioned.

"Blueberry cheesecake waffle cone, please," she said.

"How about you, Mr. Hubbard?" The young man behind the counter asked. "The usual?"

"That will be fine, Jeff. How are your folks?"

"Fine, thanks." He cocked his head toward the rear of the store. "Dad's in back doing the books." He handed Gwen her generously scooped cone and she quickly brought it to her mouth to catch the hanging overflow. The sweet, creamy flavors melded in her mouth and caused her taste buds to do a little happy dance.

"How was your first year at Purdue?"

"3.0 accumulated grade point average."

"Jeff, that's wonderful." Joel fairly beamed at the news. "Have you decided on a major yet?"

The young man shook his head. “Not yet.”

“If you need any help, you know how to reach me.”

“Thanks, Mr. H.”

“Mr. Hubbard!” A voice boomed from the backroom doorway. A bear of a man every bit as big as his voice came toward them waving his hand. “Put your money away.” He turned to his son. “This man never pays for his ice cream, you hear me, J.T.?”

“Yes, Papa.” Jeff smiled.

Joel tried to slip Jeff the money in spite of his father’s instructions. “I can’t keep letting you father do this. Jeff, please, put the money in the register.”

“You heard the man, Mr. Hubbard. You’re the one who taught me to listen to my dad. How would it look if I disobeyed him now?”

“At least let me pay for the lady’s cone,” Joel attempted to negotiate.

Jeff shook his head. “No, sir. I can’t let you do that.”

Joel sighed with frustrated resignation while Gwen quietly licked her cone and watched the lively exchange. These people obviously held Joel in high regard, but she also understood his point of view. She never liked being beholden to anyone either. Regardless of her financial situation over the years, she always managed to pay her own way.

She nudged him with her elbow and gestured with a subtle nod toward the tip jar sitting near the cash register. Joel reached into his wallet and withdrew a twenty. Folding it, he slipped it into the can with a Houdini-like slight of hand while Gwen feigned interest in the featured flavor of the week and asked for a sample.

Chapter Six

"Thanks for helping me out back there," he said as they left the shop. "I hate it when they do that. I really didn't do anything for Jeff that I wouldn't have done for any other student."

"Now why don't I believe that? You have a gift for making ordinary people feel extraordinary." She had already been on the receiving end of this remarkable ability. His attentiveness made her feel special. "People respond to that."

They walked a short distance to the park and sat across from each other at an empty picnic table. About thirty feet away a group of teenage boys were shooting hoops on a lighted basketball court.

"All I did was talk to him. I lucked out—he actually paid attention to what I had to say. I had a great deal more failures in comparison to the successes like Jeff. I'm hoping to improve my record with troubled kids by going into private practice."

"I never realized principals counseled students that way. I thought all they did was enforce the rules and regulations. At least that's all I remember them doing when I was in school."

"The troublemakers spend more time in my office than any counselor's. How could I ignore opportunities like that?"

"From the little bit you're telling me I can see why they feel the need to show their gratitude. An occasional ice cream cone seems like small compensation for turning their son's life around."

"Jeff is a smart kid and would have eventually found his way. All I did was help him find it a little sooner." Joel popped the last bite of his cone into his mouth. He crumpled his napkin into a tight ball and tossed it into the waste barrel six feet away with nothing but can.

"Nice shot," she told him.

"I still got it," he crowed, pumping his fist.

Yes, he certainly did, she silently agreed as she noticed how his attention wandered toward the action on the basketball court. She watched how his face expressed pleasure when he witnessed a good shot and twist with disappointment at a play gone wrong.

"You like basketball, Joel?" Gwen tried to channel his attention back to her, even if it meant attempting a conversation about a subject she had only the most rudimentary knowledge about.

"What? Oh, yes, I do. I coach a team at the Y and I played in college."

"Really? Samantha is determined to play collegiate softball."

"From what Nick and Davey tell me, she has an excellent chance. I understand she's very good."

"That's what everyone keeps telling me."

Joel looked a little surprised. "You mean you don't know how good she is? She throws a sixty-eight mile an hour fastball at fifteen."

"Is that fast?"

He laughed at her ignorance, not cruelly but out of amazement. "Trust me, from forty feet it's fast."

"She's been fortunate to have good coaches who have recognized her talent and helped her develop it over the years because I can assure you she didn't get her athletic ability from me."

He cocked his head and looked at her as if he didn't hear her correctly. "You don't consider yourself an athlete?"

"Heavens no! What on earth gave you the idea I was athletic?"

"You're a runner, aren't you?"

"Oh, that." She shrugged and waggled her hand dismissively. "Running doesn't take any special talent or ability. It's just putting one foot in front of the other."

"Don't sell yourself short, Gwen. Running takes a considerable amount of physical ability, stamina, and discipline," Joel pointed out. "Just ask any drill sergeant with a unit of new recruits."

"All right, all right," she laughed. "You've convinced me."

A basketball came flying off the court, took a few bouncing leaps in the grass and finally came to a rolling stop near Gwen's feet. She bent down and picked it up as a young man of about seventeen ran up to them. Expensive high tops put an extra bounce into his already cocky, urban strut.

"Thanks, lady," he said as he grabbed the ball. "Oh, hey, Mr. Hubbard," he added when noticing Joel sitting across from Gwen.

"The lady's name is Ms. Marconi, Kevin." Gwen detected a gentle hint of authoritarian. Once a principal, always a principal, she noted.

Wearing a backwards baseball cap and loose fitting jean shorts, the young man tossed a cursory nod in her direction. "Yeah, okay, how ya doin'?"

"Fine, thanks," she replied.

Just as quickly as she answered, he turned his attention back to Joel. "How about joining us, Mr. H. We could really use an extra guy for a game of three on three."

Joel vacillated purely for her benefit and she didn't make him squirm for too long before letting him off the hook. "Go," she said, shooing him off with a wave of a neatly manicured hand.

"You sure you don't mind?" Joel asked, already getting up from the table. "Quick game, honest," he promised. "Just to twenty one."

Gwen laughed aloud as she watched him jog across the grass to the lighted half court with an easy loping gait.

Not wanting to miss a single shot, she moved nearer to the action. Finding a table just off the court, she sat on the tabletop and placed her feet on the intended seat, effectively turning it into a makeshift bleacher. Having watched Samantha play ball on some out of the way, ill-equipped fields over the years she'd learned to make do with whatever seating was available, be it picnic tables, benches, tree stumps or fences.

Joel was amazingly good. Gwen really enjoyed watching him keep up and occasionally surpass kids half his age, and she cheered wildly when he really got the best of them. He matched them shot for shot and rebound for rebound. Halfway through the game, he ran breathless and laughing to where she sat and pulled his polo shirt over his head. He tossed it on the table next to her and without saying a word he ran back to the court. If his basketball ability hadn't already captured her undivided attention, his taut, muscled, hard body would have definitely done the trick. She found it exceedingly difficult to concentrate on the rest of the game.

"Taken to trolling the parks for fresh meat, Gwen?"

The raspy male voice grated across her nerves like sharp claws on a new blackboard and she shivered against the chills creeping down her spine. She tried to ignore him and focused on the game, hoping he would take the hint and go away.

"Aren't they just a little too young and tender even for you?"

"Ray Farley." She breathed his name with nothing but contempt dripping off every syllable.

"It's been a while," he said.

Not long enough. "What are you doing here? It

hasn't rained in days."

"What in the hell you mean by that?" he demanded.

"Isn't that when the worms usually come out?"

He leaned in close and whispered in her ear. "When you gonna learn that mouth of yours is only good for one thing? And smart ass comments ain't it." The smell of stale cigarettes and cheap booze followed his words and elicited a tug on her gag reflex, and her skin literally crawled from his nearness.

Refocusing her attention on the basketball court and its active occupants, Gwen gripped the edge of the table and disregarded his presence hoping he'd vanish as suddenly as he'd appeared.

A hand much too soft to rightfully belong to a man wrapped around her wrist and applied increasing pressure until she flinched from the pain he inflicted. Attempting to yank herself free from his grip, she swung at him with her free hand. She managed to land a single blow, glancing her knuckles off his bristly jaw before she was blocked and restrained. With both arms trapped in his grasp, Gwen panicked. She couldn't bear to be held against her will.

"Let go of me!" she spat, kicking and twisting.

From out of the corner of her eye, something round and orange came flying toward them. An odd, hollow thump quickly followed. Releasing her with a startled yelp, Farley ran off clutching his head.

Once free, Gwen leaped off the picnic table and placed as much distance from the scene as her shaky legs would carry her. Leaning against a drinking fountain, a rush of excess adrenaline flowed from her body. The air rushed in and out of her lungs with raspy hisses as she pressed the button on the fountain. After running her hand under the arcing stream of cool water, she patted it across her face and neck.

A hand touched her shoulder, and she nearly jumped out of her skin as she took a defensive step back. Joel held up both palms up in a gesture that indicated he intended no harm. “I didn’t mean to startle you. Are you all right?”

She nodded but couldn’t find her voice as she pushed a damp lock of hair off her face.

Two of the young men ran up to them, breathless and excited. “Sorry, Mr. Hubbard, the dude took off so fast we couldn’t get his whole plate number.”

“Thanks, guys. I appreciate the effort.” Joel remained amazingly calm. His level of composure was like a soothing balm on her raw and frazzled nerves. She was soon breathing normally and the tension in her neck and shoulders began to subside.

One of the boys questioned, “You want us to call the cops?”

“No!” Gwen exclaimed, adding more calmly, “Please don’t.” Panicked at the thought of the police getting involved, Gwen felt the tension return. Her fingers curled into fists at her side. The last thing she wanted was to explain how and why she knew that despicable character. “It’s over. I’d just as soon forget the whole thing.”

One of the young men handed Joel his shirt. He stuffed his arms into the sleeves and pulled it over his head as he said, “I’d better get you home.” Joel placed a tentative hand on her elbow and guided her across the grass to a gravel path that led them out of the park.

She stumbled in the loose stones but he was there to keep her steady as he wrapped a stabilizing arm around her shoulders. She kept her head bowed, her gaze down, and watched their feet take each step farther away from the humiliating scene in the park. Joel remained physically supportive yet stonily silent.

As they turned down her street, she finally pushed aside the expansive silence that wedged itself between them and spoke, "I suppose I owe you some sort of an explanation."

"Only if you want to give me one," he told her.

She cast him a curious and confused glance. She'd never met anyone like him, and she wasn't quite sure how to deal with someone who wasn't the least bit demanding or insistent she give him every detail. She wondered if it was because he was that disciplined or simply that disinterested, which in turn made her question if she should be flattered or offended.

She decided to be grateful and relieved. "You're a smart man, Joel Hubbard," she told him. "It's better not to get involved with my problems."

His strides came to a grinding halt. "Wait just a doggone minute," he said as he took her by the shoulders and turned her to face him. He looked her square in the eye. "I don't want you thinking that I'm not concerned about what happened to you back there. But the last thing you need right now is another difficult man getting in your face about it. Tell me, don't tell me, do it now or do it later, it's entirely up to you." He released her and started walking again.

They continued in silence and soon found themselves standing on the sidewalk in front of her house. "Ray is part of that unabridged version of my life I'd just as soon forget if you don't mind." Not that she ever would forget. His face had been the central figure in every nightmare she'd had for the last two years."

"Fair enough."

"I do want to thank you for coming to my rescue. The look on Ray's face when you whacked him with the basketball was priceless." She actually found herself chuckling as she recalled the scene.

"Inasmuch as I'd like to take credit for running the guy off, I have to confess it wasn't me. It was Kevin who made the winning throw."

"Please thank him for me the next time you see him." She turned and started for the door. Joel placed a deterring hand on her shoulder.

"Could we do this again some time?" he asked. His words were somewhat stilted and awkward.

"Sure," she answered with a lighthearted lilt. "I'll bring my pompoms and megaphone next time."

"I was thinking more on the lines of dinner and a movie for our second date." He reached out and tentatively touched her arm. She was amazed by how gentle such big hands could be as they stroked the flesh of her upper arm. Slowly his fingers slid down, caressing each inch of her flesh until he found her hand at the end of his travels. He took her long-fingered, delicate hand into his much larger one and held it with tenderness and utmost respect. She was overwhelmed.

"I...I didn't realize this was a first date," she stammered.

"I'd like to consider it one because it didn't have any of the usual awkwardness that ordinarily comes with first dates. That alone makes me think the next one should be even better.

"I'll call you tomorrow," he said.

"Actually, I'll be calling you. We have to arrange a time to get your house listed."

"I'll look forward to it." Taking her by surprise, he cupped her face and planted a soft, lingering kiss on her cheek.

Her eyelids fluttered shut as she surrendered to the slow caress of firm fingertips gliding lightly across the slope of her jaw, and she almost gasped aloud with disappointment when his touch withdrew.

"Goodnight, Gwen Marconi," he breathed.

Startled by his action and even more so by her reaction, her eyes flew open just in time to see his broad-shouldered, long-legged frame disappear around the corner. She couldn't help but notice that he whistled a jaunty little ditty, and she chuckled when she recognized the melody. She never would have guessed him to be a Toys R Us Kid.

Chapter Seven

Joel couldn't sleep. It was two o'clock in the morning and the house was too quiet. Knowing Emme wasn't around to wake up or cry out in her sleep left him feeling restless and very much alone. Yet, if pressed to bring complete honesty into the equation, he would have to admit that it wasn't just his daughter's absence or chronic insomnia that robbed him of sleep and left him tossing and turning in his bed.

He propped his hands behind his head and stared into the darkness. The bedroom hadn't felt this empty and lonely since the days following Beth's funeral. Those nights had been endless, the solitude overwhelming, and the mindless bliss of sleep elusive. His grief had been crushing and all-encompassing until his daughter's birth eased the emptiness.

What disturbed him tonight was the fact that it wasn't his wife's absence that left him sleepless. Gwen Marconi had awakened some wonderful feelings in him—feelings he thought he'd buried with his wife, feelings that had been exclusively Beth's. The guilt and confusion at their resurrection left him troubled as he dealt with the knowledge that another woman could arouse him in the same way. It seemed the years of self-imposed celibacy were finally taking their toll, although he was somewhat surprised by the intensity of his physical reaction.

He discarded the sheet with frustrated kicks and sat on the edge of the bed. Shoving his fists against the mattress, he pushed himself to stand. In spite of being dressed in only a pair of cotton boxers his body was damp with a sticky film of perspiration. The air was still and cloying, making it difficult to breathe.

The curtains at the open bedroom windows hung limp and utterly motionless. Even the trees outside stood stock-still. Not so much as a blade of dry grass or supple leaf fluttered in the heavy, humid night.

It had never crossed his mind to turn on the air-conditioning before he retired. There had been a gentle, soothing breeze coming through the windows at the time and if given the choice he'd take open windows over air-conditioning any day.

Late June was such an unpredictable time of year in Northwest Indiana. Just days after the vernal equinox, the first official days of summer could be sweltering hot or cold and rainy. There was no telling what to expect. Weather in the Midwest was a veritable crapshoot.

Born in the Southwest and raised in one warm climate after the next, he was accustomed to hot weather so it wasn't the stifling heat of the summers that bothered him nearly as much as the biting cold winters. Since heading East to college, nearly half his life now had been lived in areas with four distinct seasons and still he wasn't used to the subzero temperatures and mountainous snow banks lining the streets after a significant snowfall. Of course most native Midwesterners cursed the snow and cold and claimed they didn't like the winters any more than he did. He eventually learned that acceptance and adaptation was the key to survival in The Region.

Joel padded down the carpeted stairs and wandered into the kitchen with a restless step. He dispensed crushed ice and water from the fridge and took a long, chilling gulp. The frigid swallow hit his throat with a painful jolt. Brain freeze!

He set the glass on the counter and ran a hand across the familiar bristly crew—a hairstyle he hadn't varied much in almost thirty years. Maybe it was time to overhaul his appearance and his life. His friends and family certainly thought it was time to move on and shed the widower mantle. He was the only one who wasn't sure he was ready to get on with his life without Beth.

Wandering onto the screen-enclosed back porch, he looked around and smiled. It had been Beth's favorite part of the house. Perfectly scaled natural wicker furniture was presently shoved and crowded into an unattractive arrangement at one end to accommodate the pieces of baby paraphernalia, none of which he used for Em anymore. She was far too big for the swing and entirely too smart to be confined by the playpen.

The next thing he knew he had collapsed the mesh sides of the playpen and folded it flat, leaning it against the solid back wall of the house to be stored in the basement along with the other baby stuff she had outgrown. He then turned his attention to dismantling the swing.

Once he had both pieces deposited in the basement, he returned to the porch and began to rearrange the furniture, not exactly in the same manner Beth had left it but in a way he had always felt it should be. Standing back, he surveyed his late night handiwork. It wasn't much of a change but it was a start and he laughed to himself as he wondered what his neighbors would think if they saw him moving the furniture around in the middle of the night—in his underwear, no less.

The smile left his face as quickly as it had appeared. What was he doing? A wave of uncontrollable guilt washed over him and he took a step toward moving everything back to Beth's original arrangement. He stopped himself by sitting in the nearest padded chair in an effort to let the urge pass. The chair creaked under his weight with the typical characteristic sound wicker made when strained against its natural state. This wasn't going to be as easy as he originally thought. If he couldn't face rearranging one room how could he sell it all and let a family of strangers move in?

He turned off the lights and headed back to bed. There wasn't anything else that needed to be done that couldn't wait until morning. Major life changes needed time to evolve.

****

On the other side of town Gwen Marconi was having trouble sleeping. All the ceiling fan whirling above her bed did was move hot air across her body. She tossed and turned, the fitted sheet and underlying mattress pad bunching and wadding under her constant restlessness, leaving lumps and bumps she found impossible to ignore. When there wasn't a comfortable square inch to be found, she scooted to the end of the bed and climbed off. She slipped her feet into flat mules and ignored the knee-length cotton robe lying across the foot of her bed.

What an awful time for the central air-conditioning to break down. Then again, there was never a good time. If it was needed and it didn't work, it was a bad time. Calling a heating and cooling technician first thing in the morning was at the top of her to-do list. She would need to have her office manager rearrange her morning appointments, but that shouldn't be a problem. Bette Hauser was the most efficient human ever to walk the earth in spiked heels and stirrup stretch pants. And Gwen blessed the day the older woman wandered into her office looking for a job.

Gwen escaped the stifling confines of her room and headed downstairs to the lower level family room. Summer or winter it was always cooler down there. She was surprised to find her daughter already there watching a classic episode of *Three's Company* on Nick at Nite. Samantha sat with her feet propped on the coffee table painting her toenails an iridescent shade of coppery rose with wads of cotton stuffed between her toes. A sweating can of Mountain Dew dripped on the end table, leaving a puddle on the mosaic-tiled surface.

"You can't sleep either, huh?" Samantha hit the mute button on the remote and sat back as she screwed the cap on the bottle of polish.

Gwen shook her head as she snatched a tissue from the box on the end table and absorbed the moisture before slipping a cork coaster under the half empty can of soda.

"I'm calling a repairman in the morning."

"That's not the reason I can't sleep. Davey and I had a stupid fight."

"Most fights are." Gwen sat next to her daughter on the couch. "You want to talk about it?"

Samantha expelled a long sigh. "We had a nice evening up until Davey and his dad drove me home. Davey started telling me what colleges I should consider. Mom, you should have heard him! He was naming all the top softball programs in the country."

"It sounds like he's proud of what you've accomplished. Weren't you flattered by his thinking you could play for those schools?"

"It wasn't so much what he said as what his father added. When I laughed off Davey's suggestions and said that no pitcher from this area had a chance at any of those schools, Mr. Chapparelle offered to see what he could do for me. He said he knew a few prominent people in the sports industry who might be able to pull a few strings with some of those schools, and he'd be happy to approach them and put in a good word if I was interested."

"How did you react to that?"

"I was stunned but I managed to politely refuse his help and told him that inasmuch as I appreciated his offer, I informed them both that this had to be my decision and on my terms."

"And they had a problem with that?" Gwen was still confused.

"I didn't think so at the time. Mr. Chapparelle seemed cool with it. In fact he said he respected me for wanting to do it on my own." She turned away and pressed her hand across her eyes. "He even gave me a hug when I got out of the truck and told me that his offer was always open if I ever changed my mind."

"I'm still not hearing a fight here."

Sniffling as a fresh wave of tears filled her eyes, Samantha reached for a tissue and continued, "Mom, I never saw it coming. Davey walked me to the door and kissed me goodnight like usual. Then out of the blue he called me an ungrateful brat and said if I had any sense at all I'd reconsider his dad's offer. Oh, he said it like he was teasing, but I completely lost it. I told him that if I wasn't good enough to get a scholarship on my own then I didn't want it given to me any other way, and that I sure as heck didn't need the Chapparelle name or money to do it for me even though he apparently thought I did."

"I'm sure that went over well." Gwen was hard pressed to remain neutral in this discussion. She was tempted to tell her daughter that she agreed with her completely, but she also knew when to keep her opinions to herself. "So what happened next?"

"He just shook his head and said I was putting words in his mouth and that's when I told him..." Her daughter paused and turned away.

Samantha..." Gwen urged. "What did you say?"

"It doesn't matter what I said. All that matters

is that we had a fight and I feel terrible." She dropped her head against the couch cushions.

"Tell me."

"Fine!" She exclaimed. "When he said I was putting words in his mouth I told him that was about all he could expect in his mouth from me for a while. Then I slammed the door in his face."

"Sa—man—tha," Gwen stressed each syllable with a reproving tone only the mother of a teenager could produce. "So what are you going to do to make yourself feel better about this?"

"Call him in the morning and apologize?"

"Are you asking or telling?"

"Telling," Sam answered with an assured nod.

"That's my girl." Gwen stood and planted a kiss on the top of Sam's head. "Now I'm going to salvage what's left of this night and try to get a little sleep. I suggest you do the same."

"Goodnight, Mom. Thanks for listening. Love you."

"Ditto, kiddo."

Gwen wiped a cool, wet cloth across her face, neck, and arms before she returned to her bedroom. She glanced at the rumpled sheets and twisted blanket lying on the floor where she'd kicked them in a fit of heated frustration. She couldn't remember the last time her bed had gotten so mussed and tumbled. Too bad it wasn't for a better reason. As a matter of fact, she couldn't remember that last time for that either.

She must be getting old. There was a time when having a man in her life was every bit as important as having her first cup of black coffee in the morning. It was simply a necessity. When did it drop so low on her list of priorities?

Chapter Eight

Gwen never trusted her eyes before her first cup of coffee. She stumbled around on autopilot until that first jolt of caffeine sharpened her senses and made her feel human again. So when she opened her front door to retrieve the morning paper, she stepped one foot onto the porch, picked up the folded newspaper, and retreated. It was only after the door shut behind her did she pause and wonder what exactly it was she thought she saw.

She pulled open the door ever so slowly and peered through the gap. No amount of coffee could change what she found in her front yard. It was a veritable garden of balloons—big balloons, little balloons, single shiny silver balloons, clusters of multicolored balloons, heart-shaped, star-shaped, animal-shaped, triangles, circles, and squares—all hovering in the early morning air, dancing at the end of their weighted tethers from the playful touch of a morning summer breeze.

"Samantha!" Gwen called, beginning to chuckle. "Samantha!" she called again, loudly enough the second time to guarantee Sam's attention as well as half the neighborhood.

Her daughter stumbled out of her room and down the stairs wearing her standard teen jammies—a pair of cotton boxers and a skinny-strapped tank. Her heavy hair fell in a tangled curtain across her face and the partial imprint of a daisy was clearly imbedded on her cheek from a crewel pillow sham. "What? What's wrong? Is the house on fire?"

"Take a look for yourself." Gwen stepped aside, pulling the door open wider to give her daughter an unobstructed view of the front yard. Just as soon as she pushed the strands of auburn hair off her face, Samantha's eyes grew wider than Gwen's had at first sight. "I assume these are for you."

"Mom..."Samantha breathed in wonderment. "How? Who? When?"

"I think the who and when is fairly easy to figure out. The how isn't quite as obvious."

Wandering barefoot through her helium-filled garden of latex and Mylar, Samantha touched each balloon and read each message, some of which were hand scrawled across the colorful latex with others were brightly pre-printed against the glossy Mylar. Every message conveyed pretty much the same sentiment: He loved her, he was sorry, and he wanted her forgiveness.

"I got to tell you, Sam," Gwen remarked as she leaned casually against the doorjamb. "The boy's got style."

"I've got to call him," Samantha exclaimed as she dashed past her mother, leaving Gwen to watch the neighbors' reactions to her recently added yard decorations. Let 'em wonder, she thought with a pleasant smirk as she shut the door and headed to the kitchen for a cup of what would now run a poor eye-opening second that morning.

By five after eight Gwen had scheduled a serviceman to fix the air conditioning and called her office to let her office manager know she'd be working from home. Shaking her head and wearing an amused grin, she hung up after hearing Bette's heartfelt assurance that they would somehow muddle through the day without their fearless leader. She carried a second mug of coffee to her upstairs office and dialed Joel's home number.

"Good morning, Mr. Hubbard." Her voice was

cheerful and melodious the second she heard him pick up.

"Is it?" he rasped as he cleared his throat.

"I woke you. I'm so sorry."

"That's okay," he said through an unsuccessful attempt to stifle a breathtaking yawn.

"Go back to sleep," Gwen encouraged. "Call me back when you get up." Just as she had done when she placed the call, she hung up before he had an opportunity to respond.

She had no sooner severed the connection—the receiver was in fact still in her hand—when the phone rang. It startled her and she let it ring several more times before she answered. "Gwen Marconi."

"You hung up on me," he stated, sounding considerably more like himself this time around.

"I didn't mean for it to seem that way. I just felt bad waking you up. I figured the sooner I hung up the quicker you could get back to sleep. I forgot you didn't have a small child dragging you out of bed at the crack of dawn this morning."

He laughed. The husky resonance reverberated through the line and traveled like an electric current up her arm and down her spine. "I must admit that sleeping in this morning did have a certain tempting appeal."

"And I ruined it for you." She sounded truly regretful. "Please, as a favor to me, go back to sleep. Call me later."

"Wait!" He fairly shouted.

"What?"

"Before you hang up on me again, just tell me why you called?"

"I wanted to let you know I won't be able to get to your place until later today."

"Sounds like you're already having a bad day and it's only..." There was a brief pause. "...eight fifteen."

"Some bad days start earlier than others. Any time my day begins at the mercy of an AC repairman's schedule it's like a predictor of things yet to come. But if I have another night like last night, tomorrow morning won't be starting out any better than today's."

"Is there anything I can do to help?"

"Yes. You could ease my guilty conscience and go back to sleep. Good bye."

She logged onto a multiple listing database and started searching for properties that might fit Joel's requirements.

It was nearly ten o'clock when Samantha stuck her head around the corner. "I'm heading over to Davey's now."

"I take it you and he have made up." Gwen turned to face her daughter.

"Yeah," she said. "What can I tell ya, the boy's crazy about me..." she batted her eyes as she burst into a fit of giggles. "He says since I'm so determined to do this my way, the least he can do is help make me the best pitcher in the state." She smiled. "So he's gonna help me work on my curve ball and then we're going to spend the rest of the day being lazy by their pool. They just got a new slide I can't wait to try." Just as she finished, the doorbell rang. "That must be Davey now. Bye."

"Have fun," Gwen called out as her daughter bounded down the stairs and she returned her full attention to the computer. As much as she always gave each and every client one hundred percent, she felt an overwhelming desire to give Joel one hundred and ten. That realization caught her by surprise and caused her to frown as she leaned back, pondering this unexpected turn of events. Sometime between Saturday morning and Sunday night this had become more personal than it ever should, and she couldn't help wonder if she should just hand Joel's file over to one of her associates before she let this get out of hand.

With the back of her knuckles, she absently stroked the place on her cheek where he had brushed a kiss. There was something so remarkably undemanding and straightforward about him, she was having difficulty thinking of him as just a client, and she found herself looking for other reasons to call him. Damn that repairman. Where was he, and how much longer was she going to have to wait? She hoped he'd get there soon so she could still make it to Joel's house by early afternoon.

Instead of driving herself to distraction on something over which she had no control, she did what she always did when her mind refused to stay focused. She snatched up a pencil and started to doodle. Curlicues and fleur-de-lis, hearts and flowers, lines and circles, she never knew what path her mindless scribbling would follow. She only knew that when she was done she would find herself with an eight-by-ten sheet of paper filled with intricately designed swirls and patterns she had no real conscious recollection of creating. Her staff constantly teased her about these almost trancelike states and threatened to turn them over for in-depth psychoanalysis.

The sound of the front door opening and shutting broke her reverie. "What did you forget?" she hollered, as she glanced at her latest artwork. Her eyes grew wide with astonishment. Today she found an overwhelming assortment of complex circles and tunnels pierced by thick-shafted arrows. She didn't need Freud or anyone else to tell her what they suggested. Hell, they were a sight more than suggestive. They were downright indicative of the places her imagination had wandered. She crumpled the paper and pitched it into the waste can where it rightfully belonged before Samantha walked in and discovered her mother's erotic doodling.

"Two points!" That deep resonate voice was most definitely not Samantha's.

Gwen spun around in her chair and found Joel filling the doorway.

His appearance evoked both pleasure and suspicion. "How long have you been standing there?" she questioned, sincerely wishing she'd had the foresight to run the evidence of her fantasies through the shredder.

"Long enough," he answered as his eyes fell to the wadded ball in the chrome mesh wastebasket then back to her—long enough to see how utterly appealing she looked in her hang-around-the-house clothes of faded jean shorts and form-hugging T-shirt. Dress her up, dress her down, it didn't matter. She looked fresh and wonderful. Anything else in the room wasn't important, including whatever it was she'd hastily tossed in the trash.

"I thought you were Samantha," Gwen stated.

"I ran into her as I was coming up the walk. She told me to go right in. I hope that was okay?"

"Do you plan on stealing the silver?"

"Uh, no..."

"Then I guess it's okay."

"In fact, I come bearing gifts." He held up a white bakery bag for her inspection. "Fresh bagels."

Gwen forced a smile and reached for her empty coffee mug. "Great," she said, standing. She set the computer on standby and snatched the stack of listings from the printer tray. "I found some houses you might find interesting. Let's go into the kitchen so you can take a look." Casting an over-the-shoulder glance at the crumpled ball of incriminating evidence, she took him by the arm and led him downstairs.

"Coffee okay?" Gwen offered as she poured herself another cup. "Or would you rather have tea or juice?"

"I didn't come here to have you wait on me."

She'd been so pleased to see him that his reason for showing up without warning hadn't entered her mind. "Now that you mention it, why are you here?" She glanced at him from over the rim of her favorite mug. His military upbringing was all too apparent with the rigid back, perfect postured stance. No slouch with half a brain would dare creep into that man's spine. He stood beside the breakfast bar with his hand resting on the back of the swivel stool as if waiting for permission to sit.

"I've come to offer my services." He came around the breakfast bar and started peering into cabinets.

"Services?" Gwen questioned as she watched him make himself right at home. The man tallied major points in her book for not expecting her to wait on him, although in his case she would have done it gladly. Waiting on him would have been a pleasure.

"I thought I'd wait here for the repairman so you could go to my house and do whatever it is you have to do." He carried plates and knifes to the counter and started digging into the bag, finally selecting a bagel to his liking. Raisin, she determined, or maybe blueberry.

"Oh, no." She shook her head against the very idea. "I couldn't ask you to do that."

"As I recall, you didn't ask, I offered." She watched him smear a thick layer of cream cheese on one half of the tire-sized bagel and deplete it by a third with one clean, tearing bite.

"Semantics aside, it's not right." Distracted by a splotch of cream cheese sticking to his full lower lip, her words were stilted and unconvincing. "This isn't your problem."

He chewed and swallowed then reached for a napkin and wiped his mouth. "Have you always been this stubborn?" His question was delivered as mildly curious, not the least bit critical or depreciating.

"Why yes, as a matter of fact I have, although I prefer the term independent."

"Now who's quibbling over semantics?" he said as he tore another considerable bite off the bagel and helped himself to a cup of coffee.

"I don't mean to sound ungrateful. I appreciate the simple fact that you even thought to offer a helping hand, really I do."

"Does this mean you're changing your mind about accepting my offer?"

"No, but that doesn't make me any less grateful."

He looked at her as if he hadn't heard her correctly then began to chuckle and shake his head. He popped the last of the bagel into his mouth and brushed the crumbs off his hands. "You're really serious about not letting me help with this?"

Poised and ready to argue further, she opened her mouth, but just as suddenly thought better of it and shut it again. "Fine," she finally said. She'd learned a long time ago to choose her battles carefully. She elected not to take this one on. Seeing the pleased smile light up his handsome face convinced her she'd made the right decision.

Chapter Nine

After a cursory examination of the house's exterior and making the necessary notations, Gwen slipped the key Joel had given her into the front door lock. The door swung open and she stepped into the house that Joel had shared with his wife. How long had she been gone? Gwen thought back to the things he had mentioned. What was it he said about Emme? She never knew her mother, she remembered him saying, and the child had just celebrated her third birthday a few months ago. That would mean Beth had been gone for at least three years as well.

So why did the house still smell like the woman had just left for the day? There was the distinct feminine scent of perfume—not men's cologne, or air fresheners, or even pleasantly fragrant baby wipes. She half expected someone to step out from another room in explanation of the lingering aroma that greeted her wherever she went.

She glanced around the living room and saw the indelible signature of a woman's touch. It was obvious that Joel hadn't changed anything since his wife's death. Gwen touched the delicate petal of a silk Victorian rose artfully arranged in a crystal bowl with a dozen more of the same in various shades of pink. The room was predominately floral chintz—tasteful, quite lovely in fact, but definitely influenced by a woman who was given free rein when it came to the decorating.

Gwen was so fascinated by the steadfast tribute she almost forgot the real purpose of her being there.

She dug into her briefcase and pulled out a clipboard and an electronic tape measure and got down to work. Decorating, although often instrumental in selling a home, was not what she was supposed to point out to potential buyers. She had learned to ignore the icing and pay closer attention to the underlying cake. Unless, of course, the decorative frosting was so outrageous or bizarre that she couldn't help but broach the subject with the seller and suggest, delicately of course, to tone it down. Most peopled didn't realize a realtor's job went far beyond slapping a *For Sale* sign in the front yard and running an ad in the local paper.

It wasn't easy remaining objective as she toured Joel's house. Everywhere she looked she found another reminder of a woman who was deeply loved and dearly missed. The dresser in the master bedroom still held a number of Beth Hubbard's personal belongings—a lovely carved jewelry chest, a collection of crystal perfume bottles, an antique brush and comb set, and the most personal item of all, a silver filigreed framed wedding photo with a delicate strand of freshwater pearls draped over one corner of the ornate frame. Upon closer examination, Gwen realized the necklace was the same one worn by Joel's lovely young bride. She was a pretty, petite woman, fairly dwarfed by Joel's towering stature. A bubbly, bright-eyed redhead with a smile so brilliant and expressive it caused the rest of her pleasant features to pale by comparison.

Gwen made a mental note to tell Joel that valuable keepsakes should be removed and placed out of sight once the house was listed, ideally in a safety deposit box. As much as realtors took every precaution to safeguard their clients' homes during showings, there was always the chance that someone would see the necklace as a temptation too hard to resist. In fact, she would recommend that the entire jewelry chest be removed as well as any other irreplaceable effects.

Gwen lifted one bottle of perfume and sniffed the stopper. The scent was unmistakable. It permeated the house like a living, breathing entity. Feeling a little guilty for snooping, she replaced the bottle among the others and returned her attention to doing her job. She inspected and measured the rest of the room, trying very hard not to dwell on the king-sized bed that dominated the less than generous sized room.

When a realtor inspected a house to list it was important to recognize special features and points of interest, which meant opening closets and cabinets. She'd learned over the years to do it, but to this day she still didn't like it. There was always something so personal, so invasive, about poking her nose into parts of people's lives they purposely hid behind closed doors.

There were two good-sized closets in the master bedroom. The one that led to the attic access was long and deep with shelves lining the length of one wall. The other was a fairly large walk-in with built-in shelves, shoe cubbies and drawers. She knew from experience that people loved those kinds of features. Interested buyers would remember the closets and forget the less than generous room dimensions. The two smaller bedrooms were average sized with typical sliding door closets.

The house itself was a two-story, all brick Georgian, circa post World War II, with a narrow, single car side drive and detached two-car garage set far back on the lot. It was in good shape, solidly built, and well maintained. The screened porch was obviously added later, but judging from the look of the construction, not during Joel's eight-year ownership.

Joel was right about one thing. The back yard

was small. What there was of it was filled with toddler toys and equipment. Building any further addition was out of the question. If for no other reason than the current town codes would never permit it.

It would make a good starter home for some lucky couple, just as it had been for Joel and his wife. He had mentioned that he and Beth had always planned on moving once they started their family.

She finished in the kitchen, making notes and taking final measurements. The warm and inviting room made her want to curl up in the rocker by the window with a cup of steaming Earl Grey and an even steamier romance novel. In spite of his need for larger accommodations, this house was not going to be easy for Joel to leave. She hoped he had the strength to give it up when the time finally came. So much of his wife's influences still dominated every room, walking away could be like losing her all over again.

What to do, what to do? Dating divorced men was easy. Most of those men were eager to get on with or at the very least indifferent to their lives without partners. But widowers—they were a whole different animal, and came with more baggage than a jumbo jet heading to Florida with a load of snowbirds.

She wasn't stupid, she wasn't naïve, and she wasn't blind; she knew Joel was interested. With a little effort on her part they could slip very easily into an affair. There was just one minor problem with that. She wasn't sure if that was all she wanted from this man.

It was just so hard to separate the man she found herself attracted to from the man who lived in this house and maintained it in such a way that suggested his wife was just away and could return at any moment and find her home just as she'd left it. Was she ready to face the emotional obstacles she would eventually encounter?

By the time she locked up the house and aimed her car toward her own, she had decided to let Joel set the pace. She would let him make the next move and she would try to respond accordingly.

****

The minute Gwen stepped into her house she was greeted by the sonorous hum and cool relief of a functioning air conditioner. It felt heavenly. She dropped her briefcase and purse on the entry bench, kicked off her sandals, and headed for the kitchen. It smelled heavenly in there. She found a container of chocolate chunk cookies on the counter and helped herself. Her daughter had obviously decided to do something domestic—a peace offering to Davey for their earlier disagreement was the likeliest explanation for the treats. The way to that boy's heart was definitely through his stomach. So what if they were only the slice and bake variety, it was the thought that counted.

"Sam?" she called, taking another bite of the gooey cookie. As she licked melted chocolate from her fingers and lips, she wandered from the kitchen to the lower level family room. There wasn't any sign of her daughter. What she did find was the television on but set to a satellite music channel. She never would have guessed the man stretched out and asleep on her couch was a country music fan, and a classic country music lover at that if "Your Cheatin' Heart" by Hank Williams Sr. was any indication.

What now? Gwen wondered. If this was his next move, how did she respond to it? She knew how to handle letches, gropers and hitters—God knows she'd had more than her share of experience with those—but he wasn't like any of the men she was used to. Joel was a nice, normal man who played asphalt basketball with teens in the park, cared about the lives of past students, dealt with AC repairmen for a woman he hardly knew, and listened to classic country on satellite TV.

For the first time in her life she was stymied on how to deal with a man.

Well, for the time being it was easier to let him sleep. Besides, she reasoned, she owed him a nap.

"Hi," he said, righting his lanky frame on the couch. "You're finished already?"

"I woke you again. I'm sorry."

"I wasn't sleeping," he said.

"You were just resting your eyes, right?"

"You've heard that one before, huh?" He glanced at his watch, looking a little embarrassed.

"Once or twice." She chuckled as she sat beside him. "And in answer to your other question—yes, I'm finished. I like what you did with the bedroom closets, by the way. It'll be a great selling feature. People love that kind of stuff."

"You were in the bedroom?" he questioned.

"In order for me to list a house, I have to inspect the whole house," she told him, unsure whether she was explaining or defending herself. "If you weren't comfortable with me doing this without you, you should have waited until you could be there."

"It's not that. It's just, well, I never thought…"

She finished for him. "You never thought I'd be invading your private space, is that it?"

"Something like that."

"As long as we're on the subject, there are a couple of things I need you to take care of before the house goes on the market. First of all, you need to put away all personal belongings and valuables—jewelry, photos, things like that."

"Why?"

"Because we want people to see themselves in the house, not photos of strangers sitting around.

You need to make the house as impersonal as possible."

"That makes sense." He nodded in understanding and questioned, "Anything else?"

"Yes," she answered, wondering how she was going to tactfully broach this next subject. Mementos were one thing. The lingering scent of his late wife was another altogether. She decided that the direct approach was best. "The perfume smell in the house. It's a little overpowering."

"I meant to warn you about that. Em found a bottle of Beth's perfume in the downstairs bathroom and proceeded to sprinkle it all over the house before I caught her."

"I discovered an odor remover called *Common Scents* when Samantha pulled a similar stunt when she was little. I've used it over the years with good results. You can find it at any home improvement store."

"Speaking of Samantha, she called while you were out. She's going to Pizza Hut with Davey and his family, which leaves you free to have dinner at Kelso's with me."

"Kelso's?" she repeated. It was one of the newest, upscale restaurants in the area—and one of the most expensive. "What's the occasion?"

"Our second date," he said as he kissed her.

His lips were warm and electrifying, and without giving her action a second thought, Gwen planted an open palm on his chest and leaned into him to deepen the connection.

"Wait until you see what I've got planned for our third date," he told her as he deepened the kiss to include a little tongue and a lot of heavy breathing.

She was lost in his arms. "I can't wait to find out," she said, hoping it included less clothes and a lot more of that amazing tongue.

Chapter Ten

Gwen would have elected for the less clothes and more tongue route over Joel's idea of a third date. She hid a worried frown behind a pair of oversized Jackie O style sunglasses as she climbed into the passenger seat of Joel's silver mini van, tossing a canvas carryall into the back next to where Emme sat strapped in a booster seat. The sight of the smiling child momentarily eased Gwen's misgivings about this holiday shindig he was taking her to at Nick and Maggie's house. But for the most part, those old insecurities fluttered and bounced in her stomach, leaving her feeling similar to the time she'd eaten a batch of bad clams.

She pulled the door shut and took her time adjusting the seatbelt. "I'm still not convinced this is the right way to let your friends know we're seeing each other."

He gave her hand a reassuring squeeze as he planted a light kiss on the corner of her down-turned mouth. Her gaze settled on his strong, chiseled features and she smiled. Not a big one, but it was the best she could do while her stomach rolled and pitched.

"What better way for them to find out," he said. His breath tickled her cheek.

Unconvinced, Gwen responded with a loud sigh. "Have you told anyone about me?"

"Not specifically, no. I told Maggie I was bringing someone. I can't wait to see the look on their faces when I show up with you on my arm."

"There'll be plenty of looks all right, just not the

ones you're expecting." She shifted in her seat. The knot in her gut was getting bigger and more uncomfortable by the second. "I'm not going," she exclaimed, twisting to bolt. The click of the automatic locks dropped into place just as she reached for the door handle.

"Let me out, Joel," she said.

"Can't do that," he said as he eased the van away from the curb. "I promised Maggie I was bringing a date. You're it."

"So tell her I got sick." It wouldn't be a lie. She'd been nauseous since she woke up. "I'm really not feeling very well at the moment. Better yet, tell her I died. You can't be held to your promise if your date died." This wasn't like her. She was ordinarily a gutsy soul, ready to take on the world and anything it tossed in her path. But today she felt like a scared rabbit chased by a pack of wolves—big ones.

"You want to tell me what's really going on behind those dark glasses?"

"I've never been welcome in my client's homes except as their realtor. These people don't want me around after the ink is dry on their mortgages."

"Is that what all this is about?"

"That and the fact that a few of the women that'll likely be there today think I've slept with their husbands." Gwen tossed it out and let Joel decide what to do with it. He'd probably heard the rumors already but was too much of a gentleman to mention it.

"Did you?" he asked without missing a beat.

His immediate comeback took her by surprise. Most men would want to know but wouldn't be quite as blunt in their approach to find out. No beating around the bush for this man. That alone deserved an honest, straightforward answer in return.

"Yes," she said. "One man, one time, when I first moved here." She had to give the man credit. He didn't flinch, gasp, clench the wheel, or run off the road from her answer. There was nothing but a suffocating silence immediately following her reply. "I hope you're not waiting for further details," she finally added.

"Of course not," he answered. His gaze remained focused on the road.

"Still think showing up with me today is such a good idea?" Just once in her life she'd like to know what the view was like from the right side of the tracks. "It's not too late to turn this buggy around and take me home. No harm, no foul."

"Is that what you want?"

"Joel, I'm giving you a way out here. This ought to be what you want."

She watched him glance into his rear and side view mirrors as he pulled into a mini mart parking lot. He whipped into a slot and threw the van into park. Turning in his seat, he took her hand and rubbed a thumb across her cold knuckles.

"We all have things in our past that we're not proud of, Gwen. Some of us are just better at hiding our indiscretions than others."

Gwen barked a harsh laugh. "Yeah, well, my past in this town is an open book."

He squeezed her hand. "I don't believe that. There's more to Gwen Marconi than rumors and innuendo."

"Just ask anyone at that party today. I'm sure they'll be happy to give you all the sordid details, at least their version. The ironic thing is that one indiscretion, as you call it, is what helped me get where I am today."

He cocked his head. "I don't follow."

"I built my business on *other* people's dirty little secrets."

"Care to explain?"

"About six years ago one of those wives came

into my office and showed me some eight-by-ten glossies she thought I'd find interesting."

"That must have been awkward."

"Oh, these pictures weren't what you think. They were of several beautiful summer homes on Lake Michigan, one of which she now owns."

"I take it she got it in the divorce."

"On the contrary, they're still married and he's been a model husband ever since." She gave a husky laugh. "He can't afford to be otherwise. Everything is in her name."

Joel threw back his head and laughed. "That's ingenious. Absolutely ingenious! That is without a doubt the most brilliant means of dealing with a philandering husband I've ever heard. I love it!" He backed the van away from the store and eased into the traffic.

"I can't take the credit for the idea, just the execution. But that woman must have had a great many friends with similar marital problems because my business picked up considerably after that."

He continued to chuckle. "So what it boils down to is they don't want you around because you know what's buried in their backyards."

"That's one way of putting it. So now you know why I'm persona non-gratis at these functions. It's a little hard to rub elbows and exchange pleasantries with someone who holds the shovel."

They had no sooner started moving when they were brought to another delay by a lumbering freight train. Gwen chose to use the holdup more constructively than brooding over a past she couldn't change by playing tickle tag with Emme. Gwen reached between the bucket seats and tickled Emme's bare foot. Em giggled and wiggled her toes, daring Gwen to do it again. Over and over she walked her fingers around the seat and crept toward Em until the child squealed. Gwen couldn't help thinking that every relationship should be as easy to develop as those with children. They were so accepting and non-judgmental.

"Tickle Daddy," Emme encouraged, pointing at her dad.

"You think I should tickle your daddy?" Gwen stage whispered, snaking her finger toward his collarbone. She barely touched his skin and he cringed and faked a very convincing laugh.

"Oh, stop!" he said in a screeching falsetto. Emme tossed back her head, sending her red curls bouncing, and laughed louder at her father catching it. Gwen found his performance pretty hilarious too, and she couldn't help but toss her laughter into the mix. She hoped the rest of the day went as well. But hoping wasn't getting. What she expected was a disaster.

****

After the necessary introductions and obligatory small talk, Joel was lured away from her side to join the men around the poolside bar.

"Look for me under that tree over there," she told him. "That cushy-looking chaise is calling to me."

"Don't worry," he said with a wink as he ran his hand down her back. "I'll find you." Reluctant to let her go, his fingers lingered at her waist as she moved away. He followed her movements, watched her long-legged strides as she walked across the lawn. As he glanced around he realized he wasn't the only man studying the graceful sway of her feminine curves, and he wasn't above recognizing the stab of jealously he experienced at seeing other men appreciate her loveliness.

"Joel." Maggie touched his arm to redirect his attention. "My husband and sons seem to have conveniently disappeared just when I need some help. Do you mind giving me a hand?"

"Sure thing. How can I help?" He followed her up the back steps, through the screened porch, and finally into the kitchen where she pointed to a blue and red cooler filled with ice and assorted soft drinks.

"I need that out of here."

"You know, you really had me going, Joel." Maggie lifted a tray of assorted veggies from the fridge and slid it onto the table. "I thought you were bringing a real date today." She gave a little laugh. "Not your realtor."

"Gwen is my date," he stated, unsure of what Maggie found funny.

She tucked a lock of hair behind her ear and laughed again. "Gwen Marconi has finagled her way into too many neighborhood parties for me to believe that."

Joel stiffened at her levity. "I'm telling you, Maggie. Gwen didn't finagle her way into anything. I invited her."

Maggie studied his expression. "You're not joking?"

He shook his head. "Why is my dating Gwen so hard for you to believe?"

She shrugged. "She's just so different from Beth, that's all."

He jammed his fists into his pockets to hide his irritation. "I'm not looking for another Beth."

"Don't get all defensive on me. I just never thought you'd be attracted to someone like that."

Since she'd already detected his annoyance, he didn't see any reason to keep a lid on it. "Like what? Do you have something against smart, successful, attractive women?"

"Of course not," she returned as she busied herself at the sink and cast him a saucy grin in an obvious attempt to smooth his hackles. "There are, after all, so few of us left to go around."

Her flippancy wasn't fooling him. "Then what's the problem?"

"She just doesn't seem like your type, that's all."

He shook his head in disbelief. "Will you listen to yourself," he said. "What does *my type* mean exactly?" he queried.

She turned away from his scrutiny and collected bottles of catsup, mustard, and relish from the pantry. Her posture and reaction to his displeasure caused him to cut her some slack. She had been his wife's closest friend, after all. "Look, Maggie, I know this must be difficult for you to see me with another woman, but it has been four years since Beth passed away."

"Four years," she breathed as if the span of time took her by surprise. "A day doesn't go by that I don't think about her. I still catch myself picking up the phone to call her."

"I know." Joel placed a comforting hand on Maggie's shoulder. "I've done the same thing."

She patted his hand. "I think it's great that you've started dating again, really I do. And now that you are, I have some friends who will be thrilled to hear it."

"Whoa! Don't even go there." He snatched up the cooler and headed for the back door. "No matchmaking, Maggie. You hear me?" In spite of his adamancy, he knew she wasn't paying the slightest bit of attention to his protests. He could see the wheels turning as she mentally made out her list of eligible friends, and he knew he wouldn't have a moment's peace until he staked his claim on the woman of *his* choice. So he plunked the cooler next to the bar, snatched a beer from another cooler, and headed out to do precisely that.

****

While most of the other women lounged around the pool with their kids or spouses, Gwen wandered solo around the informally landscaped grounds before finally staking claim to the isolated lounge chair to observe the Cartwright Corners gathering from a distance. She kicked off her sandals and slipped off the open turquoise camp shirt to reveal the matching lace-trimmed tank top beneath. It was a beautiful, sunny day. No sense in wasting it.

Ordinarily at a gathering like this she would have been working the crowd, flirting with the men and flattering the women. At the very least she would have been handing out business cards, networking, and making contacts. Today, however, she didn't feel like doing any of those things. She chose instead to put a lid on her gregarious party personality in exchange for a little peace and quiet.

Gwen watched Nick Chapparelle play the congenial host and attentive husband. It was obvious that he and his wife were devoted to one another. Why they were divorced for more than four years before remarrying was a mystery to Gwen. Sitting in the observation seat, she noted their searching glances to seek the other out just to share a smile or a glance. The brief yet poignant exchanges caused a wave of envy so powerful it made Gwen gasp from its intensity and forced her to turn away to keep from staring at something she never expected to experience first hand. Nick and Maggie led a charmed life. From Gwen's point of view they had it all—a stable, loving marriage, a beautiful family, financial security, and a gorgeous home. It wasn't just a gorgeous home; it was the premier house in the neighborhood, the anchor of Cartwright Corners.

Amazed by the renovations Nick had done on the outside since she'd sold it to him four years earlier, Gwen studied the sprawling Craftsman style house with an experienced eye. She hadn't seen the inside yet but Joel insisted the interior was even more spectacular than the exterior. She sighed wistfully and leaned back, closing her eyes. She'd ask Joel for the nickel tour later.

"Penny for your thoughts."

Gwen opened her eyes in time to watch Joel drop his lanky frame on the ground beside her. He plucked a thick blade of grass from near the base of the tree and ran it through his fingers.

Gwen laughed. "They're not worth that much and I don't have change."

Joel's brows lifted over the rim of his sunglasses as he took her hand and intertwined his fingers with hers. "They must be worth enough to cause such a serious expression on this carefree day of sparklers and barbeque."

"What's the story with those two?" She gestured with a nod toward the patio where Nick wrapped his arms around his wife from behind. Maggie snuggled into her husband's embrace as he nuzzled her neck. He whispered something in her ear and she acknowledged him with a nod and an over the shoulder smile. The exchange was over as quickly as it had begun and Nick was off to fire up the grill as Maggie turned her attention to the task of covering the picnic tables with lengths of red, white, and blue checkered oil cloth.

"They're quite a pair, aren't they?" Joel brought her hand to his lips and kissed her palm. "I envy their relationship as much as I admire it." Her fingers curled against the intimate gesture and she couldn't help but wonder if anyone was watching his open display of affection.

"I look at the two of them and wonder what twists and turns their lives have taken to bring them to this particular moment in time. What is it that brought those two back together? A better question would be what caused them to split in the first place?"

"That's Nick and Maggie's story. It's not mine to tell."

"In other words, it's none of my business."

"No, that's not what I'm saying at all." He released her hand and turned to face her as he drew up one leg and rested his forearm across his knee. "Get to know them and you'll understand without being told. There are some people just meant to be together and regardless of the twists and turns their lives take, they always find their way back to one another."

He jumped to his feet and pulled her up and into his arms. The warm scent of his body, the gentle way he gathered her into his embrace, the way his slate-blue eyes danced when he laughed added up to a dangerous combination that scared the hell out of Gwen. She didn't know how to stop herself from falling head over heels for this man. Just like there were some people who were meant to be together, there were also some that shouldn't.

****

By early evening the crowd that had been there earlier had significantly dwindled. Some had other holiday obligations, others headed to the town's annual festival in the park, while only a handful of folks remained at the Chapparelles to watch the community fireworks display from the patio.

Gwen lounged in an Adirondack chair near the pool. Long bare legs with ankles crossed stretched in front of her. Her pink painted toes wiggled with lazy contentment as Em slept sprawled across her.

The child had toddled up to her twenty minutes earlier, whiny and cranky, rubbing her eyes because the older children wouldn't let her play in their game of hide and seek. She crawled onto Gwen's lap and immediately fell asleep. Certain instincts never disappear regardless of how long they lay dormant. Gwen's maternal ones sparked to life the moment the child had come to her for comfort. Without giving her action a second thought, Gwen rocked back and forth in her seat as she rubbed Em's back with slow, soothing circles.

"Here, let me take her from you." Joel came up behind her and started to reach for his sleeping daughter. "You don't look very comfortable."

Gwen raised her hand to stop him. "Don't disturb her."

Joel pulled up another chair and positioned it close beside her. He folded his tall frame into the low, sloping seat and draped his arm across both arm rests, his knuckles brushing across her arm as he fingered his daughter's curls. He eyed the way Em's head lay pressed against the rising swell of her full breast. His gaze narrowed, desire deepening his eyes to dark slate. "Lucky little girl," he murmured.

"Give Gwen a break, Joel," Maggie told him as she walked up with a couple of glasses and a bottle of merlot. "Why don't you take Emme and put her in the boys' room."

Maggie smiled congenially and sat in a chair across from the one Joel had just vacated. Gwen watched her pour the dark wine.

"Samantha is such a sweet girl," said Maggie as she handed Gwen one of the stemmed glasses. "We just love having her around."

"Unlike her mother, you mean?"

Maggie shifted in her seat and gave an uneasy laugh. "I see where Samantha gets her spunk."

"I'm flattered that you think Sam got anything from me." Gwen sipped from the glass, grateful for the pungent warmth the wine supplied.

"Davey's been moping around the house ever since Sam told him she couldn't be here today."

"The tournament she's playing in this week is an important one. A lot of college recruiters will be there," Gwen explained, sounding more defensive than she intended.

"He understands that," Maggie interjected. "But it still doesn't make it any easier when his brother and the rest of his friends have dates today and he's odd man out." Maggie took a long swallow of wine as an uncomfortable silence settled like a heavy curtain between them.

Gwen sensed that her hostess was working up the courage to say something else. Here it comes, she thought as she watched Maggie toss back the last of the wine and set her glass aside.

"You know, Gwen, you're the first woman Joel's shown any interest in since his wife died."

"And you're telling me this because...?"

"It's obvious that he's quite smitten with you."

"I'm fond of him too. He's a special man."

Maggie straightened and leaned forward. "Just how serious are you?"

"Serious enough to keep seeing him in spite of your disapproval," she stated.

"I'm sorry, Gwen, but I have to tell you I think he's making a mistake."

How could she respond to Maggie's declaration when there were times she thought the same thing? It wasn't an arguable point.

They were saved from further conversation when Joel reappeared, carrying a sleepy-eyed Emme. "She woke up the minute I tried to put her on the bed."

"Come here, baby." Maggie held open her arms to the child.

Em squirmed out of her father's arms and headed straight for Gwen. The child promptly climbed into her lap and snuggled against her. With her thumb planted firmly in her cherubic mouth, Emme closed her eyes and promptly fell asleep again.

Joel breathed a soft laugh. "Em knows what she

wants." He bent low and planted a lingering kiss on the top of Gwen's head, whispering, "As does her father."

The fireworks exploding in the distant night sky couldn't compete with the ones going off in Gwen's head. There was nothing more she could do but follow her heart until it broke.

Chapter Eleven

Exactly two weeks later Gwen figured her heart had reached its breaking point.

Joel barely rolled to a complete stop in her driveway before Gwen swung the van door open. Hoping he'd have enough sense not to follow, she hopped out and hastened to the front door as quickly as her heels would allow. She couldn't remember if this was their fifth or sixth date, all she knew was it was bound to be their last.

The ride from the restaurant had been made in a silence so thick and intentional it felt like a separate entity sat between them in the vehicle. Gwen had been grateful for the barrier and wanted it to stay since there wasn't a single word in any language that could defend her behavior.

"Gwen," Joel called out as he climbed out of the driver's side.

As she fumbled in her purse for her keys, she wondered how a bag so small could have so many dark recesses to hide stuff. When she finally found them, they fell from her fingers and landed in a jangled cluster at her feet. She leaned against the door and sobbed. All the stupid things she'd said and done snapped and flashed in her head like a bad video.

"I'm sorry. I'm sorry. I'm sorry," she cried. "Now will you please go away and leave me alone?"

"I'm not going anywhere until you hear me out."

She cringed at his determination. "Let me save you the trouble because there isn't anything that you can say to me that I haven't already said to myself."

"Really?" he questioned. "In that case I hope my apology sounded sincere."

She looked at him as if he'd just sprouted a set of purple horns and grown a green-banded tail. "Excuse me? Why would you apologize to me? I'm the one who acted like a drunken fool."

He considered her for a moment as he adjusted his glasses. "You don't appear the least bit inebriated now."

"Yeah, well, total humiliation has a sobering effect."

"You aren't drunk now because you weren't drunk then. The one cocktail you had before dinner and the glass of house wine you sipped during the meal isn't what caused you to behave the way you did." He picked up her keys and sorted through them. When he found the house key, he unlocked the door and pushed it open, gesturing for her to precede him.

"What you're saying is I don't need a reason to act like a fool?"

Joel expelled a deep sigh of frustration. "That's not what I'm saying." He tugged off his necktie and loosened the top collar button of his dress shirt with a quick flip of his thumb and forefinger.

Gwen wasn't quite sure of what she was witnessing. He gave every indication that he was settling in for what was left of the evening and had every intention of making himself comfortable in the process. The next item of clothing to come off was his suit coat, which he carefully draped over the entryway bench on his way to the living room.

"Why aren't you angry?" Gwen questioned. "I ruined your dinner party. I embarrassed you in front of your friends and colleagues."

"I am angry, make no mistake about that. I'm mad as hell, as a matter of fact." He paced around the living room rubbing the back of his neck and mumbling under his breath.

Aha! Now they were getting somewhere. At least he admitted he was angry, although she had to admit he sure had a funny way of showing it. But then again, she should know by now that this man didn't do anything in a manner she was used to men doing.

"But not at you," he quickly clarified as he positioned himself in one of the winged-back chairs by the front window. He crossed his legs, ankle to knee, and shook his foot with obvious irritation. This was quite possibly the only real indication that he was peeved.

"I'm angry at my so called friends—and myself. I should have guessed something like this would happen and trusted my first instincts about taking you to this party, but I ignored them because *I* wanted you there."

Tears sprang to her eyes as her breath rushed from her lungs. She'd never been struck so hard in all her life, and this man managed it without laying a finger on her. She couldn't speak, she couldn't even move. She'd been struck dumb and paralyzed by his words. She blinked only once and the pooling tears tumbled like fat raindrops down her cheeks. "I think you'd better leave."

"Gwen?" He acted truly surprised by her reaction as he uncrossed his legs and reached her with several long strides. He touched her wet cheek with the back of his knuckles. "What is it?"

"In spite of what some people think, I still have feelings." She sniffled and brushed her fingers across her face, angry with herself for letting him see how his words had affected her.

He frowned. "I know that. Tell me what's wrong. Why are you crying?"

How could such an educated man be so obtuse? "You tell me you knew you shouldn't have taken me tonight, and you don't think I should be upset by that?"

He was thoughtful for a moment. "No, no, you misunderstood. It was the other women who were going to be at the party I didn't trust. A couple of them are, well—to be perfectly blunt—catty bitches. Any woman I showed up with tonight was going to catch their malice. They never gave you a chance. I should have at least warned you. I can only imagine the awful things they said to make you react the way you did."

"I suppose that depends on your definition of awful. Would the comment about you getting back into the dating pool by diving head first into the really *shallow* end qualify? Or how about the crack that I shouldn't have any trouble keeping you from getting in over your head considering the amazing floatation devices I possess. How about that one? Would that meet your criteria for awful? And then there's the bets going down among your colleagues as to how soon you'll dump me when you discover there's nothing to hold your interest from the neck up."

"Who said those things?" he demanded.

She had to give him credit. He sounded genuinely horrified. "What difference does it make? It was said, isn't that enough? And I can't help wondering how much truth there is in their observations." There, now she'd said it.

He tossed his hands in the air. "How am I supposed to respond to that?"

She shrugged. "They're right, you know. We're just too different for anything to ever come of this relationship." Her head was telling her to end it now, but her heart refused to listen.

"That's what makes this relationship interesting. I like our differences...I appreciate them...I value them."

"Some differences," she snorted. "You're a highly respected member of this community. You have a PhD. All facts your colleagues were quick to point out. And that was just for starters."

"I'm sorry about the way they made you feel. They had no right to do that. And I apologize for their behavior, inexcusable as it is. But answer me this—have I ever given you the impression that I'm in any way better than you? Have I ever once treated you like an inferior?"

"Of course not. You've always made me feel good about myself, like I was your equal."

"That's because you are."

"Not according to your friends. They think I'm totally wrong for you. And I'm not so sure they're not right." The only tears she shed now were those of sadness and regret for what was never to be. They slipped slowly and silently down her face. "Tonight should have proved that to you."

"Is that what you were doing tonight?" He reached into his back trouser pocket and produced a folded, white handkerchief. Ever so gently he blotted the soft cotton beneath her eyes. "Were you trying to prove to me and the rest of the world that we don't belong together?"

"We don't. We're like stripes and plaids. No matter how hard you try to get them to go together, they just never seem to look right. If you can't see it now, you will..." She paused then added, "...eventually."

"I beg to differ." He placed his hands on her shoulders and pressed his lips against her forehead. "I think we were made for each other." He slipped his arm around her waist and pulled her closer. The swift, unexpected action snapped her head back and forced her to take a long look at him. His strong, square jaw was set with fierce determination she'd never quite seen before.

His arousal pressed hard and urgent against her belly. Only a thin barrier of silk and wool separated them from the fiery passion that had been building in her since the first day she met him. Her head was sending urgent messages of caution. She would be hurt worse when he inevitably walked away because she cared more this time. And he would. The special ones always did. But her reckless heart was hearing none of the frantic warnings. It led her blindly into the uncharted abyss to explore the dangerous depths of this ill-matched relationship.

Gwen tipped her head and accepted the kiss she'd been waiting for all her life. It was nothing like she imagined it would be. It was everything she wanted it to be and so much more. An indescribable combination of warm, caressing lips and silky, probing tongues danced within the confines of their joined mouths. Husky and trill moans partnered into a passionate duet. The heat of their desires burst into a flaming explosion. Gwen didn't need any further incentive. Without another word, she took his hand and led him toward the stairs.

Joel burst out with a nervous laugh. "Will you listen to me? I feel like a teenager having sex for the first time."

"It is your first time..." she said. "...with me."

"I, ah," he stammered. "I'll be right back!" He pulled his hand from her grasp and headed for the front door.

"Joel?" Gwen breathed, startled and wide-eyed.

He cast a reassuring glance over his shoulder as he crossed the threshold. "I'll be right back. There's something I need to get from my car."

She smiled knowing. "I like a man who comes prepared. I'll be upstairs." Her voice was low and breathless as she turned with a slow and seductive strut. "It's the second door on the left." She took each step with an exaggerated swing of her hips as her manicured fingers slid suggestively up the banister.

He hurried out the door and leaped off the stoop, all the while mumbling, "Second door on the left, second door on the left, second door on the left..." as his fingers fumbled with the keyless remote. Finally unlocked, he yanked open the passenger door and reached for the center console. He threw off the lid and snatched the crinkly plastic bag imprinted with a local pharmacy's logo. Stuffing the package into his pants pocket, he locked the car and swaggered up the front walk with a chipper whistle.

The sound of a vehicle braking close by distracted him. Instinctively, he glanced over his shoulder and discovered Samantha jumping out of a black and silver van, hauling her sports bag behind her.

"Hi, Mr. Hubbard," she greeted as she shut the van's side door and waved as it pulled away and disappeared around the corner.

His smile collapsed at the sound of a bubble bursting in his head. "Hello, Sam. I thought your tournament didn't end until tomorrow." Joel curled his fingers around the package in his pocket as he acknowledged the disappointing fact that he wouldn't be using the contents that evening.

"Yeah, so did I," she said with a disappointed scowl. "We got rained out. They canceled the rest of the tournament." She kicked the toe of her black cross-trainer into the grass. "I hate it when my plans get screwed up like this."

He knew exactly how she felt, but prudently kept his feelings to himself. Afraid Samantha would be able to read his thoughts if he dared voice his sympathy aloud, he just nodded and offered to take her bag. He hoped that lifting something heavy would redirect his energies and expend his pent up frustrations.

Thanks." Samantha gratefully handed off the

cumbersome baggage without argument. “Mom inside?” She bounded up the steps and through the open door. “Mom, I’m home!”

“So I see.” Gwen came down the stairs. She still wore the royal blue silk sheath and dyed to match heels but the waist-whittling belt was missing and her legs were now bare where there had once been flesh-toned pantyhose. A teasing glimpse of flesh-toned lace peeked out from where one front pearly button remained unfastened. As she hugged her daughter, she glanced at Joel and cast him a helpless look that expressed the same disappointment he was experiencing. “Sorry,” she mouthed with a pitiful pout.

He forced an equally pitiful smile as he placed Samantha’s bag on the floor and moved to collect his jacket and tie from the nearby bench. “I’ll say goodnight now.”

“Don’t let my unexpected appearance cut your evening short. I’m beat and there’s a bed with my name on it upstairs. Doing nothing is worse than playing all day.” She hoisted the bag’s strap over her shoulder and took the stairs two at a time. “Goodnight.”

Gwen waited a few extra seconds after she heard Sam’s bedroom door shut before she walked to where Joel stood. Wrapping her arms around his waist, she pressed her cheek to his chest and gave a weak, little laugh as she peered at him through darkened lashes. “I agree with Sam’s sentiment. Doing nothing is most definitely worse than playing.”

Joel gave a short laugh as he wrapped his arms around her. He pulled her closer and brushed a kiss against her temple as he drew a deep breath and exhaled. “I’d invite you back to my place but there’s even less privacy there. Beth’s parents stopped in for a visit and they’re staying until Sunday afternoon.”

He lowered his head and planted warm, wet kisses at the place where the dress exposed the soft flesh of her neck. "You smell wonderful," he whispered. His fingers pulled the silky fabric aside as he continued to follow the gentle slope of her shoulder with exploring lips. His other hand busied itself with cupping her breast and finding the nipple with a playful thumb.

Gwen covered his hand with her own to press it deeper against her aching breast, and she brushed teasing kisses along his jaw and neck.

Joel lowered his hand to creep the slender skirt up her thighs until he found the hem. Slipping his hand under the fabric he found smooth, naked thighs with muscles that flexed and moved restlessly beneath his wandering fingers. He found her deliciously bare and open to his bold explorations.

"My God, Gwen," he breathed. "I want you so much."

"I want you too, but I can't. Not here, not tonight. It's just something I've never done when Samantha's home. House rules, I'm afraid. I can't make exceptions now. Not even for you."

"I understand," he said.

He placed a chaste kiss on her forehead, gave a defeated sigh, and collected his jacket. He was out the door and in his van before she could change her mind.

Chapter Twelve

Less than five minutes after Joel left, Gwen was slipping a slinky, gray satin nightgown over her head. It shimmied over her skin, touching her like a whisper and leaving a trail of aching emptiness. She smoothed the slick fabric over her breasts and hips as it settled down her thighs.

The phone jangled just as she crawled between the sheets. It startled her and caused her heart to jump. Samantha's friends knew better than to call at this late hour, but every once in a while one of them suffered a temporary lapse in memory. One particularly smitten young man came to mind, who not only suffered from an occasional bout of amnesia but also an acute case of puppy love. Gwen was prone to forgive him on occasion as long as he didn't do it too late or too often. Tonight was definitely too late.

Before it rang a second time, she snatched up the phone from the nightstand fully expecting to hear Davey's youthful voice.

"I need to know something," he said.

A thrilling chill slipped down her spine as a husky, much more mature voice caressed her senses. "What's that?"

"Are you feeling what I'm feeling?"

"That depends," she replied. "What are you feeling?"

"I can't stop thinking about you, Gwen. My imagination is working overtime. Everything we didn't get to do tonight is running through my mind. I see you lying naked in my arms and I very much like what I see. I can't wait to use the rest of my senses."

Weak and breathless, Gwen collapsed against the pillows. "Unrealistic fantasies often make for disappointing realities."

"You've already surpassed my fantasies."

A glimmer of an idea began forming in her passion-fogged brain. No mature woman in her right mind would even hint at what she was about to suggest. She would plead temporary insanity if questioned about it later. "Where are you now?" she asked, hoping he wouldn't tell her he was already home.

"Sitting at the light on Main. Why?"

"Will you do something for me without asking a lot of questions?"

"Yeah, sure, I guess..." He sounded hesitant yet more than a little intrigued.

"Turn around and come back. Park your car on the street and meet me at the garage service door."

"Gwen, what are...?"

"No questions..."she cut him off in mid sentence and hung up just as she heard the distinct squeal of tires cutting a sharp u-turn.

Snatching the matching satin wraparound robe and belt from the closet, she slipped her arms into the flowing sleeves as she rummaged in a dresser drawer. Where was it? It had to be there. Although she hadn't needed it for a while, she kept the prescription current for just such an occasion. Aha! Her fingers wrapped around the diaphragm case. A little more digging produced a never been opened tube of spermicide, its expiration date still good. A quick trip to the bathroom eliminated one barrier. Or added one, she amended with a silly grin. As long as Joel was willing to be a little adventurous, the rest of her plan should be a breeze.

Giddy with anticipation, she headed down the

stairs and out the back sliding glass door into the night just as she heard a car crunch in the dirt and gravel along the street curb. A car door slammed and the heels of men's dress shoes paced hurriedly against the rough concrete driveway. "Gwen?" His familiar voice called softly. "Where are you? Gwen?"

A ghostly satin arm snaked out of the garage service entrance and grabbed him by the front of his shirt, yanking him forward. He stumbled into the darkness and into her arms.

"What the—" Warm lips pressed against his own, promptly stifling his startled outburst. He responded accordingly. He sighed as his hands found plenty to do without further prompting. Soft, naked flesh yielded beneath the thin layers of slippery fabric.

He tore his mouth away from hers and rasped, "Did you haul me back just to torture me?"

"No questions," she said as she unbuckled his belt and extracted it from the loops with a quick tug. It hit the floor, coiling soundlessly until the buckle hit the concrete with a distinct metallic clink. She backed up slowly, taking him with her, and worked her way to her sedan. She didn't stop until she felt the pressure of solid, American made steel against her backside.

With one hand she worked her way down the buttons of his shirt while she fumbled behind her to find the passenger side rear door handle. Shifting her hips just enough to open the door, she tugged him into the backseat with her. He caught himself by kneeling on the exposed doorframe and straddled her barely covered hips with his palms.

He gave a sharp laugh. "You can't be serious, Gwen. I'm a grown man. You can't possibly expect me to make love to you in the backseat of this car."

"I am and I do." She pushed his shirt off his shoulders and began to tug his undershirt from the waistband of his slacks. He gave little resistance as she slipped it up his broad back and over his head. A quick flip of her wrist sent the tee to join the dress shirt on the front seat. Her lips planted tantalizing kisses across his chest and she flicked her tongue across his nipples. He shuddered and scooted forward, covering her body with his own. Full-sized vehicle or not, there really wasn't much room for them to move. They were immobilized, unable to maneuver into any position capable of completing what she had started.

"Now what?" Joel asked, his face barely an inch from hers. His tone was gruff, yet she detected more than a hint of mirth sneaking past the sternness. He wiggled just enough to free his right arm from between them, which he slipped under her head to lend support. His left arm was hopelessly tangled between them, although its location was conveniently placed with his palm cupping her left breast. Even the smallest flexion of his trapped fingers was enough to make her nipple stand up with gratitude for the attention. He seemed to realize the happening at the same instance and wiggled his fingers again.

"If I could just scoot up a little," she strained and wiggled her way out from under his full weight. Once her arm was free, she groped between the door and driver's seat until she found the power button adjustment. Slow and steady the seat crept forward to give them enough additional room to loosen their limbs and arrange themselves more comfortably. There was, however, still much work to be done.

Gwen loosened the tie belt at her waist and wriggled her arms out of the robe sleeves.

"You're really serious about doing this?"

"You bet I am." The nightgown was next. She found the hem and began to work it slowly up her hips. The satiny fabric was slick enough to slip between them with very little resistance and once loose she pulled it over her head. "I'll save the strip tease for another time," she told him as she positioned her legs around him. Her breasts glowed pale and perfect in the defused moonlight.

"But I'm not prepared. At least let me go to the car—"

"I got it covered," Gwen assured, kissing him and positioning herself beneath him with a slip and slide and a couple of suggestive wiggles.

"That's probably a good thing because the last time I fumbled with a condom in the back seat of a car I was sixteen, forty pounds lighter and three inches shorter."

"Three inches?" Gwen gasped. "How big is it now?"

"I'll let you be the judge of that." He chuckled.

"This just isn't how I imagined our first time, Gwen," he said on a more serious note.

"But you can't tell me you're not excited at the prospect." She ran her hand up his thigh and filled her palm with his straining bulge.

Then she helped him eliminate the last barrier.

She wrapped her legs around his waist and he slipped inside her.

"You feel so good," he moaned as they settled into a mutually comfortable rhythm. She met each eager thrust with a restless tightening of her legs to pull him deeper and harder.

Stroke after luxurious stroke he brought her nearer and nearer to that elusive destination. The trip was an exhilarating combination of excitement, ingenuity, and titillation as he tensed and shuddered and finally collapsed against her with a hoarse cry. She'd come closer than ever before and she was satisfied.

She sighed and nuzzled her face against his chest. "That was by far the nicest ride I've ever taken in this car."

Joel chuckled and twisted himself to position them on their sides facing each other, she with her back against the rear seat and him teetering on the edge of the seat cushions. He peered at her through the darkness with a concerned frown as he stroked her hip and slid his fingers down her belly until they rested at the juncture of her thighs. With a gentle nudge, he parted her moist cleft and began a slow massage. The pleasant ache returned. "But you didn't—"

She cut him off in mid *didn't* and gently pulled his hand away, as if telling him not to bother. "I've never."

He pulled back and stared at her in disbelief. "Never?"

She confirmed his question with a slow shake of her head. "It's all right," she said softly as she planted a soft kiss on his jaw. "Tonight was for you."

"No, it's not all right," he declared. "This is supposed to be good for you, too."

"It was, Joel. I'm not complaining."

"You damn well should be," he stated. "I feel like I've cheated you somehow."

"Why? I did this for you, not me."

"This is supposed to be a mutually intimate connection, enjoyed by both of us. If I wanted to fly solo I could have stayed home."

She shrugged. "This isn't your fault. I'm just one of those women who can't…you know…climax."

"What kind of crap have the previous men in your life been handing you? There are no such women. There are, however, insensitive, selfish bastards who blame their inability to arouse their partner to orgasm as being the woman's fault."

"It's not that some haven't tried."

"Then they didn't try hard enough." He fell silent for long moments before adding, "Gwen, I may not be the best lover in the world, but I'll always try to be a considerate one. I want you to experience the same pleasure you gave me."

She was touched by his heartfelt declaration. "You just might be the one to crack the code, Dr. Hubbard."

"It won't be for lack of trying," he said as he leaned over and kissed her. "I'm a man on a mission now."

Positioning his long-limbed frame was no easy task considering his pants had worked their way down his thighs and now sat bunched and twisted around his legs from ankle to calf. There was something so utterly ridiculous about the whole situation, his shoulders started shaking, which transferred to his chest, then rumbled up his throat until he was laughing so hard he shook himself right off the edge of the seat. He crashed to the floor, which jammed him into an even more absurd position. He laughed all the harder.

Creeeeak... The sound of the service door inching open stifled his humor.

"What was that?" Joel questioned, pushing himself up enough to grab his pants and begin the arduous task of tugging them up. Lift and tug, lift and tug. He didn't remember it being this much trouble getting them off.

"What?"

"That noise..." Lift and tug, lift and tug. "Didn't you hear it?"

"I didn't hear anything." She reached for the hem of her robe and clutched it to her nakedness as a precaution, feeble and inadequate though the attempt was considering most of the fabric was still bunched beneath her.

Creeeeak...

"There it is again?" Joel backed out of the car feet first and finished hiking up his trousers as he touched solid ground.

There came a blood-curdling yowl when his foot hit the pavement. A screaming bundle of fur hurled itself in the air, ricocheted off the car's rear quarter panel, and lunged straight for Joel's head. The weight of the animal pushed against his shoulder as sharp claws sliced across his neck.

"What the hell," he yelped as he threw his arms up to ward off his furry attacker. Joel pitched himself back into the car, taking Gwen with him. He drew himself around her and pulled the door shut behind them, pinning her under his weight as he tucked her into the protection of his arms.

"Wha..." was all she managed to utter before he clamped his hand across her mouth.

"Shhhh," he hissed in her ear. "Be quiet. There's something out there. I think it's a wild animal."

Gwen's eyes grew enormous. Not from any fear of wild animals but from the simple fact she couldn't breathe. His big hand not only covered her mouth but totally blocked her nostrils. She struggled and fought to free herself from his smothering grasp.

"Will you stop struggling?" he whispered.

Yanking a hand free, she clawed his fingers away and gulped a lungful of air. "I couldn't breathe!" She gasped and wheezed.

"Sorry," he said. "You all right?" he asked as he lifted his head to peer out the window. He immediately ducked down again. "There's somebody out there."

"Your wild animal is probably just the neighbor's cat, Muffin. He wanders in here all the time when the door's left open."

"Unless Muffin stands over five feet tall on his hind legs there's something or somebody bigger standing in the doorway."

"That would be my neighbor, Elsie Miller. She knows her cat comes in here."

"Muffin?" The woman clucked and called for her cat. "Here kitty, kitty…Muffin, are you in here?"

A slow, cautious shuffle worked its way further into the dark garage. "Yep, that's Mrs. Miller," Gwen confirmed.

"Muffin, did you come in Gwen's garage again?"

Joel buried his face against Gwen's breast to stifle a snicker.

"Stop that?" She gave his shoulder a nudge. "We can't let her find us here," Gwen exclaimed in a panicked whisper. "I'm naked!"

"So I noticed," Joel husked as he nuzzled her neck and shifted his leg to let her know just how much he noticed. "And if you don't stop wiggling," he growled. "Muffin won't be the only one coming in your garage again."

Chapter Thirteen

Joel found Nick in the converted stables, now a state-of-the-art mechanics dream garage situated behind Nick's house. The top half of Nick's body was buried under the front end of his latest sideline project—an orangey-brown, primer-coated '57 Chevy convertible. Joel rapped his knuckles on the front fender to get his friend's attention.

Nick dug his sneaker heels against the concrete floor and rolled himself out from under the jacked-up front end. "Hey, buddy," he said as he climbed off the creeper and grabbed a rag to wipe the grease off his hands.

"I was surprised when Maggie told me you were home."

"Two blown engines during trials convinced me I wasn't supposed to race this weekend. So I packed up my broken toys and left." He gave a that's-the-way-it-goes shrug.

"So how'd your party go last night?" Nick asked as he opened a nearby refrigerator and grabbed two long necks.

Joel accepted the beer Nick handed him and twisted the cap. "Does the term fiasco mean anything to you?"

"What happened?" Nick chuckled. "Your colleagues *roast* you a little too well-done?"

"If they would have stuck to roasting me, it would have been fine. But they decided to roast Gwen as well. In defense of herself, she turned the tables and played the intoxicated vamp to the bitter end."

Nick's only response was a hissing wince.

"By the time I dragged her out she had every man in the room panting and every woman ready to plunge a steak knife into her back." With a quick toss of his head, he sucked down half the bottle in one long swallow.

"I thought she'd toned down that flamboyant side of hers since the two of you started dating." Nick leaned against the tool-strewn workbench and crossed his feet at the ankles.

"I'd never seen that side of her before last night. That was not the Gwen Marconi I know."

"Sooner or later, it was bound to come out."

"So what if her past is a little tarnished. She's smart and beautiful, and she's managed to build a decent life for herself and her daughter."

Nick held up his palm in defense. "Hey, man, you don't have to defend Gwen to me. I like her."

"Yeah, well, Maggie doesn't."

"She's coming around. Give her time. She's looking at this from a whole different perspective than you or me."

"Gwen is obviously seeing it from the same female perspective because she was ready to call it quits last night. Why do woman always think they know what's better for us than we do?"

Nick raised his eyebrows and dropped his jaw. "Have you forgotten I'm married to the queen diva of that particular song and dance? I dangled at the end of her *'I'm doing this for your own good'* rope for four long, frustrating years. I hope you were able to convince Gwen otherwise."

"Oh, I think we managed to work it out and reach a mutually agreeable compromise." He took another slow sip from his beer as he recalled their impetuous passion.

"Works for me." Nick lifted his nearly empty bottle in a salute before he downed the remainder of the brew, tossed the dead soldier into the trash, and reached for another.

"What? What works for you?" Joel didn't think he'd revealed too much by what he'd said.

"Sounds to me like you and Gwen danced to a much different tune than "Breaking Up is Hard to Do."

Wearing a sly smirk he couldn't disguise as anything but what it was, he conceded, "Well... it wasn't my dad's '64 Chevy, but we managed a pretty respectable version of the backseat tango."

"The mini van?" Nick croaked as he straightened his posture.

"The Lincoln," Joel confessed as he stared down the barrel of the bottle to keep himself from smiling outright at the memory. He knew he'd never be able to look at a luxury sedan or a two-car garage the same way ever again. Just thinking about it now was causing him some growing discomfort.

"You old hound dog!" Nick chortled.

"*Old* being the operative word," Joel interjected. "I never knew this pushin' forty body could still bend like that."

Of course, that same body that moved like a horny teenager the night before had rebelled in a number of painful ways that morning. He awoke with scraped knees, bruised elbows and an extremely tender lumbar region, any one of which would have been impossible to account for coming from a staid dinner party at the country club. The nasty scratch on his neck from Muffin's startled ambush was difficult enough to explain to his keen-eyed ex mother-in-law. It might as well have been a screaming purple hickey for all the questions he fielded from Elle Mahoney. But, in spite of it all, he'd do it all again in a New York minute if given the same opportunity with the same woman. He would, however, most assuredly prefer it without the elderly Mrs. Miller and her wanderlust tabby.

Nick lifted his beer in a toast. “Here’s to the women who keep us young and limber.”

“I’ll drink to that.” Joel clinked his bottle against Nick’s. “If they don’t kill us first,” he added as he placed the bottle to his lips.

Nick’s hearty laughter rose up and echoed off the high-beamed metal roof.

Joel’s wasn’t too far behind.

****

Joel’s next stop later that afternoon was Gwen’s real estate office. He had a plan and was eager to present it to her.

He motioned to the young woman sitting at the reception desk to be quiet and whispered that he was here to see Gwen. She nodded and gestured for him to go on back.

Joel pitched the manila envelope from the doorway. It sank like a weighted Frisbee and landed on her desk with a dull smack. Loose papers flew everywhere, some fluttering to the floor.

Startled, Gwen looked up. Her heart did a crazy lurch at the sight of Joel leaning against the partition wall wearing a lazy smile. She felt like a young girl in the throes of her first crush. It was a wonderful, scary feeling after all these years.

“What’s this?” she asked as she pushed it aside to gather and reorganize the scattered mess he’d created.

“Open it and find out,” he urged, coming nearer.

Gwen cast the large envelope a curious glance before letting her gaze wander to the sexy man resting a thigh on the corner of her desk. She pressed open the metal clip and slipped her fingers into the opening. She touched what felt like the slick cover of a magazine. Grasping it between her fingers, she cast him a suspicious glance as she slid it out just far enough to read the title, which was all she needed to know the contents of the publication—an adult toy catalog. A hot flush crept up her neck and colored her cheeks like a tropical sunburn. The suggestive publication was released and allowed to drop into its almost plain brown wrapper.

"Are you blushing?" he asked with surprise as he started to chuckle. He touched her warm cheek with warmer fingers. "I love it."

Gwen set the envelope and its suggestive contents on the desk and politely pushed it aside. "I'm so glad you find my *condition* amusing." She was humiliated, and he was laughing.

His laughter quickly faded. "I find your condition charming, arousing, and even a little surprising, but never amusing," he said as he ran the back of his knuckles across the curve of her tight jaw. "I just thought maybe a few props would help make the process more fun."

"Process? Props?" she reiterated. "I'm not a project. I don't want to be what you did on your summer vacation." She picked up the envelope and handed it to him. "Thanks, but no thanks," she told him.

"Is there somewhere we can go?" He glanced around her partitioned, doorless office. "And discuss this with a little more privacy?"

She shook her head. "I have work to do." She turned her attention to the stack of papers on her desk. The print blurred in spite of her concerted effort to focus on the swimming words and figures. The man was driving her to distraction. Correction, the man *was* the distraction.

As much as she wanted to be irritated, she was a little turned on by his offer. He had obviously given her *problem* some thought. All right, if she wanted to be perfectly honest with herself, she was more than a little turned on by his thoughtfulness. She was downright squirming in her seat. If his intention was to start her thinking about the unlimited possibilities he was offering, it was working. Big time. She never felt so sexually aware of a man before. She'd played the role of seductress many times. That she was on the receiving end of the seduction this time was a new experience for her.

"I'm not suggesting we go high tech or even battery-operated." His intimate tone sent wicked tremors down her spine. "We could start out with something simple, like massage oils or sensual body powder and a feather."

"Are you saying you're not man enough to do the job without party favors, Doctor Hubbard?"

He leaned closer, his lips at her ear, his breath hot and teasing as he whispered, "Are you tossing down the gauntlet, Ms. Marconi?" His husky tone shot through her like a lightning bolt.

"Yes," she breathed as she gripped the edge of her desk, trying desperately to control her traitorous body. This man was causing some major hormone surges, and she wasn't sure how to deal with them. Sex for her had always been about teasing and pleasing the man. The control had always been hers. Now this man was trying to take that control away. He was stripping away her power and leaving her vulnerable to his advances.

A myriad of unknown emotions battled inside her head, translating into waves of equally alien sensations to course through her body. For the sake of her sanity and self-preservation, she had to salvage at least a fragment of that control.

Gwen took a deep breath, stared into his steely blue gaze, and said, "Are you *up* for doing it the old fashioned way?"

"If this room had real walls and a door that locked, I'd show you just how *up* I am," he said. His voice was dangerously low and guttural. "Last night was just an appetizer for us, Gwen. I'm ready to serve up the main course.

"More than ready," he added as he scooted forward on her desk to give her an unobstructed view of the bulge in his jeans. With his back to the doorway, he positioned himself in a way that blocked his next action from anyone else's view. She watched as he ran a fingertip around the scooped neckline of her knit shell, stopping only to plunge his index finger into the rising swell of her abundant cleavage. He withdrew and sank it into the fleshy divide again, and again. Perspiration trickled between her breasts, lubricating his action.

She felt like Sleeping Beauty waking from a hundred year nap. His touch awakened her like the Prince's kiss, and in some very real way he was awakening something else. Every nerve ending tingled and twinged through her aching breasts and shot straight south. She squirmed in her seat like a restless child as liquid warmth pooled between her thighs. She shifted again. Something wonderful pulsed through her, leaving her feeling both weak and invigorated.

He plunged one final time, grazing the soft underside of her breast with a crooked finger, and then withdrew slowly, letting his fingertips graze ever so lightly across her pebbled nipple.

Devastated, as cool air replaced the heat of his searing touch, she shivered from the chilling gooseflesh marching across her breasts as she licked her lips and questioned, "When's dinner?"

Chapter Fourteen

"So, what do you think?" Gwen questioned in her no nonsense realtor voice as she climbed behind the wheel of her Lincoln. She'd scheduled Joel for a house-hunting afternoon just to get him alone for a few hours. This time they spent together wasn't perfect, but it was better than what they'd managed to put together in the last nine days. Ever since his promise to take her to ecstasy, they hadn't managed enough time alone for him to take her to the movies. Gwen found it difficult not to laugh at the irony. Man on a mission? Hah! It was more like mission impossible.

"I can't take much more of this," Joel groaned as he yanked the seatbelt across his chest and snapped the buckle into place. Each gruff syllable came out sounding like they were sandblasted from his gut.

Gwen's heart went out to him. She'd rarely met a man who enjoyed house-hunting. "There's just one more to see," she assured him. In an attempt to soothe his irritation, she started the car and inserted a mellow jazz CD into the player. The air was quickly filled with the soulful moans of a lonely saxophone. Joel promptly shut it off.

Gwen found no reason to comment on his abrupt action. Some people didn't like jazz. Joel was obviously one of them.

"We've seen several really nice houses today. Have you seen anything you like?"

He heaved a loud sigh. "What do you think of this last one?" His attitude was far from interested and anything but enthusiastic—two surefire signs this wasn't the house for him.

"Oh, no," she chuckled, shaking her head. "I don't offer that kind of advice to a client."

"Don't think of me as a client, think of me as the man who wants to rock your world."

The look he cast her made everything inside her turn to liquid. "All the more reason to keep my opinions to myself," she told him with a sly, sideward glance.

Joel barked a laugh. "Do you have any idea how hard it's been walking into all these bedrooms and knowing there's nothing I can do to you in any of them?"

"No," she said with a playful pout as she slid a hand up his thigh. "Tell me how *hard* it's been?" She kneaded the tense muscle beneath her fingers.

"You're not helping," he growled. "And stop that," he added. Lifting her hand from his leg, he moved it to the steering wheel.

"Stop what," she questioned as she licked her upper lip with a languid swipe of her tongue.

"If you don't stop looking at me like that I'm going to bite the buttons off your blouse," Joel told her through clenched teeth.

She could see he was fighting for self-control as she shifted the car into gear. Changing the subject might be the best course of action for both of them. She was ready to bite a few buttons herself.

"This next place just came on the market this morning. The listing sounds perfect for your needs. The house is in Cartwright Corners—just down the street from Nick and Maggie's as a matter of fact. It's a six-year-old, two-story brick Colonial with a separate entrance in-law apartment that could easily be converted into an office suite."

Knowing the owners were out of town, Gwen pulled into the driveway and opened the front door with the key from the lock box. She stepped aside to let Joel enter first and closed the door behind her. Placing her business card on the table in the foyer, she gestured to the formal living room and began her spiel.

"This house has everything you need, and more," she said. "It has three natural fireplaces—"

He followed so close she felt his breath on her neck. The heat of his body emanated through his clothes as her heartbeat thundered in her ears. She moved on autopilot—conditioned over the years from doing the same thing over and over—and managed to walk him through the dining room and kitchen without conscious effort as she pointed out features she thought he would find important.

"I have it on good authority that the owners are anxious to sell."

It wasn't until they were climbing the staircase to the second floor did she realize she'd been the only one talking. Joel hadn't uttered more than an occasional grunt to indicate he was paying attention. She forced herself to keep talking and moving. It was an effort she found more and more difficult to maintain. Without so much as a word or a single touch, the man beside her was draining her of the last shreds of professionalism she possessed. Gwen hastened her pace to place some space between them and give her a chance to catch her breath.

"Oh my," she breathed the moment she stepped into the master bedroom. She'd seen a lot of spectacular houses over the years, and it took a lot to impress her these days, but she couldn't determine if it was the whole house or just this room that captivated her and captured her imagination.

The master suite was exquisite. Designed with a couple's comforts in mind, it boasted a spacious bathroom, a separate dressing room, and huge his and her walk-in closets. The soft, indirect lighting enhanced the rich, jewel-tone hues of the room's decor.

As if in a trance, the heat of her thoughts spread through her like wildfire as she stared at the king-sized bed draped in an exquisite sapphire silk spread. Her breasts rose and fell with every labored breath she drew. She had to get out of there before she flung herself across the bed and screamed for him to take her right there and then.

"Step away from the bed," Joel whispered behind her in a grating tone that should have prompted her into immediate action. She was rooted to the spot instead, her limbs shaky and weak. His arms snaked around her waist and tugged her tight against his chest as he buried his lips against her hair.

"Why, Doctor Hubbard, this is so unprofessional," Gwen murmured as she leaned against him and settled into his embrace. The perfection of the way their bodies fit amazed her every time he held her.

"Uh huh," he mumbled as he drew her hair aside and nibbled on her neck. "It's my prescription for what ails us."

"This is a nice bedroom," she commented as her gaze fell to one of the fireplaces she'd mentioned earlier. A bedroom fireplace had always been a long-standing favorite fantasy of hers. If he didn't want the house, she just might be tempted to buy this one herself.

"Very nice," he agreed as his fingers inched her slim skirt up her thighs.

Busy fingertips slipped under the bunched hem and cupped her silk-covered mound. The heat of his touch seeped through the flimsy fabric of her panties as he slowly stroked between her legs. Gwen rocked harder against his hand. Everything inside her coiled tighter and tighter as sensuous tendrils of white-hot heat licked through her like fire dancing down the wick of a stick of dynamite. Every heartbeat, every trilling whimper pushed her nearer and nearer to the heart of the explosion.

Their phones went off almost simultaneously. They jumped apart as each cursed and searched for their respective cell.

Gwen found her shoulder bag on the floor near the bed and fished her phone out of the side pocket with trembling fingers. She glanced at the display and took a slow, calming breath before she finally answered. Samantha never called unless it was important.

"Hey, Sweetie," she breathed, smoothing her skirt down her quivering thighs as she sat on the edge of the bed and crossed her legs in an effort to stop the throbbing ache. She watched Joel drag his phone from his pocket and leave the room as he answered. He, too, appeared shaken and unsteady.

"Hi, Mom." There was a pause before Samantha asked, "You sound out of breath. You okay?"

Gwen drew a deep breath. "I'm fine. What's up?"

"Davey and his family are going to the Dells for a couple of days and they invited me to go along. Can I?"

"When?" Gwen questioned.

"They're leaving later this afternoon. Please, can I go? We'll be back in plenty of time for my tournament this weekend."

"I guess it'll be all right." This wasn't the first time the Chapparelles had invited Samantha to join them on a family outing. Gwen glanced at her watch. "I'll be home in half an hour to give you money and help you pack."

"I'm already packed," Sam confessed with a laugh. "But I'll wait around for the cash."

Gwen grinned at her daughter's cheekiness. "Brat," she said.

"Yep, that's me. Oh, got to go. There's another

call coming in. Bye." She clicked off before Gwen had a chance to respond. Some things never change. From the day she entered the world feet first, her energetic daughter was always two steps ahead of Gwen.

Gwen stood and smoothed the bedspread. The raw, nubby silk felt rough under her sensitized fingertips. The subtle scent of Joel's cologne lingered on her hair and skin and it made her smile. This sudden turn of events might be just what the *doctor* ordered.

"That was Maggie," Joel explained. "They're taking the kids to the Dells and want to take Em with them."

"They're taking my daughter, too." Gwen cast him a sly grin. "You know what that means don't you?"

A slow, wicked smile lit his face. "I finally get to bite your buttons?"

****

"Well, they're gone," Gwen said as she stood at the curb and continued waving long after the RV carrying Nick and Maggie, their four kids, Samantha and Em, and enough supplies to sustain the troops was out of sight.

"Yep, sure looks like it," Joel agreed as he shoved his hands into his pants pockets and rocked back on his heels.

Gwen grabbed Joel's hand and tugged him toward the house. "So what are we waiting for?" The second the words were out of her mouth, Gwen slapped manicured fingers across her mouth to stifle a nervous giggle. She really hadn't meant to sound so eager. Okay, if she was going to be perfectly honest with herself, maybe she had.

Joel was having none of it and wouldn't budge. He gave her hand a gentle tug and smiled. "Slow down, honey. We've got all night."

The thought of Joel lying beside her, their limbs entangled, waking up with him, turned her internal thermostat up a couple of critical degrees and the increased temperature was doing some crazy things. The heat coiled low in her belly and radiated in every direction. No man had ever made her so aware of her sexuality. Her body sizzled from the waves of current shooting through her.

Gwen took a deep breath and smiled. He gave her one in return. It was a lazy grin filled with so much promise. Gwen could hardly keep from jumping him right there in the front yard. Wouldn't that give the neighbors something to talk about?

"I thought we'd have dinner first."

Dinner? Was he serious? His suggestion was so mundane, so incredibly ordinary; it took her by complete surprise and she barked a startled laugh. For the second time in almost as many minutes, she clamped a hand across her mouth.

"You find something funny about our having dinner?" His question was delivered with a generous dose of undisguised humor. Slate-blue eyes sparkled behind steel-rimmed glasses as his grin evolved into a full-blown smile. Deep ridges creased his cheeks and framed his wonderfully expressive mouth. Swirling heat pooled between her thighs. He really had to stop looking at her like that.

She shook her head. "It just took me by surprise, that's all."

"Inasmuch as I want nothing more than to drag you off to bed and ravish that lovely body of yours, right now there's something I want even more."

How could he think about food at a time like this? While she burned for his touch, ached for his embrace, all he could think about was his next feeding. There was something so oddly ironic about the situation; she couldn't help the biting sarcasm from creeping into her tone. "What's that?" she questioned. "A medium rare porterhouse with steak fries and sautéed mushrooms?"

His knuckles trailed down the curve of her clenched jaw. The contact she'd craved helped soothe her mild irritation. She closed her eyes and breathed the clean, sharp scents of soap and musk emanating from his warm skin.

"I can fix something here," she suggested on a breathless whisper. The man was driving her to the edge of total sexual meltdown and there was nothing she could do to prevent it. On second thought, there was nothing she wanted to do to prevent it. She rather liked the state of arousal he'd awakened. The last thing in the world she wanted right then was to share him with a restaurant full of strangers and a pesky waitress.

"We'd never get past the salad," he stated.

"Why are we standing here debating the issue?" Gwen questioned.

"Because the journey can be every bit as exciting as the destination."

"Just tell me what you want?"

"I want you squirming with unbridled anticipation when I finally take you to bed," he told her in a tone so low and raspy she felt it as much as she heard it. He kissed her temple. A shiver coursed through her as his breath feathered down her cheek.

"You have that already," she said as she swallowed hard in an effort to slow her racing pulse.

"Good," was his only response as he intertwined his fingers with hers and led her toward his van. "So what'll it be, Mariano's or Keeley's?"

Gwen started to follow his lead without question. There wasn't an ounce of fight left in her, and that realization scared her. Her days of letting a man tell her what to do were long over.

Gwen yanked her hand away and started for the house as she tossed an alternative over her shoulder.

"How about having a pizza delivered instead?"

"A pizza with the works sounds good," he agreed, following her up the front walk.

"I only like cheese and sausage."

"Cheese and sausage it is—thick crust, with antipasto salad and a bottle of Chianti."

"I prefer beer with my pizza," she stated as she stepped across the threshold. "And thin crust, not thick."

As the storm door hissed shut on its hydraulic hinge, Joel pulled her into his arms and frowned as he questioned, "Are you intentionally trying to be difficult?"

"Is that what you think I'm doing?" Gwen snuggled into his embrace and secretly smiled at the way she was able to mold her soft curves to his hard, muscled planes. A perfect fit.

"As a matter of fact I do. I say potato and you insist on saying po-tah-to. I say tomato—"

"And I say to-mah-to," she finished. "I'm sorry, Joel. It's just that it's been a long time since I've had pizza with anyone other than Sam, and she won't eat it any other way. You might convince me to add some mushrooms and peppers to that pizza, but I draw the line at anchovies."

"You just made yourself a deal. Call in the order while I go get the beer. Do you have a preference for any particular brand?"

She shook her head as she scrolled through her phone file. "Buyer's choice."

"And don't bother having it delivered," Joel told her as he headed for the door. "I'll just pick it up while I'm out. Where are you ordering it?"

"Pete's Pizza on Main," she answered as she kissed him and sent him on his way.

The phone rang less than thirty seconds after she'd placed the order. Probably just Pizza Pete calling to verify her order, she reasoned as she answered.

"Hel-lo," she trilled, feeling exceptionally pleased with herself and the world around her. She couldn't hide her happiness if she tried.

"Gwen baby, is that you?"

The happiness she'd felt just moments ago slipped away like smoke in the wind. In its place there settled a sick, cold knot in the depths of her stomach as the dreadful memories connected to that voice tumbled in her head.

"Terry," she gasped.

"I knew you couldn't forget me, babe. I'll be there real soon to finish this reunion face to face."

"Where are you?" How she forced herself to sound normal she didn't have a clue.

"I'm in Indiana."

"Could you be more specific?" she snapped. She hated him for stripping away her hard-earned happiness, and he caught the full brunt of her resentment.

"I'm at a rest area on I-65 just outside of Lafayette."

It didn't make her feel much better knowing he was still a good ninety miles away. "How did you find us?"

"It's amazing what a person can find on the internet these days. Imagine my surprise when I googled Samantha Hudson and discovered our little girl has turned into quiet a star athlete?"

Gwen squeezed her eyes shut at how easy it had been for him to find them. "She's very talented," Gwen confirmed.

"Lemme talk to her," he said in that demanding tone Gwen remembered all too well. As she recalled, *please* and *thank you* were never parts of Terry's vocabulary. Time obviously hadn't improved his manners any. Somehow that didn't surprise her. One of the reasons she'd left him was because she knew he'd never change.

She wouldn't think twice about lying to protect her daughter, but she found the fact that she didn't have to exceedingly satisfying. "She's not here."

"Don't give me that," he barked.

"It's true. She left with friends for Wisconsin late this afternoon."

"I have every right to talk to my daughter."

"You gave up that right a long time ago."

"You can't stop me from seeing her."

Gwen couldn't see straight. An angry red haze swept across her line of vision. "We had a deal, Terry."

"I got a friend who's a lawyer. She told me I can fight you for custody since you're the one who took her away."

"Did you happen to mention to your friend that you signed away your parental rights when she was nine months old?"

"As a matter of fact I did. She said it didn't matter. All I have to do is claim I signed under duress."

"Duress?" Gwen choked on the word. "As I recall, you couldn't scribble your name fast enough."

"The way I remember it, you didn't give me much choice."

"You sure as hell did have a choice and you chose the one that let you off the hook."

"It's your word against mine."

"You never wanted to be a father. It's a little too late to try and be one now. If you care about Samantha at all you'll keep doing what you've been doing for the last fifteen years—stay away."

Then she hung up. She didn't want to hear his response. She didn't want to hear another word out of him. But she feared against all reason that she hadn't heard the last of him. She stared at the phone, hoping and praying it wouldn't ring again.

Chapter Fifteen

Joel suspected there was a problem the minute he returned. That Gwen never looked up or acknowledged his arrival was his first clue that something was wrong. He stood in the doorway and watched her drum manicured fingertips on the counter in an agitated tattoo as she stared at the phone with a worrisome expression that bothered him. Not wanting to catch her unaware, he cleared his throat and rustled the bag in his hand in an effort to make his presence known.

"Joel—" she said, sounding startled yet relieved. She looked at him as though he was the last person she expected to see. "I never heard you come in."

Without a word, he set the pizza box on the island counter and slid the six-pack into the fridge as he watched her lift the pizza box lid with a preoccupied frown marring her lovely brow.

"Something wrong with the pizza?"

"No. It looks great," she said. Unconvincingly, he noted.

He sidled beside her and nudged her with his hip to get her attention. All she did was cast him a watered-down smile and step out of his way. He'd enjoyed the close contact in spite of her less than enthusiastic reaction.

"A penny for your thoughts," he offered.

"I told you once before they're not worth that much," she told him as she moved to the other side of the island.

"They are to me." Coming around to close the distance between them once more, he gave another little nudge—this time with his shoulder. “Did something happen while I was gone?”

She cast him a surprised glance. “Why do you ask?”

“Well, for starters, your face is a dead giveaway that’s something is bothering you. What is it?” Then a disturbing thought hit him. “Are you having second thoughts about tonight?”

“No,” she said softly, shaking her head.

“It’s all right if you are.” He urged her to look at him. The sadness in her expression twisted his gut. He couldn’t bear to see her so upset and hoped he wasn’t the cause of it. “The world won’t come to an end if it doesn’t happen, you know.”

He fingered a strand of hair from her cheek. His knuckles lingered against her soft skin. “If I’m pushing too hard or if you feel pressured in any way, you need to tell me, honey.”

The way she looked at him, all soft and sorrowful, made his heart skip a couple of noticeable beats. He wasn’t sure he wanted to hear what she had to say, after all.

She caressed his cheek. Her fingertips lingered on his jaw. “You are such a good, kind, wonderful man, Joel Hubbard.”

“And you are a beautiful, exciting, fascinating woman,” he said as he nuzzled her neck. “What’s your point?” Her pulse quickened beneath his lips.

“I don’t deserve you.”

“What is it going to take…” he whispered as he kissed her just below her ear. “…to convince you…” He planted another kiss lower near her collarbone. “…I’m here because I want to be?”

“What I don’t understand is why when there are so many other women out there with a lot less baggage.”

He studied every smooth curve of her far-too-serious expression and wondered what had turned her from the confident, loving woman he'd left into this insecure, nervous individual he found on his return.

He pushed off the counter and paced to the other side of the room before whirling to face her. "Correct me if I'm wrong, but didn't we already have this conversation weeks ago?"

"I suppose we did," she conceded.

"Then as far as I'm concerned the subject is closed."

"You're right," she quietly conceded. "I'm sorry I brought it up."

Her passive concession pushed him to a breaking point. "Damn it, Gwen," he shouted. "I don't want an apology from you."

She flinched and backed away. "What do you want from me?"

"An explanation for starters would be nice."

"I think you should leave."

Joel took her hands before she could retreat further. They trembled under his grasp. "Gwen honey, what happened while I was gone?"

"You shouldn't be here."

"Which means what, exactly?"

She tossed her hands in the air and waved them in a frustrated gesture. "Because I'm a train wreck waiting to happen, that's why. You don't want to be anywhere near me when I derail."

Her frustration was contagious. He was feeling it too—frustrated and confused. "What are you talking about?"

"His call was an omen."

"Whose call?"

"My ex."

"Now we're getting somewhere," he muttered. "Which one?"

"Which one—" she sputtered.

Her throaty laughter made him grin. "It's a fair

question."

She bowed to his logic. "It was Terry, Samantha's father."

"What made him call now, if you don't mind my asking?"

"He wanted to talk to Samantha—or so he said."

"You don't believe he wants is to reconnect with his daughter?"

"No, I do not." With a heavenward roll of her eyes, she collapsed into a chair and sank her chin onto the heel of her fist. "Terry wanted a lot of things when we were together—having children was never one of them."

Thinking this could be a long story, Joel grabbed two beers from the fridge and handed her one. "You want a glass?" he asked as he slipped the pizza from the counter to the table. They might as well eat while they talked.

She waved off his offer as she tipped her head and took a long swallow. "What makes him think he can waltz into our lives after all these years and expect to be greeted with open arms by either one of us?"

"Has Samantha ever asked about him?"

Gwen shook her head. "Not since she was little."

"What did you tell her when she asked about her father?"

Gwen visibly stiffened. "I never bad-mouthed him, if that's what you're thinking."

"I'm just curious, that's all."

Gwen expelled a deliberating breath. "I told her he died. I figured telling her that was simpler than trying to explain why there was a man out there who would have sooner seen me abort than carry to term. If he tries to see her now, I don't know what I'm going to do."

Joel took Gwen's hand and gave it a reassuring squeeze. "You're going to tell her the truth.

Samantha's a bright, young woman. She'll understand why you did what you did."

Tears glistened in her eyes. "He threatened to take her away from me." Real fear wrapped around her every word.

"That's not going to happen. You might not be able to stop him from seeing her, but I can't imagine there's a judge in the world who'd grant him custody at this late stage. I have an old army buddy who specializes in family law. I can give Rick a call if you'd like."

She shook her head against the idea. "Let's wait and see what happens."

****

After three beers and enough pizza to leave her blissfully mellow and teetering on the brink of uncomfortably full, Gwen managed to dump all residual thoughts of Terry Hudson into the outside trash can with the empties.

Appreciating the peace and quiet of twilight settling over the neighborhood, she lingered in the driveway. Lightning bugs twinkled in the bushes as the pesky drone of mosquitoes buzzed around her head. She shooed them away with a swipe of her hand and a lazy flick of her wrist.

Clouds of black smoke billowed over the neighbor's fence, informing Gwen her bachelor neighbor was attempting to dazzle his latest lady love with his masterful barbequing skills again.

Joel snuck up on her from behind and wrapped his arms around her. "Trying to decipher the smoke signals?"

She relaxed into his embrace and chuckled. "It's the same old story. And it's not a pretty one."

"That sounds ominous." He took her hand and led her to the two-seater swing sitting in the front yard.

"There's nothing ominous about a man turning a

choice cut of beef into a piece of charred shoe leather."

Joel shuddered. "But it should be criminal," he pronounced as he drew her down beside him and wrapped his arms around her. Settling her against his chest, he locked his hands around her waist.

She snuggled against him and rested her head on his shoulder. She felt his breath in her hair, the beat of his heart at her back, and she closed her eyes and sighed as she folded her arms across his and melted into his comforting embrace.

"This has always been my favorite time of day."

"It is nice," she mumbled around a sleepy yawn. The gentle swaying of the swing nudged her closer and closer to the brink of slumber.

"Am I going to have to carry you to bed?" His voice was heavy with innuendo, shooting a jolt of desire through her from head to toe. She suddenly wasn't tired any more. On the contrary, her body thrummed with awakening. There wasn't a part of her that didn't tingle from images flashing through her mind's eye. Carrying her to bed was just the opening scene of what she hoped was a long-running play.

Shielded from prying eyes beneath their overlapping arms, he caressed the underside of her breast with slow, lingering strokes. She'd never considered that part of her body particularly sensitive before, but under his tender explorations, she found his touch especially arousing.

The close by slamming of a vehicle door momentarily distracted her from Joel's subtle seduction and she slowly glanced toward the street. She stiffened in Joel's arms and sat up to get a better look. "I don't believe it."

"Terry Hudson, I presume," Joel murmured as he released her.

Gwen could only nod in response as she stared

at the man coming up the walk. She stood and crossed her arms with fists clenched in a defensive, self-protective stance.

In spite of the animosity she felt at seeing him again, she was surprised by the rising curiosity she also experienced for the man who'd once been her husband.

From what she could tell as he approached, the years had been kinder to him than she'd ever thought possible knowing the path he'd been heading down when they split. His tall frame appeared a little leaner, and his once pretty-boy handsome features had developed sharper angles and a few creases, but all in all he was still a devilishly handsome man. She'd always expected the booze and bimbos to take their toll, and she had to admit that she was a little disappointed that his excessive lifestyle hadn't caused more visible damage. There was one all too familiar thing about him that hadn't changed. Beneath a layer of none-too-subtle men's room, two-squirts-for-a-dollar cologne he was so fond of, there lingered the unmistakable hint of cheap whisky and even cheaper women of which he was even fonder.

"I told you to stay away."

Terry flashed a smile she didn't recognize. Some serious dental work had taken place in that mouth. "Is that any way to greet your long, lost husband?" he questioned as he spread his arms open wide. "Come here, darlin', and give me a proper welcome."

"That's *ex*-husband, if you don't mind, and don't come any closer." Joel came up behind her and rested his hands on her shoulders. She welcomed the strength and support his gesture offered and she cast the man behind her a grateful glance before refocusing her attention on the man standing in front of her.

Terry stopped in his tracks and glared at them.

"I see how it is. I always knew you couldn't make it on your own."

"I've changed. I'm nothing like the woman you married."

He barked a sharp laugh and jerked a nod in Joel's direction. "I sure as hell hope so, for his sake. You didn't know the first thing about pleasing a man as I recall. Just laid there expecting me to do all the work."

Gwen's cheeks burned, not so much from what he said but that he said it in front of the one man whose opinion she valued the most. She wasn't the same woman he remembered in more ways than one, and she refused to let his remarks get to her. "For your information, I have made it on my own. Oh, and just for the record, I've learned a thing or two along the way about men, too." she said, casting Terry a sloe-eyed smile. "The hard part is finding one." He was standing right behind her.

Joel snickered and gave her shoulder an encouraging squeeze. "Good one," he whispered.

His approval was a bonus. Watching the bluster fall from Terry's face as he struggled for a comeback that never quite materialized was the real reward.

"Still shooting off that big mouth, I see."

"Maybe you'd better leave before she reloads," Joel suggested.

"I don't see a ring on her finger so I'm guessing you got no place in telling me nothing."

"Then I'll tell you. Get out of here, Terry, and don't come back."

"I'm not leaving until I see my kid." He started toward the house. "Samantha! Y'all come out here and say hello to your daddy."

Gwen flew at Terry with fists flying. "I won't let you do this to her!" She pummeled him around the chest and shoulders. He ducked and dodged her blows, blocking most of them, but she managed to land at least one decent jab to his jaw. She found great satisfaction in hearing his phony mouthful of teeth snap together.

Joel gripped her around the waist and dragged her off. "You didn't want her when she was born," she shrieked, still kicking and swinging. "You don't deserve to see her now." She continued to struggle against Joel's restraining grasp.

Terry narrowed his gaze and sneered with contempt as he raised his fist.

Inasmuch as he did everything he could, Joel wasn't quite quick enough to avoid contact. He'd managed to swing Gwen out of harm's way but not himself. Terry's blow caught him across the side of the face and the following seconds transpired in a slow, crazy blur as he recoiled. He stumbled and fell, taking her down with him. They hit the grassy slope in a wild flailing of arms and legs and sputtering oaths.

With the agility of an athlete, Joel recovered and jumped to his feet, taking an immediate defensive stance against any further aggression. Without taking his eyes off his assailant, he reached out a helping hand and pulled Gwen up. Then he dug into his pocket and handed her his cell. "Call the police. Tell them I've been assaulted."

Terry took a surprised step back. "You can't prove that."

"I can and I will."

"She attacked me first," Terry argued. "I was defending myself. You just got in the way."

"That's not the way I saw it. Who do you think they're going to believe—a member of the town board or an unwelcome drifter with no ties to the community?"

To Terry's credit, it took him barely a heartbeat to realize he didn't stand a chance against Joel's logic. He blathered and blustered a few seconds longer for effect before retreating with his pricked ego stuffed in his back pocket and his tail tucked between his legs.

To Gwen's credit, she refrained from laughing until the taillights of Terry's pickup were two red specks rounding the corner.

Chapter Sixteen

"Sit," Gwen instructed as they entered the kitchen.

"I'm fine," Joel assured her as he touched the tender place on his face. "It's just a scrape."

She faced him with an expression that brooked no further debate. With a groan of resignation, he did as he was told.

"You never mentioned you were a member of the town board," Gwen remarked as she collected the medical supplies she thought she'd need to tend to Joel's poor, battered face.

"I'm not," Joel confided as he slumped in the kitchen chair.

She doused a gauze pad with antiseptic and tenderly touched it to the abrasion on his right cheekbone. Thankfully it wasn't nearly as bad as she'd feared. "You lied?" She found his ploy amusing and couldn't help the smirk tugging at the corners of her mouth as an unladylike snort quickly followed.

"I bluffed," he corrected as he snatched the pad from her fingers and swiped it across the scrape with what she recognized as typical male impatience at her pampering. "If you recall, I never specified myself as the board member or for that matter him as the drifter. I simply presented a possible scenario. I can't be held responsible for what he unwittingly assumed."

Gwen chuckled as she reached for an adhesive bandage, which he promptly refused with an impatient wave and a glance that dared her to try.

"You're my hero," she said softly as she planted

little kisses all around the wound instead.

"Why's that?" He gripped her hips and pulled her closer.

A fierce yearning flared deep inside her, leaving her breathless and longing for his touch. "No one has ever *taken* a hit for me before." She kissed him again, this time near his ear, and whispered, "How can I ever repay your chivalry, kind sir?" She straddled his knee and arched toward him. She'd give him a lap dance right there in the kitchen if he wanted one.

"Oh, I'm sure we can negotiate a suitable way for you to show your gratitude." He drew his lips across her breast until his face was nuzzled between the two ample mounds. He moaned her name like a starving man suddenly discovering a feast beyond his wildest dreams now within his reach.

"I'm counting on it," she purred as she urged him to his feet. "How about we take these negotiations upstairs?"

The schoolboy grin he cast her turned her weak with desire.

Her provocative steps were slow and deliberate as she drew him up the stairs and into the darkened bedroom with eyes hungry with anticipation. She was ready to give herself to him in ways she'd never wanted to give herself to a man before, wholly and completely. This was the moment she'd been waiting for all her life. The very thought of disappointing him made her insides quiver.

Even under the cover of the deep shadows engulfing them she could see his frown. "You're shaking," he said, taking her into his arms.

She curled into his embrace like a frightened kitten seeking warmth and protection as she pressed her cheek against his chest. "I can't find the words to tell you how much I want you."

"Honey, you just did." The raggedness of his

voice combined with the racing beat of his heart and the rapid tempo of his breaths managed to calm her fears and quell her tremors.

He painstakingly removed each piece of her clothing, taking his sweet time, savoring each inch of flesh he exposed with a stroking caress or a lingering kiss. When she tried to reciprocate, to touch him in return, he gripped her hands to stop her. “Tonight is for you—touching you, pleasing you, loving you.”

“But that’s not—”

His fingertips covered her lips and stilled her protest. “Shhh,” he breathed as he positioned her on the bed to shimmy her panties down her long legs. He rolled her to her stomach and parted her legs to leave her spread eagle on the center the bed. Gwen sighed and curled her arms beneath her head as she closed her eyes and submitted to his tender explorations.

It struck her that she trusted him without a single reservation or moment’s hesitation. The security he engendered could be her undoing. The sudden realization caused her to tense as she attempted to make herself a little less vulnerable by rolling away.

“You need to relax,” he said. Taking her foot between his hands, he slowly massaged each toe, kneaded the sensitive curve of her arch, and rubbed his thumb up the cord of each Achilles’ tendon.

Relax was far too mild a word for the boneless condition in which he lulled her. She moaned and sighed as his hands wandered freely, branding her wherever he touched. She gasped from the roaming caress of his fingertips against the smooth, sensitive skin of her inner thighs. His hand delved between her legs, his fingertips stroking and teasing everywhere but where she craved his touch the most. Desire sparked and danced across her flesh. She squirmed and tensed muscles to lift her hips in an effort to position his hand where she wanted. She moaned and writhed; she trembled and sighed.

When she heard his soft chuckle, she quickly realized he refused to let her efforts step up his pace. If anything, he slowed his touch and added his mouth to the mix of exquisite torment he wreaked across her body. He kissed the tightening muscles in her buttocks and thighs and oddly enough she felt herself relax beneath his gentling lips. His breath was a cooling balm against her fevered flesh.

Only after he'd kissed her from ankle to neck and every square inch in-between did he roll her over and start all over again. But not before he left her side where he stood at the edge of the bed and slowly removed his clothes under her unwavering, intense cobalt gaze. Gwen licked her lips in anticipation of the places she planned on planting them when her turn came to pleasuring him with her tempting kisses and teasing tongue.

Her breath grew shallow and labored, causing a dizzying lightheadedness that left her exposed and defenseless. She opened her heart to him even as she opened her thighs to his intimate caresses.

"Joel, please," she rasped as his warm mouth closed over a taut nipple. "I can't take much more—"

"Tell me where you want me to touch you next," he said against her breast as he pinched and rolled the nipple between his fingers. A deep, aching desire coursed through her. He sucked the hard bud and flicked his tongue back and forth until she arched and pressed herself into his oral assault. The depth of her longing rolled through her like fire down a mountainside.

"Every part of me wants you," she cried. "Take your pick."

He slithered down her body until he kneeled at the foot of the bed. Pulling her forward, he positioned his mouth and parted her with warm, gentle fingers as he slid his tongue over and around each feminine fold. Her hips jerked off the bed and she gasped aloud from the jolt that shot through her.

Without missing a beat, he held her steady and continued to lick and tease as the tension mounted and everything inside her ached with an unbearable, indescribable need she knew he wouldn't deny her.

The climax was so powerful it shook her to the core and she cried out as she shattered under him. She was stunned by the sheer magnitude of her orgasm.

"Wow," Gwen whispered as the shudders rolled through her. Every molecule in her sated body was doing a happy dance.

"The pleasure was all mine," Joel said as he climbed onto the bed, positioned himself over her, and entered her as her final twinges pulsed around him.

In an agile movement so quick she didn't have a chance to protest, he rolled and had her on top and straddling him. Gwen braced her hands against his chest to catch her balance and settled her thighs around him as she reveled in the way the new position opened and exposed her to greater friction. Holding her gaze, he gripped her hips and rocked her against the base of his erection until she started moving to the pace he'd initiated. He held her tightly against him, maintaining the pressure and keeping the contact between them constant. She panted in rhythm with their thrusts. The tighter her body coiled, the quicker she moved and writhed against him. He pulled her down, holding her hands against his chest as he met her final, desperate thrusts. She welcomed this orgasm with a triumphant cry and tightened around him as she carried him with her over the edge and into mutually ecstatic gratification. She collapsed against him, breathless and content.

"That was pretty incredible," Gwen panted. "How soon before you think we can do that again? I've got a lot of catching up to do."

"Just give me a little time to recharge my battery."

"Anything I can do?" She snuggled against him and draped a leg across his naked thighs.

She sighed and drew curlicues through his chest hair with a fingernail. She couldn't quite believe the contentment settling over her.

"You're already doing it." He pressed a soft kiss against her hair. "You mind if I ask you something?" He shifted a little and wrapped his arm more tightly around her shoulder. She found something warm and wonderful about the way his fingertips rubbed leisurely circles on her skin as he held her close.

"Sure. Shoot." This pillow talk and cuddling was yet another new experience for Gwen and she reveled in their shared closeness almost as much as the sex itself.

He cleared his throat. "It's rather personal?"

"What could possibly be any more personal than what we just did?"

"True enough," he agreed. "I'm just curious about something, that's all."

"My failure to ignite before tonight, you mean?"

Joel chuckled. "It's obvious there's nothing wrong with your ignition switch. Why didn't you just do the job yourself?"

"That, I'm afraid, was never an option for me." Gwen blessed the darkness and silently congratulated herself for not pulling the sheet over her head when she answered. *Having* sex had never been the problem for her; it was *talking* about it that made her uncomfortable.

"Are you going to tell me why or are you going to make me play twenty questions?"

When he hugged her a little tighter, it made her

feel like there wasn't anything she couldn't tell him.

"My daddy raised us with a Bible in one hand and a belt in the other. He caught my older brother "doing the job" behind the barn and beat J.T. in front of the rest of us. By the time he finished he had me believing God would strike me dead if I so much as thought about touching myself down there. No matter how hard I tried, that was one childhood memory I couldn't overcome."

"What happened to your brother after that?"

"We woke up one morning and he was gone. We weren't allowed to mention J.T. after that. We heard months later from one of his friends that he'd joined the Army."

"How old were you when that happened?"

"Old enough to know I couldn't wait to follow in his footsteps, fourteen or fifteen maybe. The Army was J.T.'s means of escape, Terry Hudson was mine." Gwen breathed a depreciating laugh at that. "I guess that tells you how desperate I was to get the hell out of there."

"It explains a lot," he said thoughtfully. "I'm surprised you've managed to have any semblance of a normal sex life after having that kind of propaganda drummed into your head."

"So what's your diagnosis, doctor? Is there hope for me?"

He kissed her on the forehead and grinned. "Absolutely," he said with another kiss on the cheek this time. "But it could take years of intense therapy under me—" His mouth kept moving southward to her anxiously waiting lips. "I mean under my care, in order to make a complete recovery."

"Sign me up," she murmured as she snuggled against him. "So tell me, how did your parents handle the subject?"

Joel barked a laugh. "You have to remember I was raised on Army bases around the world. My brother and I learned pretty much everything there was to know about sex from very young ages—and in a number of different cultures, I might add. Playing with ourselves was the least of our parents' problems. They were cool with it as long as we didn't do it on the good furniture or in front of guests."

Gwen giggled as she asked, "Tell me about your brother?"

"Jake's fifteen months older and a head shorter, but when we were kids people always thought we were twins. Even now we look a lot alike."

"My sister Grace and I were like that. People were always confusing me for her. Sometimes I didn't correct them."

"Why'd you do that?"

"Gracie was the perfect child from the day she was born, and my folks never let any of us forget it. Since we looked so much alike our daddy always called us two sides of the same coin. I figured since she was the good side, I was, of course, the bad. But every once in a while I'd let people think I was Gracie just to know how being the good one felt."

"Poor Grace. Those are tough expectations to live up to. What ever happened to her?"

"I have no idea what happened to any of my brothers or sisters. My father wouldn't allow me to have any contact with them after I left."

"How many kids were there in your family?"

"There were eight of us—five boys and three girls." Gwen had enough of talking about a childhood it had taken all of her adulthood to overcome. "Are you and your brother close?"

"As close as two people can be living seven thousands miles apart. Emails help us keep in touch and we call each other occasionally."

"Where does Jake live?"

He's currently in Saudi Arabia. I think. He moves around so much, it's hard to keep track."

"Another military man?"

"No, actually, he's a civilian engineer for an oil company, but he might as well be in the Army for all the traveling he does."

"Is he married?"

"Nope. He's a vagabond through and through. Never could settle down in one place or with one woman."

"When was the last time you saw him?"

He was quiet for a moment. "Four years ago," he said as he tossed back the sheet and swung his legs over the side of the bed. The muscles across his back and shoulders tensed as he braced his palms against the mattress, looking very much like a man ready to bolt. "At Beth's funeral," he added on a barely audible murmur.

Chapter Seventeen

Gwen thought about what he'd just said but no matter how she tried to make sense out of it, to make the numbers work, there was always something wrong with her calculation.

"Your wife died *four* years ago?"

He nodded his response.

"But Emme is only three, isn't she?"

This time he glanced over his shoulder. "That's right."

"I'm sorry, I just assumed that Beth was her biological mother."

"She is."

"How is that possible?"

"Em was conceived in vitro and carried by a surrogate. Em was born after Beth passed away. When we couldn't get pregnant the old fashioned way, Beth had her eggs harvested to see if we could make a baby through one of the less conventional methods." He gave a slow sigh. "We'd failed at the one thing we wanted more than anything else in the world—making a family. That little part of her she left behind turned out to be her greatest legacy."

Gwen was stunned into thoughtful silence. What could she possibly say to a man whose desire to give his wife a child transcended the grave. Joel drew into himself right before her eyes. She wasn't sure how she should respond to this display of selfless devotion, but she knew if she let it pass without saying anything she would regret it—if not now, surely later.

She scooted across the bed and curled next to

him. When he didn't make a move, she took it as a good sign. "Tell me about her," she urged. If she wanted him to consider her a part his future, he needed to know she was willing to embrace his past. "What was Beth like?"

"She was funny and smart, as unpredictable as a firecracker one minute and as guileless as a child the next. Every day with Beth was like the Fourth of July and Christmas rolled into one. She burned bright but briefly, like a shooting star, and every time I look at our daughter I feel blessed all over again."

"She sounds like a remarkable woman."

"That's just it. She really wasn't. The only thing that made her truly remarkable was her indomitable spirit and that she chose to share her short stay on this earth with me."

Gwen wrapped her arms around him and drew his head to rest against her breast, not in a sexual way but in a comforting one.

"I'm so tired," he said with a heavy sigh.

Gwen pressed a kiss to his shoulder, letting her lips linger against his warm skin as she ran her hand up and down his back in soothing, circular strokes. She felt him relax under the repetitious motion and soon he rolled to his side and fell asleep.

She moved to the other side of the bed and pulled the top sheet over them, all the while wondering if he would ever think of her as anything more than a bed partner. He was linked to a past love she wasn't sure he wanted to sever.

****

Not knowing exactly what it was that jarred her awake, Gwen opened her eyes and tried to focus on the bedside clock. Its glaring red numbers informed her she'd been asleep only a couple of hours. With a contented sigh and a pleased grin, she stretched and reached for the man who'd brought that wholly satisfied smile to her face. Until, that is, she discovered the place beside her cold and empty. Then her smile turned into a disturbed frown.

Unsure of what she expected to find, she sat up and looked around the room. She found Joel standing by the open bedroom window, his posture slouched and braced by his forearm against the window frame. Seeing him standing there sent a sizzling jolt of arousal through her like a shot of pure energy. She couldn't believe how just the sight of the man turned her weak with desire. What a difference the right man made.

"Joel?" she said around a hoarse, sleep-laden whisper. It took a moment for him to react. She was just about to call him again when he turned. It was too dark for her to see his shadowed expression, but a sensation she couldn't describe crept down her spine and caused her to shiver. She tucked the sheet around her and scooted to the side of the bed where he stood. "Are you okay?"

He rubbed the heels of his palms across his eyes before he answered. "Yeah, I'm fine," he said, adding, "I can't sleep, that's all." In spite of his reassurance, he didn't sound the least bit fine. His usual deep, commanding tone sounded strained and weak.

She trailed a finger down his arm. "You were exhausted just a few hours ago."

"I guess I forgot to mention I'm a chronic insomniac. I haven't slept through the night in years."

Since his wife died four years ago was Gwen's guess, but she kept her diagnosis to herself.

He reached for his pants and shirt from the floor. "Go back to sleep. I'll go downstairs so I don't disturb you with my nocturnal stirrings."

As he moved toward the bedroom door, a silvery shaft of moonlight momentarily cast its beam across his naked back and shoulders before another step shifted him into the cover of darkness.

"Why don't you come back to bed and hold me until I fall asleep." She patted a place beside her and let the sheet slip around her waist. One way or the other, she hoped to entice him back to bed.

He faltered and glanced over his shoulder, his expression obliterated by heavy shadows. "What did you say?"

It bothered her that his tone was a bit too sharp and demanding for a simple query. "I said come back to bed and hold me until I fall asleep. What did you think I said?"

He shook his head as if he didn't understand. "It's just that—well—you sounded like..." He shook his head again. "Never mind, it doesn't matter." He flung open the bedroom door and left, leaving Gwen to stare into the empty hall long after he'd made his departure.

His recent behavior bewildered her. Maybe the sex wasn't as wonderful as she thought it had been. She was, after all, no expert on the subject. Maybe he was having second thoughts about continuing their relationship, and who could blame him after Terry's surprise visit. A man would have to be crazy to get caught up in the middle of that mess. Then again, maybe she was just being her usual paranoid self where men were concerned. Gwen gave a derisive snort at that realization. Who'd have ever guessed her paranoia would be the lesser evil of her choices?

Letting her imagination run amok wasn't going to resolve a darn thing, she told herself as she climbed out of bed and reached for a robe. She cinched the tie belt around her waist and smoothed her hair behind her ears as she padded barefoot from the room.

When she couldn't find him immediately, she

thought he'd left and her heart plummeted. Just when she was about to give up looking, she spotted his shirt draped over the back of a kitchen chair and the back door open. It was then she discovered him sitting at the picnic table in the backyard. He sat with his back to her and she trekked across the dry, summer grass to join him. The night air was warm and a balmy breeze tickled her exposed skin.

He didn't seem surprised when she ran her hand across his shirtless shoulders as she sat on the bench next to him.

Bracing her elbows on the table behind her, she leaned back and studied his pensive features with a thoughtful pout. "I guess it's my turn to offer you the big bucks for what's on your mind."

Her words made him smile, and she took that as a good sign. She didn't take him for a man who'd smile just before handing her the "*it's not you it's me*" speech. She'd been forced to use the phrase once or twice as a last resort, and she distinctly remembered *not* smiling when delivering it.

"You don't know what you're asking. Sleep deprivation can cause some pretty deep, often disturbing thoughts to run through this mind."

"I hope I'm not at the root of those disturbing ones?"

He took her hand and intertwined their fingers. "Never. You bring me nothing but the most pleasant thoughts."

"I was having a few disturbing thoughts myself when you left the bedroom like that. I was afraid I'd said or done something wrong. I really didn't expect to find you still here when I came downstairs."

"I'm sorry about that. It's just that what you said, how you said it, sounded like Beth. She'd said a similar thing to me the night she passed away."

Gwen pressed her forehead against his shoulder and ran a finger down his arm. "I'm sorry too."

He gazed at her over the rim of his glasses. "What do you have to be sorry for?"

She wasn't sure exactly, but replied anyway, "For reminding you of a painful memory, I guess."

"I can think of a way for you to make it up to me." He fingered the knotted belt at her waist and worked it loose. The silky wraparound fell open and he filled his hands with her unbound breasts. His thumbs worked the nipples to hard, aching buds before his fingers trailed lower. They slipped between her legs as he leaned in and began a trail of tantalizing kisses across her flesh.

Gwen tossed her head back and surrendered to his thrilling touches. "This is a good start," she gasped. A whispery sigh evolved into a throaty moan as she moved restlessly against his busy fingers. She really didn't want to climax alone. She wanted him moving inside her, stroking her, filling her as they built their excitement together.

"Come with me," she said as she pulled him to his feet and led him toward the house.

"I'm sure that can be arranged," he replied.

Chapter Eighteen

Gwen fumbled for the phone without bothering to open her eyes and proceeded to clunk herself in the head as she dragged the receiver to her ear. "Hello," she croaked.

"Gwen?"

Gwen's eyes flew open at the sound of her office manager's voice. She immediately shut them again from the blinding glare. The room was much too bright, which meant only one thing—it was later than she usually got up.

"Bette…" she breathed through a yawn as she pushed a lock of hair from her face. "What time is it?"

"It's after ten. Why? Are you still in bed? Oh my God, what's wrong? Are you sick? Are you hurt? Do you need the paramedics? Should I call an ambulance?"

"No, no, don't do that," Gwen promptly replied to stop Bette from doing any of those things. "There's nothing wrong."

Quite the opposite, actually, thought Gwen with a furtive grin as she swung her legs over the side of the bed and searched high and low for a robe that was nowhere to be found. "I was up late and must have forgotten to set the alarm, that's all. I'll be in just as soon as I can."

"Take your time. I've already rescheduled your morning appointments. You don't have anything now until the Morgan closing at three. And if anyone asks how you're feeling, give a little sniffle and tell them 'better', got it?"

Gwen gave a grateful chuckle at Bette's quick thinking. "I think I can manage that."

"I'll just bet you can," Bette chuckled as she severed their connection.

Not that 'better' came anywhere close to describing the way she really felt, but since she couldn't very well tell her staff she'd been up late having earth-moving sex, the sniffles would have to do. And she had the man currently running his hand up her spine to thank for that better than better feeling.

The mattress dipped as Joel shifted into position behind her. On bended knees, he straddled her with his thighs. His hands traveled around her ribcage and stopped as he cupped the underside of her breasts. The thrill of his touch sent tremors of pleasure to churn low in her belly and pool between her legs.

"I—I really don't have time for this," she murmured as she swayed into his embrace.

"Uh huh," he wholeheartedly agreed, as he marched a trail of kisses across her back from shoulder to shoulder and back again.

"I have to get ready for work," she announced on a breathless whisper as she braced her palms on his knees and tipped her head to give him greater access to her neck. "I should have been there hours ago."

"I know." He drew her more tightly against his chest.

His erection poked against her spine. The heat of his need excited her and left her panting in quick, needy gasps of desire too urgent to ignore. Maybe they had time for a quickie.

With a cry of surrender, she turned in his arms. All thoughts of work flew right out of her head as passion ignited and flared in its place.

****

It was quarter after one when Gwen tore into

the municipal parking lot like one of the Duke boys pulling an evasive three-sixty. As it turned out, Joel wasn't familiar with the term *quickie* and she hadn't the heart to explain it to him.

She was ready to forego her usual Starbucks, but her body and brain screamed for caffeine. She needed her morning—correction, afternoon—fix.

"Hi, Gwen," greeted the barista, glancing at her watch. "You're running kind of late today, aren't you?"

"So I've been told."

"What'll it be? The usual?"

"You bet," Gwen replied as she scanned the case of mouthwatering pastries and wondered if she should eat something. Joel hadn't allowed her time for breakfast either. Her stomach gave a low, rumbling growl in response. "Give me one of those blueberry muffins, too. In fact, bag up a dozen assorted." She might have to toss them at the curious mob, also known as her co-workers, to make it to her cubicle. Maybe if their mouths were munching on pastries, they'd be too busy to give her the third degree about her out-of-character tardiness.

She was never late for anything. Regardless of the job, Gwen had always been a model employee and led by example now with her staff. Showing up late or calling off simply wasn't acceptable in her mind, not for her or anyone who worked for her. She doubted she'd be allowed to live this one down for quite some time.

She entered the storefront office of Marconi Realty waving the bag stamped with the familiar coffee shop logo. At the jingle of the door chime, all heads looked up from their desks. Here goes, she told herself as she plastered a brilliant smile on her face and squared her shoulders in preparation to run the gauntlet.

She swept into the reception area with an attitude that defied anyone to challenge her afternoon appearance. What she got in return were mumbled, half-hearted greetings and not a snicker, eyebrow lift, or knowing grin more.

She eyed each member of the staff with a curious glance, but looked to her office manager for explanation. "What's going on?" Gwen demanded, loud enough for all to hear as she plunked the bakery bag next to the coffeemaker.

"There's someone waiting to see you." Bette pointed a blunt, unpolished nail in the direction of Gwen's cubicle. "He says he was your husband."

She kept a careful grip on her coffee cup as a cold, twisting knot settled in her empty gut. She should have known the previous night wouldn't be the last time she'd see Terry. "Get Randy Meyers on the phone and ask him to get over here as soon as possible." A seed of an idea began to form, and she figured having a little muscle to back up her plan couldn't hurt.

"*Chief* Randy Meyers?" Bette questioned.

"The same," said Gwen. When Bette didn't immediately reach for the phone to make the call, she added, "Now!"

Gwen marched around the partition and into her office where she found Terry lounging in her padded, leather office chair with his tooled leather boots propped on her desk like he owned the place.

She smacked his feet off the furniture, sincerely wishing it was his face. "You've got thirty seconds to get the hell out of my chair." There were times, this being one of them, that she longed for a real office with a real door so she could have some real privacy. It was so quiet on the other side of the partition; if she didn't know better she'd think everyone had gone to lunch.

He pushed himself out of the swivel chair with

the speed of a snail and moved around the desk with an equally slow, lose-limbed swagger he hadn't altered one bit since he'd assumed it at seventeen. His actions reminded her of a past-his-prime rooster strutting around the barnyard just before winding up in the stock pot. Oh, how she'd love to be the one to dunk his body into a boiling caldron and be done with him. It was then she realized she wasn't the least bit afraid of him any more, just a little leery of his motives, and that was okay. Leery would keep her on her toes.

"Looks like my little Gwenny's done real well for herself," he said as he ran his fingers across the polished surface of the teak credenza. "Your chair, your office, your business..."

And her building, she silently added, thankful she never made her ownership of the prime property common knowledge. Her staff had no way of knowing Terry was a two-bit, bottom-feeder bent on pumping them for information. They couldn't tell him what they didn't know. Not even the tenants, her staff, or daughter knew she owned the strip of connected Main Street storefronts, which she bought just months before the town's massive restoration plans were revealed. Buying the property when she did had been one of the few times in her life that her timing couldn't have been more perfect. Practically overnight the property value had increased tenfold and was still going up with every passing day.

Gwen wanted him out of her office, the town, and her life once and for all. "What are you doing here?"

He heaved a pathetic sigh as he collapsed into a hard-backed chair near the doorway and hung his head.

Gwen rolled her eyes. "You know, Ter," she said as she leaned a hip against the corner of her desk. "If I didn't know better, I might almost believe this poor-pitiful-me performance of yours." She took a slow sip from her coffee and narrowed her gaze, searching for anything that might give her a clue as to his agenda. She braced herself for another demanding request to see Samantha.

"It's not an act, Gwenny, I swear. The last few years have been rough for me."

"I've had more than my share of rough patches over the years as well, but I've never resorted to conning old ladies out of their savings to make ends meet. Does your parole officer know you've crossed state lines?"

All the color drained from his face. "You know about that?"

She crossed her arms and stared him down. "I've had a private detective tracking your whereabouts and activities for quite some time."

He straightened in his seat, which only made him look slightly less pathetic, and lowered his voice. "I'm not here to cause trouble, Gwenny. I was just hoping maybe you could help me out a little."

"I should have known," she spouted. "All that crap about wanting to see your daughter was just that, wasn't it?" She pushed off the desk, angry at herself for even thinking for a moment he might have changed.

"I could maybe arrange to stick around for a while to see her, if that's what you want me to do." He lifted his gaze to meet hers. There wasn't anything resembling sad or pitiable in his expression now, just contempt and greed. He knew she'd do just about anything to get rid of him, and he was right.

She crossed her arms and met his gaze. "Okay, Terry, how much?" Her pitch was low and guarded, and she hoped he didn't mistake it for a furtive whisper instead of the intimidating query she intended.

"Huh?"

She could see her question caught him by surprise. He obviously hadn't expected it to be this easy. "You heard me. What is it going to take to convince you to leave? And before you quote me a number, keep in mind this is a one time only offer. When you walk out that door it's for good and forever."

He never hesitated, and looked surprisingly more like his old self. "Twenty-five grand ought to do it," he stated.

Gwen sustained her poker face as she settled herself behind her desk. "You'll get five and be grateful."

"Make it ten, and I'll be gone before you can blink those big blues."

"Ten it is," she agreed. Little did he know she would have paid a lot more for the privilege of getting rid of him, but she wasn't about to tip her hand just yet.

The intercom on her desk buzzed once and Bette announced, "Randy's here."

"Send him back." Gwen pulled out her checkbook and started to write.

Randy poked his shaved head around the partition. "Hey, Gwen. What's so urgent you couldn't wait until I finished my lunch?" Randy Meyers was a formidable man in every sense of the word. Well over six-foot in stature, he carried enough muscled bulk to intimidate without uttering a single word. But when he did speak, his booming baritone could shiver timbers and cause the most belligerent hombre to cower in his presence. Terry didn't have a chance.

She motioned for him to come in. "I need you to witness a transaction."

He looked rightfully puzzled by her odd request. "Isn't that what you've got a staff full of notaries for?" Randy was quick to point out with a hitch of his meaty thumb in the direction of said staff.

"I needed somebody not affiliated with the business," she explained as she signed the check with flourish and dotted the final *I* with a definitive punch of her pen. She cast Terry a sideward glance and noted the heightened color retuning to his cheeks. She smiled benignly and made the introductions.

"Randy, I want you to meet Terry Hudson."

"Hudson?" Randy queried with a wide grin. "Sam's dad?" On Terry's mute nod, the big man grabbed Terry's hand and pumped it vigorously. "It's nice to finally meet you."

Still smiling, Gwen wondered how friendly Randy would be if he knew the man whose hand he was shaking was shaking her down to the tune of ten thousand big ones.

"Randy's one of Samantha's coaches..." she explained as she slipped the check into an envelope and sealed it. "...and the town's chief of police." Gwen had to force herself not to laugh out loud as Terry's eyes shifted in her direction and widened with comprehension.

She extended the envelope in Terry's direction. "Here you go, Ter. Signed, sealed and delivered." She turned to Randy in explanation, "I'm helping Terry out a little."

"I can't take that," Terry said as he adamantly shook his head against the proffered check and backed away. His forehead beaded with perspiration.

"I'm only trying to help."

"I appreciate your offer, Gwen, honey, really I do, but you know I can't take your money. It wouldn't be right."

Gwen feigned appropriate surprise by Terry's change in attitude.

Randy patted Terry on the back like they were old buddies. "Look, man, I know how you feel, but sometimes you just got to swallow your pride and take the help when it's offered." Randy snatched the envelope out of Gwen's outstretched hand, folded it into neat thirds, and stuffed it into Terry's shirt pocket. He gave the bulging pocket and Terry's chest a couple of solid pats for good measure.

"I don't want it," Terry shouted as he ripped the envelope from his pocket and pitched it across her desk. "I told you I can't take it." He backed toward the exit, practically falling over his own feet in his haste to get the hell out of there.

"I don't understand," Gwen said. "I thought you said you needed the money."

"I—I changed my mind. I don't need it after all." He turned and hightailed it out of there.

Gwen clamped a hand over her mouth to hold back her laughter as she stood in the doorway and watched Terry make his retreat.

Randy came up behind her and questioned, "You want to explain what exactly I just witnessed?"

"That, my friend, was Terry Hudson making the most expensive mistake of his life—underestimating his mark."

Joel walked in just as she started to explain to Randy.

"What are you doing here?" Gwen questioned.

"I called to find out when you'd be finished for the day and Bette told me who was waiting for you when you arrived." He gripped her shoulders and tipped his head with a gentle expression of concern. "I came by to make sure you were okay."

She was touched by his concern. "Everything's fine," she assured as she noted his doubtful glance in Randy's direction. "Do you know our chief of police?"

Joel nodded and extended his hand. "Randy and I are old friends. School principals and the local police department often find themselves working hand in hand. We've worked together on a number of committees, as well. How've you been, Randy?"

Randy waggled his finger between Joel and Gwen. "You two are dating?" At their nod, he added, "That's the best news I've heard in ages. Congratulations." He shook Joel's hand with appropriate enthusiasm.

Gwen was pleased to hear that at least one person in town thought so. She ushered both men into her cubicle and attempted to bring them up to speed. She heard the shuffling of chairs and the not-so-quiet jockeying of her staff for position outside her office to eavesdrop. At this point, she didn't care what they heard.

"I realized what he wanted when he showed up." She turned to Joel. "I'm sure he would have hit me up for money last night if you hadn't been there. All that posturing about wanting to see Samantha was just to make me all the more eager to be rid of him." Then she turned to Randy. "Terry is a convicted felon recently out on parole."

"What was he in for?" Randy was poised and ready to go after the one that got away.

"He's not dangerous, just despicable—he successfully wooed several rich, lonely old ladies and relieved them from some of their ready cash and jewelry. He would have gotten away with it, too, if one of the women hadn't gotten past her embarrassment and turned him in."

"How do you know all of this?" It was Joel who jumped in with a question this time.

"I'm sure you're familiar with the Templar-Stone Agency?" Gwen directed her question to Randy. Upon his nod, she continued, "I've had Angel on retainer since before she added the hyphen to her name. She's been keeping tabs on Terry for me for quite some time."

"You took quite a gamble," said Randy. "How did you know he wouldn't keep the money?"

"I didn't," she said as she picked up the discarded envelope from her desk and wave it between her fingers. "Terry likes his transactions quick and private. The last thing he wanted was a witness to him taking the money, let alone an officer of the law. What he didn't know was I wouldn't have stopped him from cashing it if he'd had the balls to keep it in his pocket."

"How much was it for?" Randy tried to grab the check from her but she ripped it into pieces before he or Joel could see what lengths she was willing to take to eradicate her past.

She glanced casually at her watch. "Now if you gentlemen will excuse me, I have a closing in twenty minutes and if I don't leave now I'm going to be late." She reached for her purse and turned to Randy with a grateful smile. "Thanks for responding to my call so quickly. Your timing was impeccable."

Then she cast a gentle gaze on Joel and waved the pieces of check in the air. "Dinner's on Terry tonight." With a wink, she turned on her heel and made her exit.

"What a woman," she heard Randy say.

What warmed her heart was Joel's reply. "You got that right. And I was smart enough to see it first."

Chapter Nineteen

Joel selected a hotdog from the cardboard tray in front of him and handed it to her.

"You know," said Gwen as she accepted his offering. "When I said dinner was on Terry, I meant we could afford someplace better than a street vendor."

"I know," he said as he deliberated over the tray to make his own selection. He snatched the one with the most kraut. "But I thought this was more appropriate for a two-bit hustler." Joel tore open a packet of mustard and squirted the contents over his ordinary fare with extraordinary savoir faire. "Besides, there's nothing better than this." He grinned and took a big bite of the fully loaded hotdog.

Gwen chuckled at his enthusiasm as she plucked a cucumber slice off the top of her dog. "I think even Terry would appreciate the irony."

"Hopefully..." he said as he chewed and swallowed. "...we'll never get the opportunity to find out."

"As much as I'd like that to be the case, I don't think I've heard the last of him. Tenacity is one of his finer attributes. So, I've decided to tell Samantha the truth to take away his leverage."

"I know you were young and eager to get away from a strict home life, but how'd you hook up with somebody like that?"

She shrugged and sighed slow and deliberately. "He was the first guy willing to take me farther than the motel on the outskirts of town. We made it all the way to Vegas, where we decided to settle down. We got married, found jobs, and for a couple of years we actually lived a fairly normal life. Then I got pregnant. You pretty much know what happened after that."

"You do have a knack for condensing the facts."

"I don't see any point in talking about the *whys* and *what ifs* of past events and circumstances. It's not like I can change anything. I much prefer dwelling on my future."

He stroked her knuckles with gentle fingertips. "I was hoping by now you'd be comfortable enough to share some of those circumstances with me. They are, after all, what made you who you are today."

She tossed the last bites of her hotdog into its fluted paper boat and brushed the bun crumbs off her fingers. "What do you want to know?"

"Tell me something about your second husband. You never mention him."

Her expression softened at the mention of Vic Marconi. "Our divorce was amicable."

He looked at her for a moment, his expression a mixture of surprise and disbelief, then exclaimed, "That's it? Just four little words to sum up the end of your marriage? Do you think you could you elaborate a little?"

She grinned at his reaction. "Why? It only took half that many words to begin it. But since you insist, Vic and I were great partners—in the business world. We quickly learned we never should have tried to extend that partnership into our personal lives. And that, as they say, is that."

Joel just shook his head, a faint smile playing on his lips.

"You've got mustard on your cheek." Gwen wadded a paper napkin and reached across the picnic table to wipe the blob of yellow from the corner of his mouth. She caressed the place she'd just cleaned and he rewarded her with a kiss on the fingertips. The intimacy of his gesture intensified with a lingering gaze.

There was nothing the slightest bit romantic about sharing a tray of hotdogs and bag of shoestring potatoes from a street vendor in the middle of the community park, but Gwen never felt more cherished and wanted in her life. Candlelight and champagne had never been this effective in turning her thoughts to romance and making love. Just as she'd always suspected, the right man made all the difference and Joel had been absolutely right—the journey was indeed every bit as exciting as the destination.

Every glance, every gesture, every touch he displayed aided in elevating her awareness of the man sitting in front of her currently stuffing the last of his third hotdog into his wonderful mouth. The longer he made her wait the more she wanted him, a fact she suspected was his main objective. If the way she felt at that moment was any indication of things to come, they were in for one hell of a passionate night.

"Stop looking at me like that."

She locked gazes with him, her eyes wide and innocent. "How am I looking at you?" she questioned as she guided her drink straw between her lips and sucked.

He curled his knuckles against his lips in an attempt to hide a smirk as he spoke in a voice dripping with seduction. "Like a woman who knows how her evening is going to end, that's how."

"Are you telling me I *don't* know how it's going to end?"

He leaned in, braced his elbows on the table, and brought his lips near enough to cast a tickling breath across her cheek. "You may think you know how it ends, and you'd probably be right, but you don't have a clue as to how it's going to start." He winked and sat back in his seat.

Gwen tried to swallow as she held his gaze and hoped he didn't make her wait too long. She wasn't a patient woman when it came to wanting this man.

She gathered their garbage as an indication that she was ready to leave and take their show on the road.

"Let's move closer to the gazebo before all the park benches are taken?"

Gwen glanced around and was surprised by the number of people setting up lawn chairs and blankets around the park's newly erected performance gazebo—just another of the town's leaders efforts to get the residents more involved in the community.

She pitched their garbage into the nearby refuse container. "Is there a concert in the park tonight?" She'd seen the schedule displayed in her realty office front window for weeks. Maybe she should have taken the time to actually read it.

He folded her hand into his as they walked toward the crowd. "It's an up and coming jazz ensemble from Indy. I've read nothing but good things about them."

"But you don't like jazz," she blurted.

He frowned at her definitive pronouncement. "What ever gave you that idea?"

"Well, for starters, the way you punched off the CD I played yesterday."

He tossed back his head and laughed. "As I recall I was already in a highly...uh... agitated state at the time. I didn't need any further stimulus."

Gwen motioned to an empty bench near enough to hear the performance but far enough from the masses to enjoy a small amount of privacy. "Stimulus?"

Joel nodded at her choice and pulled her down

next to him. He draped his arms across the back and she settled beside him like she'd been doing it forever. "Jazz, at least to me, is sensual and arousing," he explained.

"Why didn't you just say jazz makes you horny?"

He hooked his arm around her neck, pulled her near, and placed a lingering kiss at her temple. "*You* make me horny," he whispered against her hair. "Jazz merely heightens the whole experience."

She warmed in his embrace and turned in his arms. "I'll keep that in mind," she returned as she snuggled against him and rested her head on his shoulder.

"Joel Hubbard?" A woman squealed as she made a beeline across a grassy expanse.

He quickly removed his arm from around Gwen and stood as the leggy redhead flung herself into his arms. "I thought that was you," she squealed. "I'd been hoping you'd be here."

He hugged the woman with equal enthusiasm then held her at arm's length. "It's good to see you again, Jackie. What are you doing in my neck of the woods? Your lungs need a break from that L.A. smog?"

"I figured mom would have kept you in the loop. I represent the group performing tonight."

"Elle didn't say a word. But I've heard they're good."

"Good? They're flipping fabulous. Wait until you hear them. So where's my little Mary Elizabeth?" She whirled around expecting to find the child in question. "Isn't she here?"

Joel shook his head. "She went away for a few days with Nick and Maggie and their whole gang."

"A world traveler already, huh?"

He laughed at that. "No world this trip, just Wisconsin. I insisted she wait until she's as least five before she leaves the country."

"I'm glad to hear the little squirt's social life has expanded beyond daycare." Jackie peered around Joel and gazed curiously at Gwen, who sat quietly taking in the reunion. "I'm even more pleased to see yours has too." She extended her hand to Gwen. "Hi, I'm Jackie Mahoney, promoter extraordinaire and once upon a time Joel's fabulous sister-in-law."

Gwen got to her feet and took the woman's hand. "Gwen Marconi."

"That's Gwen Marconi, realtor extraordinaire and Joel's fabulous date," Joel interjected.

Jackie laughed at his embellishment. "Nice to meet you, Gwen."

"Same here." Gwen saw the family resemblance. Jackie had the same fiery red hair and infectious smile as the woman in the wedding picture on Joel's dresser.

Jackie turned to Joel with a sly wink and a subtle elbow jab to his ribs. "The folks mentioned they thought you had a girlfriend. She lowered her tone and added, "Mom said you tried to pass off a love bite as a cat scratch. Way to go, big guy."

"It was a cat scratch!" Gwen declared with a tad more emphasis than necessary.

"Your secret's safe with me," Jackie assured them both. "You are planning on sticking around for tonight's concert, right? These guys really are phenomenal. And I'm not just saying that because I'm trying to build their fan base. I actually like the stuff they do—especially the sax."

"I don't believe it," Joel gasped. "You've finally developed an ear for the good stuff. But are you sure it's the music you've learned to appreciate and not just the one playing it?"

"You planted the seed a long time ago, bro. It just took a while to take root." Jackie dug into the back pocket of her very form-fitting designer jeans and produced a thin leather card case. She snapped it open and handed them a glossy, neon blue card with *Soul Strokers* in bright yellow script. She also passed out a slightly more conservative pastel rose card with her name and contact information.

"This guy is almost as good as you once were, if you can imagine that." She turned to Gwen. "I'll bet he didn't tell you he used to play a wicked saxophone when he was younger."

Gwen smiled. "You'd win that bet. He's never said a word. It explains a few things though."

"Like what?" Joel queried.

"Your amazing breath control, for one," she deadpanned.

"Ha! I love her already. She's a keeper, J-Man." Jackie threw her arms around Joel's neck and kissed his cheek. "You take care, big guy, and give Emme a big kiss from her Aunt Jackie."

"Why don't you do it yourself? She'll be home tomorrow."

"Can't. I'm heading back to the coast first thing in the morning."

"Do you ever slow down?"

"In my business if you slow down they say a eulogy and toss a handful of dirt in your face. You gotta keep moving." Jackie laughed as she spun on her heels to leave. "Enjoy the show," she called out with a wave. Six feet into her departure, she paused and tossed a wink over her shoulder. "I hope the jazz is every bit as hot as your new lady." She vanished into the crowd as suddenly as she had appeared.

The opening notes of a moaning alto sax cut through the sultry night air like the desolate call of a male searching for its mate.

"Okay, I've heard enough." Joel grabbed Gwen's hand and pulled her toward the car.

****

The ride home started in electrified, anticipatory silence. Gwen reached across the console and stroked his hand gripping the steering wheel. He flexed his fingers and grinned without ever taking his eyes off the road.

"Will you play your sax for me some day?" The thought of his beautiful lips pursed around the instrument's mouthpiece and his long-boned fingers manipulating the valves intrigued her, aroused her.

"I haven't played in years. I'm not sure if I remember how."

"Why did you stop?"

She couldn't read his expression in the dark interior, but his lengthy pause before answering "I don't remember" gave her the distinct impression that the topic was no longer open for further discussion. She sighed in resignation, knowing more than anyone that some things were better left alone.

****

Joel dropped the deadbolt when they entered her house and turned to her. With a sly grin and a heated stare, he produced a long, slender scarf the colors of a fiery sunset from his back pocket. He slid the shimmering fabric through his hands and finished by twirling the beaded fringed ends around his long fingers. She heard the delicate tinkling of the beads as the light glistened off the shiny bugles. What should have delighted her with its sparkling beauty struck terror through her instead.

Gwen panicked at the sight of it. Her eyes grew wide with anxiety and she took several wary steps away. "What do you plan on doing with that?"

He grinned with devilish amusement. "That depends on you."

"You're not planning on tying me up with that, are you?"

"Not if you don't want me to," he replied with an evenness she didn't believe.

Her eyes widened as her fear escalated and her breathing grew shallow and rapid. Lightheadedness washed over her and she staggered to the living room sofa and sat down before she found herself on the floor.

"Take it easy, honey," he soothed as he tossed the scarf aside and took her into his arms. "What brought this on?"

"Please don't use that on me." She clutched at his shirt and buried her face against his chest. "I—I don't like to be restrained."

He took her hand and attempted to rub some warmth into her trembling fingers. The gentle strength he imbued was enough to calm her. "Tying you up was never my intention," he said as he wrapped his arms around her shoulders and pulled her close. "I thought it might be fun to blindfold you, however."

She pushed out of his embrace and eyed him with a dark, wary frown. "Why do you want to do that?"

"Sensory deprivation can heighten other senses, particularly that of touch. But in order for me to do this you need to trust me."

She couldn't believe she was having this conversation, let alone considering his suggestion. Yet she found herself saying without reservation, "I do trust you." She stood, scooped the scarf off the floor, and handed it to him. "Whatever you want is okay with me." She had to get past this thinking that all men were out to hurt her.

He shook his head against the idea and stuffed the length of silk into his pocket. "I don't want you doing this just to please me."

"I'm doing this for me as much as for you."

"This trust goes both ways, you know," he said as he turned out the downstairs lights and led her to the bedroom.

He never bothered with the lights when they reached her room. He felt his way in the dark as he undressed her. In spite of him having seen and explored every inch of her the previous night, she still felt more at ease and relaxed under the cover of darkness. By the time he removed her bra and panties and urged her to sit on the edge of the bed, she actually found herself enjoying the attention he lavished on her—except for that scarf she knew he had in his pocket. She still wasn't too sure about that part of his seduction. Maybe he'd be content if she promised to keep her eyes shut. She had her answer when he withdrew the scarf.

"Trust me," he said as he placed the scarf across her eyes and tied it. "And relax."

"That's easy for you to say," she murmured. "You're not the one naked and blindfolded." Her vulnerabilities were exposed right along with everything else.

"This'll be fun, I promise," he whispered near her ear.

A doubtful huff escaped through dry lips as she tried to predict his next move. She felt strangely disoriented and off-kilter, although she was surprised to discover the sensation not entirely unpleasant. In fact she was more aroused than she'd expected to ever be by this unforeseen turn of events. She licked her lips and gasped. The grating rasp of a zipper tore through her brain as she imagined him stripping off his clothes with a clarity she found amazingly vivid.

"You're not being fair," she pouted as she tried to touch him.

"Patience," he said as the soundless swish of air and cloth brushed past her groping fingers. The soft, clean fragrance of laundry detergent briefly wafted past her nostrils before it was replaced with the sharper, headier scent of him. Her breathing grew more shallow and erratic as her need for him built with each passing moment.

She reached out and found his waist, naked and smooth and in an instant she pictured all of him looming in front of her. She stroked his hip and fingered the smooth swell of his muscled buttock, knowing exactly where to take her wandering fingers next.

When she discovered his erection, she stroked it from base to tip then wrapped her fingers around the hard shaft and playfully thumbed the fleshy head. The musky scent of him reached her nostrils and she breathed deeply. He moaned and braced a knee against the mattress, gripping her shoulders for support as she took him into her mouth. His breath exploded around her. She smiled as she ran her tongue around and down the length of him.

The familiar click of the bedside lamp startled her. She froze in mid stroke and pulled away. The very thought of him watching her pleasuring him was too much.

She fumbled with the scarf's knot. "If you get to watch, then so do I."

"Don't," he said as he kept her from removing the blindfold and urged her to lie down with hands that never touched any part of her remotely erogenous. "It's my turn to pleasure you. I want to explore every inch of you, discover your secret desires and arouse your passions." Shoulders, hips, and thighs warmed beneath his gentle restraint.

The thought of giving any man that much freedom with her body left her weak and fearful. Once again he'd taken away the control she ordinarily wielded during a sexual encounter.

As if sensing her hesitance, he drew her into his arms and kissed her with a passion that would have knocked her socks off—had she been wearing any, of course.

A single fingertip, thick and rough, drew circles around her areola but never touched the budding nipple. Gwen gasped as a tightening need shot through her and caused her to arch and squirm in an attempt to better position herself beneath his sweet, teasing touches.

She tried to envision where he'd touch her next. Every move he made was with such slow deliberateness, it allowed her too much time to anticipate where his next move would be. The mere thought of what he might do next caused her to gasp with short, panting breaths as her imagination ran rampant with aching need and burning desire.

Her guesses were never right. If she thought she'd feel his caress on her thigh, he'd stroke her shoulder. If she was sure he'd kiss her needy breast, his lips would stamp a damp trail of kisses up the soft flesh of her inner thigh from knee to groin. She held her breath as big, warm hands braced her legs open and his tongue laved a slick path through her feminine folds to find her pink nub swollen and glistening.

And just when she thought she'd explode from wanting him, he covered her body with his and kissed her, drawing her tongue into his mouth as he filled her with a deep, slow thrust and a pleasure-filled moan.

And finally, he pushed off the blindfold to look deep and long into her eyes. He held her gaze as he withdrew and plunged again, stroking deeper and harder until together they developed a sensuous rhythm of profound gratification.

Gwen gasped and cried out as her body trembled and quaked beneath him in the tightening grip of her orgasm. She arched and let the pleasant pulsing after shocks ripple around him as he sought his own explosive finish. A breathless cry punctuated his final penetrating thrust and she felt him spasm and release inside her.

He withdrew and collapsed beside her, his

breath hot and panting against her cooling flesh. His fingers curled around her breast as he settled himself next to her with a leg and an arm tossed over her to keep her close as he drifted off to sleep.

Chapter Twenty

Gwen woke to the comforting yet still unfamiliar warmth of another human being in her bed. The previous morning didn't count because she hadn't had a chance to appreciate the cozy familiarity of the moment. To save herself from a similar morning wake-up call, she'd rearranged her schedule and took a personal day. She hadn't taken a day off in the middle of the week in what seemed like forever. Sometimes it was good to be boss, she thought, as she snuggled against the man sleeping next to her.

It had been a long time since any man had stayed the whole night. Hell, it had been a long time since she'd had a man, period. That thought made her grin as she wondered what the folks in this town would think if they knew the whole truth about the infamous Ms. Marconi—that for the last two years she'd lived more like a nun than the home-wrecker so many considered her.

In truth, she'd shared her bed with very few men, and two of those she'd married. Her 'bad girl' image had always been considerably more fiction than fact. Except for that one slip-up she'd made with a married man, albeit unwittingly, most everything else was nothing more than an illusion she'd created and developed over the years to get people's attention.

Outrageous behavior, she'd discovered, was always easier than revealing her true vulnerabilities. Until now, that is. The part she found most amazing was nothing about her past, fact or fiction, had ever mattered to Joel. He'd accepted her for who she was from the very beginning.

She stretched and yawned and slowly rolled to face the man sleeping beside her—the man she'd grown to love.

Love.

Her face grew soft with amazement, as if an angel had just appeared at the side of her bed and whispered the revelation in her ear. Her heart thumped in confirmation as her body weakened from the sweet realization that she was experiencing real, honest-to-goodness love for the first time in her life. The thought terrified her as much as it thrilled her.

Lying on his side facing her, the blanket barely covered the lower half of his body. She was grateful that most of him was gloriously naked and that she was free to admire at her leisure all the places she had touched and explored the night before. So completely engrossed in her visual admiration, she never noticed him peering at her through barely open eyes until her gaze traveled upward. Only then did she find him looking back through a myopic scowl.

She smiled and restrained herself from throwing her body over his to smother him with abundant hugs and kisses. "Good morning," she whispered through the sleepy fog still lingering in her throat. She knew there was nothing she could do about the blatant look of love shining from her eyes.

Throwing caution right out the window, she drew a deep breath to gain the courage to say what was on her mind and in her heart. She touched his cheek, caressed his bristly jaw, and declared, "I love you, Joel Hubbard. Will you marry me?"

When he didn't immediately respond, she studied his expression. She knew that look. She'd caught him in the headlights.

He gripped her hand and pulled away. "Marry?"

He reiterated the word like it was in an obscure language and he was attempting to process the translation into something he could comprehend.

Her heart skipped a couple of beats then started up erratically, almost hesitantly, as if it wasn't quite sure it wanted to continue beating. How much easier it would have been if it had stopped all together. It would have saved her from this massive case of humiliation and his forthcoming rejection.

The air around her disappeared and she struggled to draw a deep enough breath. Gasping and panting in an effort to stop herself from hyperventilating, she quickly extricated herself from the tangle of limbs and blankets and sat up. *Breathe, damn it, you've got to breathe.*

Unable to verbalize a response to his silent, though no less obvious rejection, she tossed back the covers and scooted to the end of the bed. He might just as well have peeled the skin from her naked body and ripped her heart from her chest. Stinging tears coursed down her flushed cheeks. She swiped them away, determined not to let him see how badly this affected her.

As she snatched her robe from the foot of the bed, she mumbled, "You can leave while I'm in the shower. It'll save us both from making awkward small talk across the breakfast table." Gwen stuffed her arms into the flowing sleeves and bounded for the bathroom.

"Gwen, don't—" Joel could have saved his breath. She wasn't interested in anything he had to say.

She stepped into the hottest, hardest pulsing water she could bear and used the loofah sponge to scrub her body. She wanted to punish herself for being such a fool to think a man like Joel Hubbard could possibly want her for anything more serious than an occasional romp between the sheets. When she was finished, her skin stung and glowed angry red from her abusive treatment, and both shins bore multiple nicks from the hasty razor she swiped across her legs. She really wanted to kick and scream and pitch a global-size temper tantrum, but that wasn't how she handled personal disappointment. Not when it was easier to take it out on herself.

Dressed in running attire, she exited her bedroom determined to run enough miles to clear her head. Her hair was still wet and pulled off her face, held tightly in place with a clip. Not one speck of makeup touched her freshly scrubbed complexion and the faint smattering of summer freckles she usually kept covered with foundation and blush appeared across her nose and cheeks like dandelions after a spring rain.

Coming down the stairs, she smelled fresh brewed coffee and... what else? Was that burnt toast? He must have discovered her temperamental toaster.

She found Joel sitting at the kitchen table with a mug of steaming, creamy coffee in one hand and studying what looked like a hunk of charcoal in the other. She sincerely hoped he wasn't planning on eating that. On second thought, she hoped he'd choked on it.

"I'd recommend getting yourself a new toaster, unless, of course, you're into offering burnt sacrifices."

How civilized, she thought, casting him a withering glance. She wasn't in any mood to respond to him or his attempt at casual banter. "I expected you to be long gone by now." Her tone was frosty and stripped of all emotion. "In fact, I was counting on it."

He adjusted the steel-framed glasses as he peered at her. "Gwen, we need to talk."

"Really?" she questioned as she made her way around the counter to pour a cup of coffee. "What about?" The straight up black brew was bitter and hot on her tongue as it seared its way down her throat and splashed into her empty stomach. Delicious. Just the way she wanted it.

Closing the distance, he came up behind her. "Well, for starters, how about that bombshell you dropped on me this morning."

She choked on the hot coffee and barked a cruel laugh. "Oh, that. Just chalk it off to post-orgasmic hormones. I've heard they can make a woman blurt all sorts of crazy stuff. You're the first man to experience that side of me." She closed her eyes and bit her lower lip, turning away from his nearness. If this was what real love felt like she wanted no part of it.

"Please try to understand, Gwen. You really took me by surprise. I've never been in a position like this before."

Her smile was coy and compelling as she looked at him through thick lashes and darkening bedroom eyes. "I'm sure there were a number of new positions you'd never been in before. I hope you enjoyed at least one or two of them. I know I did." Her voice was husky and suggestive. If she couldn't be the woman he wanted, she might as well be the woman every other man expected.

"Stop it, Gwen." He spoke with sharp authority. "There are so many emotions churning inside me right now I don't know which one to take out and examine first."

"Why don't you start with lust and desire? Those worked pretty well for you last night." From open collar to waist, her fingers trailed down the buttons of his sport shirt and stopped only when she reached the buckle on his black leather belt where she let her fingertips linger ever so suggestively.

"Cut the act, Gwen."

"How can you be so sure that this isn't the real me and all the rest has been just an act?"

"Because I've seen too many things in your behavior to the contrary, that's how. Every time I take you in my arms and you give of yourself so completely, it never fails to take my breath away. The intensity of what I feel during those times with you scares the hell out of me."

"Do I understand you correctly? The sex is great but anything beyond that is out of the question because you can't deal with the way I make you feel?"

He turned away and bowed his head, as if what he was about to say was almost too painful to confess. "When Beth died something inside me died too. I never wanted to feel the same way about a woman again. I've got to be honest with you, Gwen. Marriage never crossed my mind until you mentioned it this morning. I don't know if I'll ever be able to commit to someone so completely again."

A choked breath escaped from her lips. "I'm sorry. I didn't mean to put you on the defensive like that. It's just that...well...I thought we were good together, that we made a pretty good team..." She still wasn't ready to give up, and added, "You know, for someone who plans on helping others work through their emotional difficulties, you'd think you'd be able to get past this widower façade and move on." She remembered something she'd heard once and mumbled, "Physician heal thyself..."

"I wish it were that simple," he said on a depreciating note.

Gwen was trying very hard to be understanding and considerate of his feelings, but she felt like she was struggling up a muddy slope against a gale force. "It's never easy giving up one life to start over with another. Believe me, it's scary, I've had to start over more times than I care to count. And I'm sure it's even more difficult for you because you loved the life that was taken away. But if you don't stop dwelling on what you lost and start living for what's right in front of you, you're going to lose a lot more." She was upping the ante with everything she had. She pushed it into the pot and prayed it was enough.

"I can't give you any more, Gwen. Not now, maybe never. I'm sorry and I hope that's enough for you."

It was time to show her hand and lay her cards on the table. "No, Joel, it's not. It's not nearly enough. Not any more. There once was a time I would have settled for that and considered myself a lucky woman, but if I've learned nothing else from you during our time together I know this much, I want more from a relationship. I want it all. I want what you and Beth had. I want what Nick and Maggie have. And what's more, I know now that I deserve nothing less. So if you can't give me what I want—what I deserve—I'm going to keep looking until I find someone who's willing to love me with his *whole* heart—inside the bedroom and out."

"Gwen…I don't know what to say." His voice was ragged.

"There's only one thing left for you to say—" Closing her eyes, she pressed a lingering kiss to his bristly, unshaven cheek and breathed the scents of their final night together, a distinctive, earthy mixture of her cologne and his, of dried sweat, and sensuously uninhibited sex, and the passionate heat that melted it all into a fusion of poignant memories that would stay with her forever. It was nearly her undoing but she managed to finish by adding, "Goodbye.

"I'm going running. Please don't be here when I get back."

She was out the door and halfway down the

street before Joel found his voice. “Goodbye, Gwen…”

****

Gwen ran for miles. She followed all her usual paths around town plus several new ones, and yet when she slowed down to catch her breath, she realized she’d come full circle. She was just a few short blocks from her house.

A glance at her sport watch told her she’d given Joel more than enough time to get out of her house and her life. At the thought of him, she gasped for breath against the hollow ache radiating in her chest that had nothing to do with finding enough air to fill her lungs. She was heartbroken and knew it would take more than a long run to heal the hurt and disappointment.

“Good morning, Gwen dear.”

Gwen pushed an errant strand of hair from her face as she whirled to find her neighbor, Elsie Miller, dragging a grocery-filled, two-wheeled wire cart behind her. One wheel emitted an intermittent squeak with every step the elderly woman took in Gwen’s direction.

“Morning, Elsie. How are you?” Gwen’s words came in shallow, breathless pants as she wiped perspiration from her forehead and upper lip. She took the cart handle from the woman’s arthritic fingers and fell into a slow pace beside her neighbor.

“I appreciate your help, Gwen. The walk to the store is getting harder every week. I don’t know how much longer I’m going to be able to live alone.”

“Maybe it’s time to start thinking about an assisted living center. I’ve heard the new one on Arthur Avenue is a lovely facility.”

“Yes, I’ve heard that, too, but they don’t allow pets. What would I do with my precious Muffin?”

Gwen knew where this conversation was leading. Mrs. Miller had broached the subject on several occasions and Gwen's answer was always the same. She was fond of her neighbor, but agreeing to take custody of her elderly cat was a tad more neighborly than she was willing to go. If Elsie's daughter wasn't willing to take Muffin, Gwen didn't feel compelled to do so either. She felt bad, guilty in fact, but not enough to change her mind. She had to draw the line somewhere.

"We've already had this conversation, Elsie. You know I can't take Muffy."

"I know, but I keep hoping you'll change your mind since Muffin likes you so much." The elderly woman cast Gwen a sly sideward glance. "I'm finding him in your yard or garage more and more lately."

Gwen tried not to think about the last time she'd seen the wanderlust tabby but failed miserably at the attempt. Every image, every sensation, every moment, of that night was indelibly etched into her heart and head, and she doubted if those memories would soon be forgotten. Especially since they were all she had left of her and Joel's short-lived relationship.

"Looks like you've got company," Elsie noted as they rounded the corner.

Gwen had been so steeped in her thoughts, she hadn't noticed the hulking recreational vehicle parked in front of her house, or the group of people standing in her yard—Joel among them.

Since it was too late to turn tail and run away, she heaved a long-suffering sigh and relinquished the cart to Elsie Miller as she plastered a smile on her face in preparation to greet her guests and ignore Joel.

"Mom!" Samantha broke away from the group and ran toward her mother. Gwen's smile was genuine at the sight of her tanned and happy daughter. "I was just about to head up a search party. Mr. Hubbard said you left to go running hours ago."

Gwen forced a self-deprecating laugh. "I decided to take a different route today and found myself in an unfamiliar part of town. Took me a little longer to find my way home." Her excuse didn't even sound plausible to her. She hoped her daughter and the others weren't paying too close attention to her ramblings. As it turned out, only Joel cast a curious glance in her direction, which caused her heart to flutter erratically as a heated flush crept across her cheeks.

"Did you have a good time?" Gwen asked no one in particular, but the kids all started talking at once with tales of their mini vacation.

Emme tugged on Gwen's fingers to get her attention. "'Mantha rided with me down the lady ribber."

Gwen crouched to the child's level. "What's the lady ribber, sweetie?" She glanced to Samantha for an explanation.

"She means the lazy river," Sam translated with a laugh as she wound the little girl's red curls around her finger. "We had a good time, didn't we, Em?" The child nodded vigorously and grinned at Samantha with blatant adoration shining in her bright blue eyes.

Maggie glanced right past Gwen and said to Joel, "Emme insisted Samantha sit next to her on the drive up and barely left her side the rest of the trip. We all thought it was cute, except for Davey, of course."

Maggie's intentional slight didn't bother Gwen nearly as much as it would have once, but she took a couple steps back nevertheless, in an effort to distance herself from the affront. She was tired of fighting the world; she was tired of wanting what she couldn't have. She was just plain tired of it all.

A wave of sadness poured over her.

She felt Joel staring at her and she found herself wondering what was going through his mind. Her mistake was glancing in his direction. Their eyes locked briefly, and in that split second she caught a glimpse of every intimate moment they'd shared reflected in the depths of his steely gaze. She couldn't do this. Not again.

"Excuse me," she stammered as she hurried up the walkway and into the house.

She ran into the upstairs bathroom and slammed the door just seconds before there came a gentle knock from the other side.

"Gwen," Joel said. "Please come out and talk to me?"

"No. Go away." She cranked the sink faucets to high with the hope of drowning out the sound of his voice. "There's nothing left to talk about." She hated this. She hated being in a situation she couldn't control. She pressed her back against the door and slid down the flat, wood panel to the floor. "Please go away," she implored. "Please."

"All right, Gwen, I'll go. But I want you to know how sorry I am about all of this. I never meant for it to end this way. I never meant to hurt you."

There was a lengthy pause followed by his footsteps down the stairs and out the front door.

For someone who never meant to hurt her, he did one dandy, bang-up job of doing exactly that.

Chapter Twenty-One

"Are you sure you want to go through with this, Mom?" Samantha stood beside her mother and prepared herself for the upcoming race with a series of warm-up stretches.

Gwen was depressed and heartbroken. So no, she wasn't sure she wanted to be at an event co-chaired by none other than the man responsible for her miserable state. Just because she'd been the one to call it quits didn't make the breakup any less painful or regrettable.

"Today isn't about me," Gwen stated. With one hand braced against a tree for support, Gwen gripped the top of her foot from behind, and pulled her heel toward her butt to stretch her quadriceps. She changed legs and repeated the stretching exercise. "I refuse to let my feelings keep me from doing what's right." She'd trained for weeks for this race and raised nearly three thousand dollars in pledges. For that reason alone she couldn't back out. She wouldn't because of its importance to her, her daughter, and every other woman on the planet. "Quitting or giving up is not an option."

"I'm really proud of you for following through with this, Mom. Did I ever tell you you're everything I aspire to be when I grow up?"

Her daughter's out-of-the-blue declaration broke through her emotional barriers and brought tears to Gwen's eyes. She swallowed against the lump in her throat and forced a depreciating laugh. "Just promise me you'll make better choices when it comes to the men in your life."

She raised her gaze to the vivid blue August sky sliced by a snapping plastic banner announcing: *Beth Hubbard Memorial Moving Toward a Cure Benefit.*

She turned just in time to see Joel take his seat on the pink bunting-draped stage rising from the center of the town square. Her breath hitched and her chest constricted as she pressed a fist against her twisting gut. He looked so handsome and commanding, in spite of the pale pink T-shirt hugging his chest. There wasn't another man sitting on the dais, except for maybe Nick Chapparelle, who managed to carry of the pastel shirt so well.

She finished stretching and melted into the crowd of participants to watch the opening ceremony. Among those numbers there were survivors, family members of those who had succumbed, and some were only observers, but all of them, regardless of their reasons for being there, were brought together with one common goal—finding a cure for the devastating disease that robbed families of mothers, sisters, wives, and daughters. Most women, including Gwen, believed there were only two kinds of women in the world—those afflicted with breast cancer and those who feared the affliction.

"May I have your attention please," requested a woman wearing a pink and white jogging suit. The microphone gave out an ear-piercing screech and she waited for a young man to adjust the volume before continuing. "Hello, everyone, my name is Monica Brady, as co-chair of this year's event I want to thank you all for coming out today.

"As most of you know, each year we choose one woman from our community who has lost her battle with breast cancer. The committee unanimously selected Beth Hubbard nee Mahoney as this year's honoree. And now, without further ado, it is my pleasure to introduce my co-chair and Beth's husband, Joel. Many of you remember him as Principal Hubbard." She stood aside and joined in the applause as Joel stepped to the podium.

"I cannot tell you how pleased my wife would have been to see all of you here today. Beth was only thirty when she was diagnosed with breast cancer. She was thirty when she died." Joel paused to allow the crowd to absorb what he was telling them.

"It took less than a year for this disease to take her life. Because she was *only* thirty, she didn't take the lump seriously and put off telling her doctor. And because she wasn't concerned, I made the biggest mistake of my life by not insisting she have it checked. That's why I'm telling every single one of you that this is one time you're allowed to harass, pester, threaten, and yes, even nag your loved one about getting themselves checked because until there is a cure, early detection and treatment is the best course of action for successful, long term survival." He raised his fist high over his head and shouted, "Be a nag, save a life!"

Everyone seated on the dais jumped to their feet and joined Joel in his chant. "Be a nag, save a life! Be a nag, save a life!"

Gwen found herself caught up in the frenzy of the crowd and started reciting the slogan, not perhaps as enthusiastic as most, but it was the best she could muster considering her heart wasn't in a lot of things lately.

Nick Chapparelle joined Joel at the microphone and raised a starter pistol over his head. "Ladies and gentlemen, start your feet." He fired the gun and the participants took off.

Gwen ran like she'd never run before. She'd needed this outlet for all the emotional turmoil that had been churning inside her for the last week and she hoped the physical exertion would do the trick because she wasn't capable of shedding one more tear. Her emotions had been stretched and twisted and battered, but now she needed to find her way back from that wretched place.

She'd made a mistake. No matter how hard she tried to make this all Joel's fault, she couldn't do it. She was just as much to blame. The phrase "It takes two" translated into more than just making love. It was every bit as much the explanation behind their inability to make it as a couple.

As she neared the finish line, Gwen cast a quick glance at her watch and realized her time was pushing a personal best. Feeing pretty good about it, she focused on tearing up the last fifty yards.

Gwen should have known better. She wasn't a novice, for crying out loud. When she first started running, she'd lost her concentration for just a split second, mis-stepped, and took a bad tumble. She'd been fortunate not to break anything but the fall had left her with a nasty case of road rash down the side of her left arm and leg and wearing long sleeves and pants for weeks.

This time all she'd attempted was a quick U-turn when she spotted Joel standing at the finish line. She cut a sharp left, hopped over the curb, and headed into the park. She didn't get very far. Not ten feet into her escape, her feet tangled in a pair of discarded warm-up pants and down she went.

More embarrassed than anything else, she found herself face down in the grass staring at a large pair of familiar white sneakers.

"Are you hurt?"

At the sound of his voice, her heart gave a couple of excited beats and she was forced to take a deep breath to settle the cardiac irregularity. She rolled to her back and shaded her eyes to get a better look at the man who caused her heart to do another crazy dance against her ribs. A week hadn't diminished her feelings for him, she realized. Like she expected otherwise?

"No," she finally answered as she sat up and disentangled the pants from around her feet. "I'm fine." She hoped her words were firm and final sounding enough to make him go away.

When she didn't immediately get up, he joined her on the ground and started feeling her grass-stained knees. The heat of his touch sent tremors through her body and made her wonder how she could still want a man with every fiber of her being when the feeling wasn't returned. No, in all fairness, that wasn't quite the whole truth. He never denied he still wanted her. It just wasn't the way she wanted him to want her. Therein lay the distinction of their differences of opinion.

"What are you doing?" she asked, sounding more wary of his action than hopeful.

"I'm just checking to see if you're all right," he said as his hand rubbed her leg with a soothing stroke from knee to ankle and up again.

She couldn't draw a deep enough breath. Such an easy, comforting gesture shouldn't cause these kinds of emotional spikes, she told herself as her breathing took on a life of its own.

"Well stop it," she said as she drew up her knees and wrapped her arms around them in an effort to keep from flinging herself at him. "I'm fine." She didn't trust herself to say more.

"Gwen..." He leaned toward her, with his hand open to cup her face, but froze the second she cringed and withdrew. He dropped his hand and groaned, "Please don't do that."

She didn't want him showing her any tenderness. She couldn't bear it. "I'd just as soon you didn't come any closer." She was surprised at how firm her voice issued her desire, although it felt incredibly brittle, as if it would break under the strain. She buried her face in her hands. "Will you please just go away?"

He dragged her hands away and stared into her eyes. "I've missed you."

She jumped to her feet and he quickly followed. Her features softened as she stared at him. "I've missed you too." Missed, and ached, and even reconsidered, but refused to relent.

His expression brightened. "Are you having second thoughts?"

"Second thoughts, yes," she admitted, though *second* didn't come close to the times she'd thought about taking what he offered.

"Really?" he said, sounding encouraged.

"But not enough to change my mind."

"Oh." His one word response spoke volumes of disappointment.

"You apparently haven't changed your mind either."

"No."

"Then it looks like there's nothing more to say. It was nice to see you again, Joel. Have a nice life." Gwen was amazed at the calm that settled through her and gave her the strength to walk away.

"Have dinner with me tonight."

"Sorry, no." She kept walking and concentrated on placing one foot in front of the other.

"Tomorrow then?"

Gwen shook her head against his persistence.

"Gwen, please, we had a good thing going. I don't want to lose that. I know you still have feelings for me."

She pinned him with a level stare, studied every chiseled feature, and breathed, "That's precisely why I can't see you again."

Chapter Twenty-Two

Bette poked her head around the office partition. "Uh, Gwen, there's a couple of detectives here to see you."

Gwen looked up from what she was doing. "Detectives? What do they want?"

Bette shrugged. "They wouldn't tell me. Said they needed to talk to you. Now."

With a wave of her hand, Gwen said, "Then I guess you'd better send them in."

Two men walked single file into her partitioned office space. The only thing missing from their rigid postures and stoic expressions was matching khaki uniforms. Although, on second glance, Gwen realized their mode of dress *was* fairly uniform with identical short-sleeved, white dress shirts, similar dark pants, and conservative neckties. On their belts they carried holstered guns, mace, and cuffs. They sure looked like plain-clothes cops. Their manner of dress couldn't get much plainer.

Gwen stood and shook their hands. "May I see some identification, please?"

Without hesitation, they reached into their pockets and produced identical black leather holders. Flipping them open, they exposed their gold shields and photo IDs for her inspection. She took her time, matching the picture with the face—Dan Riley on the left and Ken Leland on the right. Yep, they were legit all right.

Once convinced they were who they said they were, Gwen gestured for them to have a seat. "What can I do for you, detectives?" She closed the folder in front of her and rested clasped hands across the top.

Leland spoke first. "We're interested in knowing the last time you had any contact with Joel Hubbard."

"Joel? Oh, it was weeks ago, earlier this month, I think." She knew the exact time and date, it was the day of the charity run, but until she knew more of what this was all about she wasn't about to offer any information, substantial, specific, or conclusive. "Why? Is he in some kind of trouble?" Her eyes darted from one stony face to the other. Oh, they were good. Not a smidgen of expression gave away their agenda.

"Why do you ask?" Riley piped up. "Do you have reason to believe he could be in trouble?"

"Why else would you be here asking about him?" she answered with another question. She'd watched enough *Law and Order* over the years to know a few things about interrogation tactics and how they worked. "I'm not thinking you're looking for Joel because he has an outstanding parking ticket."

Detective number one glanced at his partner. "We were called to investigate Mr. Hubbard's possible disappearance. He's been reported missing. None of his family has been able to get in touch with him in more than a week. We were informed that the two of you were close friends and we thought you might have some idea of his whereabouts."

"Missing? What do you mean missing? He's a grown man, a responsible adult, with a home and a small child. People like that don't just turn up missing. And what about his daughter Emme? Is she missing too?"

"No, we've already established that she's with her maternal grandparents in Michigan. They, however, haven't heard from him since he dropped his daughter off ten day ago."

"Are they the ones who contacted you?"

"Actually, no. It was his father, Martin Hubbard."

The retired Army colonel, as Gwen recalled, or *The Colonel*, as Joel respectfully referred to his father. The Colonel had spent most of his career in military intelligence. Considering that, his suspicions were certainly justifiable though hopefully unwarranted. To him missing meant *MISSING*!

"I really wish I could help, but like I said, I haven't had any recent contact with Joel. We stopped being close friends, as you put it, weeks ago."

Then it dawned on her and she abruptly pushed back her chair, taking both detectives by surprise. "I'll be right back," she explained as she walked around the partition to the nearby, presently unoccupied, desk of Leon Washburn, the agent she had prudently handed Joel's file to after the break-up. She'd needed to make it abundantly clear to Joel that she wanted no further contact with him. A clean break was best for both of them. She sorted through Leon's stack of client folders and found the one she was looking for near the top.

Returning to her desk, she opened the folder and began thumbing through the file in search of one specific piece of paper. "If you don't already know, Mr. Hubbard is also a client. We document every communication we have with our clients, dates, times, and any other pertinent information." Her fingers finally located it. "Here," she said, glancing down the recorded entries. Her heart plummeted. "We haven't had any recent communication with him either." She glanced at the open appointment calendar on her desk. "It's been almost two weeks." Two weeks! She couldn't believe that no one had had any contact with Joel in nearly two whole weeks.

"Is there anything else in that file that could

help us?"

"According to this, he's already closed on his new house in..." Oh, God. "...Cartwright Corners." This was the first time she'd paid attention to his file since she handed it over. He bought THE house. She closed her mind to anything connected to that particular house and forced herself back to the immediate task at hand. "And there appears to be an offer currently pending on the house we're selling for him, contingent on loan approval. Nothing unusual or out of the ordinary, I'm afraid. Its all pretty standard real estate stuff."

"The sale that's pending, that's the house on Parkview Drive?"

"That's right."

The detective on the left leaned forward with renewed interest. "Realtors have keys to the properties their selling, don't they?"

She nodded and eyed them warily. "I have a key to the lock box that gives me access to the house key, yes." She knew where this was leading and she wasn't sure she wanted any part of it. "But I can't just hand it over to you."

"We understand that. But getting into his house could give us some clue as to what we're possibly dealing with here."

A cold knot clenched in her gut. "Surely you're not thinking foul play?"

"We're not sure of anything yet, Ms. Marconi. We're just starting our investigation." The older detective, Dan Riley, stood and his partner quickly followed suit. "Will you give us access to his house to help expedite our investigation, or will you force us to get a warrant, which will only delay it?"

"I'll let you in, but I stay with you every step of the way."

"That's not advisable," said Detective Leland.

"Or standard procedure," said his partner.

"This is my butt and reputation you're asking me to put on the line. I have an ethical, not to mention legal, obligation to protect my client's assets in their absence. It's either my way or the long way." She stared them down. "What's it going to be, gentlemen?" She surprised herself by how calm and resolute she sounded considering her insides felt like nothing remotely resembling either of those things.

****

Gwen's hand shook as she slipped the key into the lock box. Joel's house key dropped into her open palm and she clasped it in her fingers to keep from dropping it. She was terrified of what they might find inside. Her fearful state didn't go unnoticed.

"Are you sure you want to go through with this, Ms. Marconi?" Detective Leland seemed genuinely concerned by her hesitance. "Maybe you'd rather wait for us in the car?"

"I'm sure," she said as she drew a deep breath and jabbed the second key into the deadbolt. The door swung open.

Leland moved her aside. "Wait right here and don't venture anywhere on your own."

As her eyes adjusted to the darkened rooms, Gwen glanced around the once homey Georgian. Pictures were down and leaning in piles against one wall and she found packed and tagged boxes carefully stacked in a far corner of the living room.

She couldn't immediately put her finger on it but something wasn't quite right, and she seriously doubted it was just the bare walls and cardboard boxes that brought about the uneasiness she experienced. The drapes were drawn against the late afternoon sun, yet the house wasn't in the least bit hot or stifling as houses usually are when closed up for extended periods. It was surprisingly cooler than she would have imagined. Then it dawned on her. The air-conditioning was running.

That fact in itself wasn't particularly unusual. She knew lots of people who left the thermostat set to a consistent temperature even when they weren't home. The air would only kick on if the temperature in the house reached above a certain level. She walked to where the thermostat was located and glanced at the setting. It was adjusted to a slightly higher than normal setting. What bothered her is that she knew Joel wasn't particularly fond of air-conditioning, and he ran it more for his daughter's comfort than his own. If given a personal choice, he preferred open windows and ceiling fans. If Em was in Michigan and Joel wasn't home, why was it running at all? What the hell was going on?

Realizing the detectives were busy investigating the rooms on the main level, she ignored their directive and took the staircase that led to the bedrooms. She passed Emme's room and gave it a cursory glance as she headed for the master bedroom. The door was partially closed. Her heart thumped in her throat as she pushed on the creamy white six-panel door.

She screamed and fled the sight of the body sprawled face down across the king-sized bed. Gripping the banister for support, she stumbled down the stairs, and met Detective Riley at the bottom.

"The bedroom…" she choked as he ran past her with gun drawn. Taking the stairs two at a time, Ken Leland followed close behind.

Once both men had passed, she forced herself to move and collapsed into the nearest chair. She heard voices, first loud and demanding, then softer and muffled. Hard as she concentrated on the sounds, she couldn't make out what the two detectives were saying. She was curious, but not enough to go back upstairs and face the possibility that Joel was… No, no, it wasn't true. He was sick, or hurt, or worst case, unconscious. But she wouldn't let herself believe he was dead.

Gwen buried her face in her hands in an effort to wipe the dreadful image from her mind.

Chapter Twenty-Three

A gentle hand touched her shoulder. "Gwen…"

Joel crouched to face her and pulled her hands away from her face. "Look at me. I'm fine. This has all been a terrible misunderstanding."

She stared at him and touched his cheek with tentative fingers. He was warm and very much alive, and she cried tears of relief until the reality of the situation finally sunk in.

"You bastard!" With the heel of her palm she gave him a sharp shove to his shoulder. He lost his balance and landed soundly on his ass. "Where the hell have you been?" Relief had evolved into rage. She leaped to her feet and began to pace in an effort to settle down. Her emotions had fluctuated so rapidly, she wasn't sure what she was feeling at the moment.

He picked himself up and sat on the edge of the couch. "I needed some time alone so I dropped Em off at her grandparents and headed to my cottage in Dowagiac. It was the last chance I had before we moved."

When she finally determined which emotion was the most predominant, she whirled around and faced him. Anger flashed, deepening her eyes to cobalt. "What were you thinking? How could you go off like that without letting anyone know where you were going? There were people worried about you, although God only knows why since you obviously don't care about anyone but yourself."

"Excuse me," said detective Leland who stood in the archway between the foyer and the living room.

"We're going to head back to the station and close this case." He leveled his gaze on Joel. "Can I count on you to call your father and in-laws to let them know you're still alive and kicking, or would you like us to do it for you?"

"I'll take care of it," said Joel, visibly contrite for his temporary lapse in judgment and total lack of consideration for others.

"Can we give you a ride back to your office, Ms. Marconi?"

"Yes, thank you." She moved to join them.

"I'll see that she gets back." Joel interjected.

"That acceptable with you, ma'am?" The detective questioned, obviously sensing the tension between them.

"No, it's not." She didn't want to be left alone with Joel. There really wasn't anything more she had to say to him.

He took her by the elbow to keep her from leaving. "I said I'd drive you," he stated.

Gwen leveled her gaze on the hand that gripped her arm then slowly raised her eyes to meet his. He released her immediately.

"Gwen, please," he said softer this time. "I'd really like you to stay."

Glancing at the detectives then back to Joel, she waved Riley and Leland off. "You can go. I don't live too far from here." Then she cast a chilling glance in Joel's direction. "I can walk home if necessary."

Once the detectives were gone, Joel poured two snifters of brandy and handed her one. "You look like you could use this. I know I do," he said as he swirled his glass and tossed back a healthy swallow.

She cupped the crystal snifter in her palm and brought it hesitantly to her lips. The smell alone made her stomach lurch, which prompted her to set the glass down and push it aside. She was getting a sick headache and rubbed her temples to ease the throbbing.

"Excuse me," she gagged, as she ran to the powder room off the main hall with one hand clasped across her mouth and the other clutching her churning stomach.

He was waiting just outside the door when she came out. She cast him a quick glance then looked away. She didn't get migraines often but when she did the ceaseless pain always left her nauseous and weak. And no one looked their best after heaving their guts out.

"Let me take you home."

Eager to get out of there, she nodded, growing increasingly uneasy under his scrutiny. She wanted to get home before she made an even bigger fool of herself.

The short ride to her house was made in total, exceedingly uncomfortable silence. It seemed they were nothing more than intimate strangers forced to occupy the same space through a series of questionable circumstances. Gwen was grateful for the peace and quiet. There was nothing worse than attempting to civilize a love affair gone wrong with senseless chatter. Opening her window, she leaned against the headrest and closed her eyes. The fragrant evening air blowing across her face helped clear her head and settle her stomach. The tension flowed from her body and her eyes grew heavy. What a day, she thought as she drifted asleep two blocks from her house.

Joel pulled the mini van into the middle of her driveway and cut the engine. He released the seat belt and turned to face her. He found her sound asleep, her breathing even and peaceful.

He studied her in the amber twilight, his gaze lingering briefly on each attractive feature from hairline to chin. She was by anyone's standards a beautiful woman. His gaze fell on her eyes. Although now closed, he didn't need to see them to remember the deepness of the blue, the reflective sparkle when she smiled with that incredibly expressive mouth.

From the very beginning, there had been something so profoundly simple and uncomplicated about their relationship. It had started so amazingly easily and developed so naturally, he wondered why he didn't see that her feelings were developing faster and deeper than his own. But he had enjoyed her company. Even more importantly, he had enjoyed the effortless companionship she offered him. He'd missed that most of all when Beth died—that unspoken acceptance of one another that didn't require constant chatter to sustain it. He'd been selfish in that respect, and wondered why he hadn't seen it sooner. In an effort not to lose the one part of their relationship he cherished, and yes, their physical compatibility was certainly part of the overall equation, by not telling her he wasn't ready for a long term relationship he'd allowed her to believe it would progress into a deeper permanence. He'd certainly never given her reason not to think otherwise.

He knew she still cared. Her behavior today when she thought something had happened to him proved it. And on some distant emotional level, it pleased him to know it.

She breathed an audible sigh and her head rolled gently across the padded headrest. He touched her pale cheek with the back of his knuckle and a curious expression crossed his features. He missed so much about this woman. Aside from the obvious, he missed hearing about her day and having her listen to him about his. He missed telling her about Emme's newest discovery and hearing her boast about Samantha's latest achievement. Emme had instinctively sought Gwen's attention when a father's touch wasn't comforting enough, and she looked at Samantha with the eyes of an adoring little sister.

Like it or not, however loosely shaped, their individual lives had been woven into some obscure pattern of a family. Maybe he had seen it all along and just didn't want to acknowledge that which he wasn't ready to accept. It made him take pause and seriously wonder if they could negotiate a compromise—something more than what they had before but not quite what she had in mind. He'd never know unless he asked, he reasoned as he got out of the car and came around to open the passenger door.

"Gwen, honey. You want to wake up? You're home." He reached across her and released the seatbelt and she slumped forward into his arms like a loose-limbed doll. An elusive mixture of sweet, clean scents, warmed naturally by her skin and transferred to her clothes and hair, caught him by surprise and caused him to take a startled breath and inhale deeply. He stood motionless for a few lingering moments and allowed himself the luxury of feeling her once again in his arms.

She awoke slowly and disoriented. When it dawned on her where she was, she pulled back and pushed him away. "What are you doing?"

"Holding someone I've missed very much."

She eyed him suspiciously and spread an open palm against his chest to keep him at arm's length. "Don't even think about it, Dr. Hubbard. I'm not known for giving second chances."

"Is there no room left in your heart for a little friendly negotiation?"

"Sorry, doc, my heart's still closed for repairs from the last time I let you in." She moved forward while she continued to exert steady pressure against his chest in an attempt to escape from the confines of the van. He wouldn't budge and stubbornly held his ground.

"I know I hurt you, Gwen. And I know I don't have any right to ask for another chance, but I'm asking anyway. Surely we can find a common ground, a comfortable compromise that we both find agreeable."

"Just what exactly are you *proposing*," she asked, intentionally emphasizing her final word. She couldn't wait to hear what he had to say on that subject.

Her choice of words was not lost on him. "Like I said, I'm willing to kick this relationship up a notch. Sure, why not? We could get engaged. Engaged is okay. We'll go ring shopping tomorrow." He leaned forward, as if to seal their bargain with a kiss and God knows what else.

Exerting addition pressure on his chest with her hand, she stared at him for a long, incredible moment with an expression that clearly questioned his sanity. "You've got to be kidding," she exclaimed. "I've been propositioned with more enthusiasm, and a damn sight more conviction." She blinked hard twice, telling herself that she wasn't going to get angry. She was further amazed by the overwhelming confusion contorting his features which were similar to that of a puppy that'd just been kicked. He was good, she had to give him that, but she wasn't falling for it. Not this time.

"You have two choices—get out of my way or pick yourself off the ground." Her voice lacked any human emotion. It was dull, low and brittle. This time he moved.

"I thought this was what you wanted."

"What I want is for you to get the hell out of my way."

She was barely out of the van when she turned violently. "I'm not asking for moonlight and roses, but that sounded more like you were debating between a Big Mac and a Whopper." She pushed past him and was halfway to her back door when she whirled around with more to say. "Even my first husband managed a more charming proposal than that. And he was a first class asshole. So take a wild guess where that puts you on my jerk-o-meter." She turned her back on him again, took two steps, and then looked at him for what she hoped was the very last time.

"Did you really think that sweetening the deal with a diamond would be enough to make me take you back? I told you once what I wanted. It hasn't changed. But let me add this one last thing before I kick your sorry butt to the curb, you'd have to be the last man left on the face of this earth and I was the last female before I'd even think about giving you another chance. So find some other unsuspecting blonde to peddle that poor pitiful widower routine on because I'm sick of it and I'm sick of you!"

This time she was gone for good. Thankfully the door was open because her exit would have lost its effectiveness if she'd needed to dig around in her purse for her key.

Especially since she didn't know where the heck her purse was at the moment.

No. It wasn't. It just couldn't be. She cast a quick glance over her shoulder. Shit. There he stood with her purse swinging from his finger by the sturdy leather strap. She felt the air slowly release from her sail when she realized he was going to make her go to him. If it were anything else—a sweater, an earring, a shoe—she'd have told him exactly what to do with it. But her life was in that unstructured sack of leather. Cell phone, electronic organizer, wallet, credit cards, lipstick and tampons...the list went on and on. She needed that purse.

She stiffened her backbone, turned, and

marched down the walk. When she reached for the purse, he whipped it out of her reach.

"Will you please give me that?"

"Not until you explain that widower crack."

"You're the college graduate, you figure it out." She grabbed for the purse and missed again.

"I think you owe me an apology."

"I owe you..." she sputtered. "For what?"

He held up an index finger and added additional fingers as he ticked off the reasons. "One, the widower crack, two, the jerk-o-meter, three, the last man on the face of the earth... Need I go on?"

"Forget it. I'm not apologizing for anything. I meant every word." Her migraine was starting to rear its ugly head again. On a scale of worst days lived by Gwen Marconi, this one was definitely in the running for top honors. She'd have to think real long and hard to find a worse one, and right now her head wasn't about to cooperate with her search. It hurt just to blink and she was starting to feel sick again.

Inch by miserable inch, she felt herself crumble and collapse into exactly the kind of woman she didn't want to be—a teary-eyed, quivering-lipped, weak-kneed, spineless female. "Just keep the stupid thing," she said. "I don't care any more." Hanging her head, she began to weep, loudly and wholly undignified.

He didn't know how it happened. She was screaming and yelling at him one minute and crying the next, and damned if he wasn't feeling like the grand prize winner on her jerk-o-meter.

"Gwen, honey," he said. "Please don't do this." As he tried to put his arms around her, she sniffled loudly, sparked to life, and shoved him away.

"Get away. Don't touch me!" She snatched her purse out of his hand and took three steps back. "What's it going to take to get through to you? I'm through. It's over. I never want to see you again." On that final note, she whirled on her heels and made a mad dash for the door.

Joel was smart enough not to go after her.

Chapter Twenty-Four

Joel sat at the family-sized trestle table in the middle of the warm surroundings of the kitchen Nick had designed and lovingly built for the woman he loved. The inviting room would be what some considered the heart of the house but Joel knew it was the two people sitting across the table from him that gave the structure its real warmth and lifeblood. Was it any wonder why he sought their company at this particularly low point in his life?

From where he sat, he could see Em playing on the floor in the next room with Nick and Maggie's daughters, two-year-old Kaitlyn and ten month old Tally, short for Taledega, naturally. Only another NASCAR enthusiast would understand naming your daughter after a racetrack.

Nick shook his head in wholehearted commiseration. Maggie, however, wasn't the least bit sympathetic to his plight. She rolled her eyes as she reached for the coffee pot and said, "I'd give her some time to get over that *charming* proposal before you try to talk to her again."

"I don't think there's enough time in the world for her to get over that." Joel kept his head lowered and stared into the depths of the nearly empty coffee mug, afraid of what he'd read in the faces of his friends. He knew he was an idiot. He didn't need them to confirm it. "I've got to face the simple truth of the matter. The reason that proposal came out the way it did is because I'm not ready to make that kind of commitment. I was desperate and grasping at anything to keep her and she saw right though it.

It was wonderful while it lasted, but it's over. Gwen made that abundantly clear."

"Are you hearing what you're saying?" Maggie questioned. "How many more chances at wonderful do you think you're allowed in this lifetime?"

Joel looked at Maggie like she was a stranger. "I expected you to be jumping for joy over this. You're the one who didn't think we were right for each other from the beginning."

"I was wrong," Maggie confessed.

"So was I," Joel retorted. "Remarrying would be like burying Beth all over again. I'm not ready to do that."

Maggie turned to her husband. "How about taking the girls outside for a while? I need to talk to Joel—alone."

"Sure," Nick agreed, pushing himself from the table. "Tally, Kait," he called as he left the kitchen, "Let's get your shoes on. You too, Emme. We're going to the park."

The park to Nick and Maggie's children was an oversized sandlot located directly outside in the backyard. This veritable toddler's paradise, surrounded by a three-foot high white vinyl fence, was filled with the most imaginative playground equipment carried by Toys R Us. If it weren't for the abundant love and discipline Maggie and Nick doled out to counter balance the excesses, their children would be spoiled rotten beyond belief. But, as anyone who knew them could testify, the Chapparelle brood were indulged by loving parents who taught their children to appreciate what they have, never take any of it for granted, and above all else, never, never demand or expect it because it could vanish just as quickly as it had appeared.

After Nick and the kids were gone, Maggie left the room. When she returned, she held something in her hand. She stood beside Joel and placed her arm around his shoulder as she handed him an envelope.

Joel recognized his wife's familiar scrawl, which was a distinctive combination of printing and cursive. It was a little shakier than normal, he noted, and some of the letters weren't quite as sharp, but it was unmistakably Beth's handwriting.

"What's this?" he asked, flipping the sealed white No. 10 over in his hands.

"Something Beth asked me to give you when and if I determined you needed it. I only wish I'd given it to you sooner."

"What's in it?"

Maggie shrugged. "I have no idea. It was sealed when she gave it to me with specific instructions to give it to you if ever I saw you behaving... well, the way you are now."

"I don't understand. What do you mean the way I am now?" It had been more than four years since Beth passed away. What was so important now that wasn't then? "When did she write this? All we did was talk at the end. Why couldn't she have told me whatever it is she said in this?" He cracked the edge of the envelope on the table with increasing confusion.

"I think you might find all the answers you're looking for in there. I'll be in the other room if you need me."

"Wait." He took a deep breath. "If Beth trusted you with this in the first place, then I think she'd want you to be here when I read it. I'd like you to be here, too," he added.

She conceded and sat across from him, but not before grabbing the box of tissues from the counter behind her and placing it between them.

He broke the seal and lifted the flap. There was nothing fancy about the stationery she used. In fact it was nothing more than a few sheets of plain, ordinary printer paper. How typical, he thought with a sad smile, practical to the very end. His heart beat a little faster as he unfolded the contents.

Hi Big Guy!

I'll bet you never expected to be hearing from me again. I guess I just couldn't resist the opportunity to nag at you one last time, even if it is posthumously. Well, here goes…

Damn it, Joel! Picture me frowning and color me angry, because if you're reading this you're not the man I expected you to be by now. But, knowing you as well as I do, I also knew there might be a need for just such a letter. You're having trouble getting past this whole me dead you still alive business, aren't you? Don't even try to deny it. You never could fool me. Your loyalty and devotion is commendable, however misplaced.

You've met someone else, haven't you? And you're feeling pretty guilty about it, right? I know things must be pretty bad if Maggie found it necessary to give this to you. In spite of the fact that the hopeless romantic in me would like to imagine you grieving over me forever, I am also a diehard pragmatist. The practical part of me would hate to see such a good man as you go to waste. And you are, Joel. You're a damn good man.

Inasmuch as I expected your grief to be appropriately heartfelt—I did, after all, give you the best ten years of my life – I also wanted it to be brief so that you could get on with what's left of yours. Grief is something to get through and get over, not something to hang on to like that awful plaid flannel shirt you refused to let me throw away. I got a gold harp riding on the fact that it's still hanging at the back of your closet. Am I right?

I wasn't perfect, Joel. But then again, you and I both know neither were you. Please don't remember me as a saint just because I happened to draw the short straw. That would really piss me off if you did. I prefer thinking of it as not being the last one picked for the team for once.

Try to remember me as the whole, imperfect person I was: a short-tempered, green-eyed, redhead who constantly struggled with controlling her big mouth, her unruly hair, and her spreading hips.

Remember me as the sorority house cut-up who was quick to laugh at a dirty joke even when I didn't always understand it at the time. (Did I ever thank you for explaining the really gross ones to me?) Remember me as the wife who fought with you like an alley cat and told you off innumerable times when you deserved it and countless others when you didn't. And don't forget that fire-breathing bitch who, when provoked, was known to throw an occasional thing or two at your head, though never anything hard enough to cause permanent damage because I'd never do anything to intentionally hurt you. And every time you hold our son or daughter in your arms, please don't forget the mother I never got the chance to be. But most of all remember me as the woman who loved you with all her heart and wants nothing more than for you to live long, be happy, and love again.

It was signed simply,

Beth

Only after he'd finished did he realize the pages were splattered with his tears. He cleared his throat and removed his glasses as he handed the letter to Maggie. Then he helped himself to a tissue from the box she'd had the foresight to place within his reach. He pinched the bridge of his nose and closed his eyes in an attempt to staunch the steady flow.

Pushing away from the table, he walked to the greenhouse window over the sink. Through the delicate foliage of Maggie's carefully tended herb garden, he watched the charming little girl with her mother's unruly red hair; sweet, infectious laugh; and bright, intelligent eyes. They might not be the color of her mother's, but they definitely had the same fiery sparkle and uncanny ability of seeing things and people as they really are. His chest tightened and his eyes glistened with a fresh wave of tears, painfully aware that his reluctant heart was keeping him from so many things that made life worthwhile.

"Why do you suppose she wanted you to wait to show me that letter?"

Maggie sniffled as she folded the pages and carefully slipping them into the envelope. "I think she'd hoped you'd find your own way. You know, physician heal thyself."

He cringed as if a handful of ice cubes had been slipped down his shorts and he rolled his eyes heavenward. "What is it about that hackneyed phrase that makes every woman I know think it applies to me?" He jabbed a thumb into his chest for emphasis. "Just because I'm a licensed psychologist doesn't make dealing with my personal problems any easier. It just makes it all the more frustrating when I can't help myself."

"Would you like me to talk to Gwen?"

"And tell her what? That everything is okay now because I was given permission from my dead wife to carry on without her. Beth's letter is all well and good, Maggie, but it doesn't change a damn thing. You and I both know that."

"There's something else holding you back from this relationship, isn't there?" Maggie questioned, never leaving her place at the table. Although to Joel, it wasn't posed as a question at all. Because of the guilt that he'd allowed to fester for so many years, it sounded more like an accusation.

She'd been such a good friend to him and Beth through the years. He glanced again through the window at his daughter. He had Maggie to thank for his beautiful child. Her offer to be his and Beth's surrogate when they'd exhausted every other possible means of conceiving had come at a critical turning point in his life. He couldn't repay the debt he owed her. At the very least she deserved the unconditional explanation of his recent behavior. He'd heard confession was good for the soul. He hoped that was true because his tortured soul needed something to ease the hurt he caused as well as felt. In spite of his determination to *come clean*, as it were, he found it difficult to formulate the preamble to his confession.

"Joel, what is it?"

He gave a disconcerted shrug as he grabbed his mug from the table and refilled it. When he gestured with a lift of the pot, Maggie nodded her answer to his offer and held her mug for him to fill also. Her patient silence was his final undoing.

There was no easy or right way to say what he was about to tell her, so without preamble, he blurted, "I cheated on Beth."

"The Educators' Conference in California."

Again, he heard a statement of fact, not a question. Maggie's words hit him like a baseball bat right between the eyes. "Beth knew?"

Maggie nodded. "She suspected. She knew you weren't happy when you left."

"I wasn't any happier when I returned."

"She realized there was something different. In her own words, you were moody and distant when you returned."

"Her obsession with getting pregnant was making me crazy. I resented her for making me feel like nothing more than an on-demand sperm donor but at the same time I felt overwhelming guilt for feeling that way because I wanted a child as much as she did. When I was approached by a female colleague looking for pleasure not procreation, the temptation was too great." His face twisted with agonizing remorse as a fresh wave of tears clogged his throat. "The guilt I felt before that trip was nothing compared to what I carried after I returned."

"It sounds like you're still carrying it."

"Damn right I am. I loved my wife. What I did was indefensible and unforgivable. Her death didn't automatically wipe the slate clean."

"And you think this emotional flagellation is the only way to pay penance for your momentary lapse in judgment? Is keeping yourself from falling in love again part of your ongoing punishment for those transgressions?"

Joel stared at Maggie, as if he couldn't quite believe what she'd just said to him. "I'm the psychologist, damn it, so back off. You're not qualified to analyze me or my actions."

"Who better to delve into the deepest, darkest corners of your psyche than one of your nearest and dearest?" It was obvious to him that she wasn't about to back down.

"You got me there," he admitted with a defeated sigh and a rueful, teary-eyed glance.

Maggie stretched across the table and patted his hand with the same soothing, maternal tenderness he'd seen her display with her children. "Seriously, Joel, maybe it's time to see someone who *is* qualified to help you work through this." She waved Beth's letter under his nose. "She did this to let you know she forgave you. She wants you to be happy. Now you've got to find a way to forgive yourself."

"There's only one person's forgiveness I want, and she's made it very clear she never wants to see me again."

Chapter Twenty-Five

Barefoot and hardly dressed for company, Gwen answered the door sincerely hoping she'd find nothing more than a Bible-beater peddling door-to-door religion so she could tell them she already knew God loved her. It was the rest of the world she wasn't too sure about these days.

Well, well, speak of the devil. She wouldn't have been any more surprised if it had been Satan himself standing on her stoop.

"Maggie," she said, her voice cracked with a prickly combination of suspicion and confusion.

"Hi, Gwen." Maggie Chapparelle smiled brightly. "Mind if I come in?"

Gwen stepped aside and waved her hand in a hesitant gesture of invitation. "Of course," she drawled. She was, to say the least, leery of this unexpected visitor marching through her door like Sherman descending on Atlanta.

Maggie stepped into the foyer and casually glanced into the living room.

"Pardon the mess." Gwen studied the room, trying to see it as someone else would for the first time. The vacuum stood in the middle of the room where all the furniture was pushed away from the walls into a jumbled collection of wood and upholstery fabric. The curtains were down from the just washed, sparkling windows and currently on gentle cycle in the washer. All that remained was the decorator rod stretched across the bowed picture window like a thick, ugly uni-brow.

Maggie smiled and said, "I clean when I'm upset

too. The boys have told me more than once to stay out of their room because it's supposed to smell that way."

What's this, Gwen wondered with a wary glance at her guest. Was Maggie actually trying to be friendly? No, there had to be more to it than that. "Why don't we go into the kitchen? I haven't torn that room apart yet." She led the way. "Coffee?"

"That would be great." Maggie pulled a Windsor-backed chair away from the table as she placed what she had been carrying in the center of the polished oak.

"If you're here to sell Tupperware let me save you the trouble, I'm not interested. I've got a cabinet full of it already."

Maggie forced a nervous laugh and tapped the plastic lid with her index finger. "They're toffee bars. I remembered how much you liked them at the cookout."

Just one thing popped into Gwen's mind: Beware of strangers bearing gifts. "Thank you," was all she could murmur as she collected mugs and spoons. After pouring the coffee, she carried the stoneware mugs to the table where she had already placed a creamer and both sugar and artificial sweetener. Most people she knew used the latter, but she wasn't about to presume anything where this woman was concerned.

She watched Maggie take a tentative sip of the steaming dark brew then proceed to add sugar and a generous splash of half and half. She was relieved that she'd offered both options.

The silence that hovered between them was palpable.

"This is awkward," Maggie said, setting her cup on the table.

"To say the very least," Gwen retorted. "So why don't you just tell me why you're here and why you felt it necessary to sweeten the visit with a container of toffee bars."

Maggie took another sip and said, "I'm sorry, Gwen."

"What exactly are you apologizing for?"

"A lot of things, I guess. I haven't been very friendly toward you for a long time."

Gwen stared into the dark depths of her coffee cup. She'd never been one to beat around the bush, and she didn't feel like starting now. "You've never been remotely friendly toward me—ever. At best you've politely tolerated me for the sake of our children's friendship."

"I have no defensible argument for my behavior. I'm asking that you accept my apology. I don't expect your forgiveness in return."

"I'm a little confused, Maggie. I don't understand this change of heart in you." Gwen said curiously. "I mean, it seems a little late to make amends now that Joel and I aren't together anymore."

"I feel terrible about the way I treated you. I let unsubstantiated rumors and insinuations cloud my opinions. But it was something my husband said to me that made me realize how unfair I've been."

Gwen's only reaction was a raised brow. She remained silent otherwise.

Maggie pressed forward. "When Nick asked me how I thought someone as wonderful as Samantha got that way, it got me to thinking. Good or bad, children are more often than not a reflection of their upbringing. Samantha is an exemplary young woman because she's obviously had an exemplary role model. Joel was smart enough to recognize those qualities in you."

"Thank you for that," said Gwen.

"I can't help wondering if I'd been more supportive of Joel's decision to see you, this might have turned out differently between you."

"Joel is a grown man. I doubt if anything you said or did had any effect on the outcome of this relationship."

"Isn't there any chance for a compromise?"

Gwen shook her head. "No. Not this time. I've compromised all my life, always settled for less because it was pounded into my head that I didn't deserve anything better. Joel showed me differently. And for once in my life I wanted all or nothing. I took a gamble." Gwen paused to collect emotions that were getting away from her before adding, "Just because I lost this time doesn't mean I will the next time." She helped herself to a cookie and cast Maggie a sad smile.

"He still cares about you, Gwen."

"Not enough apparently or he would have been knocking on my door instead of you." She paused and gazed at Maggie with a thoughtful pout. "He doesn't know you're here, does he?"

Maggie shook her head. "No. In fact, he asked me not to get involved. But I thought maybe I could help."

Gwen breathed a bitter laugh. "It's over, Maggie, accept it. I have."

"That's pretty cold, Gwen. Maybe I wasn't so wrong in my assessment of you after all."

"Think whatever you want," she said as she snapped the lid onto the cookie container and shoved it toward her guest. "Joel can't let go of his memories and I can't compete with that, no woman could. It's as simple as that."

****

The Fates were conspiring against her because like it or not, Gwen was going to have to see Joel again. If her suspicions were correct, and she had every reason to believe they were, she would be intrinsically tied to the man forever.

Gwen sat in her office absently rocking a pencil between her thumb and index finger as she stared into the confines of her office. The normal, every day flurry of realty activity persisted—phones rang, computer keyboards clicked, and conversations between realtors and clients continued—yet she was oblivious to every bit of it.

The notion gnawed at her, eroding her peace of mind and left her tossing and turning into the wee hours of the morning until total exhaustion swept her into a restless slumber that left her more and more tired with each passing night.

The signs were there, yet she refused to acknowledge them with more than a frightened denial. Frightened? She was downright terrified of the very idea that it might be true. There had to be more than one explanation for the symptoms she experienced. She wracked her brain for alternative explanations and tried to convince herself that one of them was the reason she was nauseous, tired, and irritable, not to mention more than a month late.

As each day passed, she kept telling herself that it couldn't be possible. She just couldn't be pregnant. Women her age didn't get pregnant under these circumstances. Only naïve, inexperienced teenagers got pregnant by accident. What would she do if her suspicions were correct? How would she explain it to her daughter? She'd been preaching responsible sex to Samantha from the time her daughter was old enough to understand the serious ramifications of irresponsible sexual behavior. How did she tell her daughter that it's possible she and Joel had been careless once or twice?

"Oh, God," she groaned, dropping her head into her hands.

Drawing a sharp, determined breath, she reached for her purse and pushed away from her desk. This wasn't getting her anywhere. She needed answers.

She smoothed her ivory linen skirt as she stood and ran a hand around the belted waistband to assure the teal silk shell was still neatly tucked. Gliding around the upholstered partition on heeled sandals into the main area of the office, she stopped briefly at her office manager's desk situated near the entrance.

"I need to go out for a little while, Bette." She hoisted the strap of her bag higher on her shoulder.

"Don't forget you've got closings scheduled at three and six at South Region Mortgage." Bette handed Gwen two manila envelopes and sounded a little surprised by her boss's unscheduled departure.

Dismayed at her recent absentmindedness, Gwen acknowledged the appointments with a nod as she took the proffered documents. "I'll head over to the mortgage company just as soon as I take care of something." She scurried out the door before her curious office manager questioned her destination.

In order to maintain anonymity, Gwen drove fifteen miles north into an area she felt reasonably secure she wouldn't run into anyone she knew. She'd given Sherwood enough to talk about over the years without adding this to the list.

She pulled into a busy Walgreen's and whipped into the first vacant slot she spotted. In and out of the store in less than five minutes, Gwen steered her car toward the nearest gas station she knew had a reasonably clean restroom.

After waiting the required time, Gwen stared at the plastic wand clutched between her fingers. Overwhelmed, she braced herself against the white porcelain sink and tried to grasp the results.

She stuck the stick in the box, wrapped it all in the bag, and stuffed it deep into the restroom's trash receptacle. Then she stood there, staring at the garbage as if there was something she'd forgotten, something else she needed to do. Now she remembered, she still needed to cry. And then she did, in spite of the negative results.

****

Gwen felt the air leave her lungs as she gasped, "What did you say?" She felt her body sway and gripped the edge of the examination table to keep from falling off.

The doctor laughed. "I said congratulations, Gwen, you're pregnant."

"No…no, that can't be right," she argued with a vigorous shake of her head. "I…I took a test. It was negative."

Aaron Jansen gazed at her over the rim of his Buddy Holly glasses. "Gwen, you came to me for a reason. You must have still had suspicions."

"Yes, but when the test came up negative, I chalked the symptoms off to nerves, or hormones, or menopause."

"What's been going on in your life since your last appointment, Gwen?" He opened her file and scanned her records. "You've obviously become sexually active again."

"This is the first man I've been with since…" She paused. "…since that night I was mugged."

He peered at her through his bifocals this time, with a look that told her he wasn't buying it because he knew better. "You were raped that night, Gwen." He pulled sheets of photos from her file and waved them in front of her. "Two years ago you were assaulted, pinned down, and forced to have sex against your will. That's called rape by anyone's definition."

"I was mugged," she insisted, pushing the pictures away. She didn't want to look at them. She never wanted to see them again. She didn't need to see them to remember. "That's what the police report says. It's what everyone was told, including my daughter. That was my story then, and that's what I'm telling you now."

"That doesn't change what really happened." He poked at the pictures with his index finger before shoving them into her file. His tones softened as he patted her on the knee and added, "I'm just glad to see you're finally getting your personal life back on track."

She choked back a bitter laugh. "An unplanned pregnancy isn't exactly the way I planned to get my life back."

He stared at her for a long moment. "You don't want this baby?"

"Yes… I mean no. Oh, I don't know what I mean."

"What about the father? How does he feel about it?"

"He doesn't know." She gave a resigned sigh. "We're not together anymore."

"That certainly makes things more difficult, but not impossible." He gave her a reassuring hug. "Single women are having babies all the time."

"It's just that I thought this part of motherhood was behind me. Samantha's going to be sixteen." Gwen suddenly gasped and clutched her forehead. "Oh, God, what am I going to tell Sam? What's she going to think?"

"Well, I'll tell you what I think…" he said as he pulled a pen from his lab coat breast pocket and reached for a prescription pad. "I think you need to go home, put your feet up, and decide your course of action."

"Is there anything special I need to do?" She hopped off the table and stepped behind a modesty screen to dress.

"I'm sure you remember the drill. Exercise, eat right, get plenty of sleep…"

"The only exercise I get is running three or four

times a week. Is that safe for the baby?"

"I wouldn't suggest any marathons, but a moderate amount of running should be good for both of you. The best advice I can give you is listen to your body, stop before you're exhausted, and be sure to stay hydrated." He handed her a prescription for pre-natal vitamins. "I want to see you again in a couple of weeks."

"Why so soon?" She came around from behind the dressing screen as she finished the last buttons on her blouse.

"Well, for one thing, you're older this time around."

"I was wondering when you were going to get around to pointing that out."

"You're a healthy thirty-five year old pregnant woman. I don't foresee any problems, but I want a baseline ultrasound and additional blood work just the same." He headed for the door, then paused and gazed at her over his shoulder. "I'm an old man set in my ways so just humor me, okay?"

Gwen cast him an amiable grin and he winked at her in return. If only all men were as easy to please as Doctor Jansen. That thought quickly evolved into wondering how pleased Joel would be when she told him about her news—their news.

****

"Pizza's here!"

At the sound of her daughter's call to dinner, Gwen forced herself off the bed, where she'd been ever since returning from the doctor's, and dragged her sluggish, pregnant body down the stairs to the kitchen.

Another reality of her condition came to light when Gwen noticed the beer her daughter had automatically set by her place at the table. There would be no alcohol in her diet for a while. "You know, I think I'll have a soda with dinner tonight," she said as she snatched the beer bottle and exchanged it for a can of root beer.

Her choice of beverage was the least of her problems she quickly realized. One look at the greasy, cheese and sausage fare caused her stomach to rebel. But the real deal breaker was the heavy scent of spices lingering in the air. Gwen stifled a gag, pushed away from the table, and made a scrambling dash for the bathroom.

She cranked the faucet to high in an effort to mask her retching just seconds before she lost her lunch in the toilet. There was only one thing left to do, actually two things—first telling Samantha, then Joel. Gwen braced her hands on the vanity counter and stared at her pale reflection and tried to formulate the proper delivery of her news.

"I'm pregnant," she said to her reflection. That was quick, clean, and to the point.

"I'm having a baby." Maybe she should make that, "*We're* having a baby." That at least made it sound like she wanted him to share in the responsibility. Just because they weren't a couple didn't mean she didn't want him involved with his child. She'd raised one child without a father; she'd rather not do that again if she could help it.

Oh, what's the use, she lamented. It didn't matter how she delivered the news. She had to face facts; there was no good way to drop this bombshell.

She could always wait a few months to tell him. Yeah, that could be effective. Then she wouldn't have to say a word—just stand in profile wearing a Madonna-like smile and let him reach his own conclusions. The only option she didn't have was not telling him. He deserved to know.

She hadn't seen him in weeks, not since the night she told him she never wanted to see him ever again. Now didn't that declaration reach out like a cobra and bite her in the ass?

"Mom…?" Samantha rapped on the bathroom door. "Are you okay? You've been in there forever."

Gwen breathed a chuckle at her daughter's impatience. Only a teenager could think ten minutes was forever. Gwen cupped her palms under the running faucet and splashed her face with cold water. "I'll be right out," she said as she patted her face dry.

"Are you sick?" Samantha questioned with concern pinching her youthful features.

Gwen took a deep breath. "No, I'm not sick, I'm pregnant."

Samantha's eyes grew enormous. "Really?"

Gwen responded with a nod. "How incredibly dumb and careless you must think I am. Thirty-five years old and still too stupid to prevent getting knocked up."

Samantha shook her head against her words. "I don't think that, Mom."

"I don't know why not. I've been preaching to you for years about taking responsibility of your future." Gwen choked a bitter, self-recriminating laugh. "It would seem that I don't have the brains to practice what I preach."

"Is it Mr. Hubbard's?"

"Yes, it's Joel's. I haven't told him yet so I'd appreciate it if you didn't say anything to Davey or his folks until I do."

"Are you happy about it?"

Gwen considered Samantha's question as if the concept had never crossed her mind. She'd been so busy worrying and wondering how Joel would react, she hadn't given her own feelings a thought. Now that the question was put before her, she had to go with her first reaction. "Yes, I think I am." For the first time since Doctor Jansen gave her the news, Gwen smiled a genuine, no-holds-barred smile. It was at that very moment she realized how much she wanted this baby.

"That settles it then, if you're happy about it so am I." She wrapped her arms around her mother and gave an enthusiastic hug. "If this had to happen, I'm real glad Mr. Hubbard is the father and not one of those losers you've dated. With his genetic code and yours, this baby should be something really special."

Not nearly as special as the child she already had. Gwen laughed through her tears, grateful for a daughter who always saw the glass as half full. She wondered what the chances were that Joel would be just as optimistic.

Chapter Twenty-Six

Dreading what he had to do yet knowing he couldn't put it off any longer, Joel stood in front of the bed stacked high with Beth's side of the closet and confronted his past. Of all the moving chores left to tackle, sorting through Beth's things kept getting shoved to the bottom of the list. Everything was exactly the way she'd left it, but he had run out of time and excuses. He had to get this finished. The movers would be there first thing in the morning.

He straightened his posture and drew a fortifying breath as he snatched the top article from the pile. His heart constricted when realizing what it was in his hand. His fingers curled around the soft pink, bulky-knit cardigan Beth had worn with everything near the end whether it matched whatever else she was wearing or not. She'd laughingly called it her security blanket and dragged it with her everywhere. Either wrapped around her shoulders or clutched tightly in her arms, it went with her to every chemo treatment, every hospital stay, and every doctor's appointment. He remembered it being clutched in her hands the morning she passed away. He would have buried her with it had he been able to find it at the time. He'd found it weeks later at the bottom of a seldom-used clothes hamper in the downstairs bathroom, apparently tossed there by some well-meaning relative or friend who'd come to lend their help and support in the hours and days following his wife's death. He hadn't been aware of much in those first days, only that his wife was gone and she wasn't coming back.

He fingered the pink sleeve and brought it to his nose expecting to refill his memory banks with the scent of her. It caught him by surprise that it didn't smell like Beth anymore, but what he found even more unexpected was he wasn't that upset over the fact, just a little sad that the memory of her had faded.

Still clutching the sweater, he sank to the bed and pressed the soft wool to his face as he glanced to the corner of the dresser where their wedding picture always sat. It startled him when he didn't find it there. Then he remembered he'd put it away, along with other personal effects, at Gwen's suggestion. *"Make the house as impersonal as possible. People need to see themselves in the rooms, not the current residents,"* she'd told him when she'd listed it.

Gwen. The thought of her caused his heart to do a crazy, painful spasm, leaving him feeling empty and aching and so dreadfully lonely. He'd grieved over the love he'd lost, but the pain of losing Gwen was still fresh and raw and more than he thought he could bear. He'd been blessed with loving not one but two wonderful women. Cancer had claimed the first. There was nothing to blame but his own reluctance to love again for losing the other.

There was nothing he could do to bring Beth back, she was gone forever. But Gwen—his beautiful, loving Gwen—was still very much alive. Even more than that, she'd made his life worth living as a man and a lover again.

He dropped to his knees and prayed for a way to get her back.

He climbed to his feet and carefully folded the sweater. A shuddering breath rattled deep in his chest as he resolutely placed it in the box marked for charity. He found a measure of peace in the knowledge that the garment might bring another woman the same warmth and comfort it had given his wife, which in turn gave him the strength to reach for the next article of clothing from the pile, and the next, and the next. Piece by piece, memory by memory, he worked his way through the stacks and as the piles diminished he felt his heart begin to heal.

At the halfway mark, he heard his daughter waking from her nap. He was grateful for the disruption and decided he could use a break. He tossed one last shirt into the box and headed for Emme's room. He found her lying in her race car youth bed—a present from her Uncle Nick and totally out of place in the otherwise frilly pink and purple room—and singing to her beloved Cabbage Patch doll.

Joel chuckled as he listened to his three-year-old singing the lyrics to "I Love NASCAR." Yet another Uncle Nick influence. For a man who hadn't immediately warmed to the idea of Maggie as surrogate for Joel and Beth's child, once she was born Nick turned into the little girl's biggest fan and remained so even after his own daughters were born. Joel's biggest regret was that Beth hadn't lived long enough to hold their child even once. She hadn't even lived long enough to know the in vitro process had been successful.

The second Em spotted her father in the doorway, she squirmed and scooted over the side of her bed and ran to him. He swung her into his arms and hugged her tight. She was still warm with sleep and smelled of peanut butter and strawberry jam—remnants of her lunch smeared down the front of her shirt.

After a quick potty stop, he changed her for the third time that day before carrying her into the kitchen. As he slipped her into her booster seat, he asked, "What'll it be, Punkin, strawberry or chocolate milk with your animal crackers?"

"Juice," she said with a stubborn pout.

Only three and she already knew what she wanted. He chuckled and reached for a juice box.

He knew well enough not to argue over something as trivial as the great juice versus milk debate. There would be plenty of time for him to assert his fatherly authority down the road, like when she reached puberty and came home with purple hair and her belly button pierced. The very thought of raising a teenager by himself stabbed him with a terror the likes of which he'd never known. It made him realize and appreciate the amazing job Gwen had done as a single parent. Samantha was a wonderful tribute to Gwen's parenting skills.

"Done," Emme announced as she plunked her empty juice box on the table and lifted her arms for assistance from her seat.

He hoisted her out of her chair and swung her to the floor. She immediately marched to the back door and said, "Wanna play outside."

Although there was still so much to be done before the movers showed up, he nevertheless followed his daughter's dictate without argument.

Their backyard wasn't anything like the over-the-top play yard at the Chapparelles, but there was a swing set, sandbox, and a colorful playhouse to occupy his little girl. Em ran to the red slide and climbed the yellow rungs to the top of the ladder. Joel took a seat in a patio chair and watched his daughter enjoy her independence.

Em toddled toward him and frowned as she peered into his face. "Daddy mad?"

Joel breathed a sigh and shook his head against his daughter's observation. "No, Punkin, I'm not mad," he assured her. Just heartsick and miserable, he silently added.

"Daddy sad," she pronounced without a doubt as she mimicked his solemn expression.

Joel nodded in agreement this time as he picked her up and set her on his knee and kissed the top of her silky head.

"Unka Nick!" Em squealed as she squirmed off her father's lap and ran across the grass to greet him with her arms open wide.

"Hey there, Scooterbug." Nick swung the little girl into his arms and gave her a tight squeeze and a smooch on the cheek. He shifted the child to rest across the crook of one arm as he faced Joel. "Hey there to you, too, stranger."

Joel cocked a brow and narrowed his gaze. "You have that Maggie-sent-me look on your face."

"She's worried about you," Nick confessed, adding, "We both are. You haven't been around in a while."

"I've been busy," was all Joel said in defense of his recluse-like behavior. He hadn't been in the mood to socialize.

Nick set Emme on the ground. She headed for her sandbox, armed with a shiny red plastic bucket and shovel. Nick took a seat at the picnic table across from Joel.

"She also wanted me to ask if you needed any last-minute help."

"I'm just about done, actually. I've set aside a box of Beth's high school mementos that I thought Maggie might want. There are even a few old Illiana Speedway programs you might find interesting. There's one with a cocky, young upstart by the name of Chapparelle on the cover."

Oh, man," Nick chuckled. "Those should've been archived in the Smithsonian by now. Talk about ancient history."

"She even got his autograph. Think it's worth anything?"

"About a buck o' nothing on eBay, maybe," Nick chortled. "And not even that much when word gets out that I didn't renew the racing clause of my contract with Morgan Enterprises."

"How'd Mandy take that bit of news?" Joel remembered Mandy Morgan from Nick and Maggie's second marriage ceremony. She was Nick's sponsor's daughter and, as far as he knew, still Nick's business manager. She was also one of the most stunning blondes Joel had ever laid eyes on, with the exception of Gwen, of course. Mandy had also been a sore subject with Maggie during the years she and Nick had been divorced.

"I haven't had a whole lot of contact with Mandy since she crossed over to the dark side of racing and married that Grand Prix hot shot, Alejandro Albrici." Nick looked like a life-sized version of his NASCAR bobble head as each syllable of the Italian's name rolled emphatically off his tongue. "Her greatest accomplishment since moving to Italy is keeping her buns and ta-tas from burning under the Tuscan sun."

Joel gave a little laugh at that before smacking his palms on his thighs. "That's more than I'm accomplishing at the moment. Come on, Em, playtime's over, it's time for us to get back to work."

"Tell you what," said Nick. "Why don't I take Em back to my house to play with the girls for a while? You'll get more done without a three-year-old under foot. You can pick her up later and stay for dinner."

Joel glanced at his watch to give himself a moment to formulate a polite refusal.

Instead of giving Joel a chance to refuse the invitation, Nick took the situation into his own hands and made the decision for him. "Hey, Emme, You want to go play with Kait and Tally?" The little redhead abandoned her sandbox and ran to Nick, her curly pigtails bouncing as she squealed with delight at the prospect of playing with her little friends.

"Well, I guess that settles it," Joel remarked as he watched Nick carry his only child away. He wasn't sure he appreciated being outsmarted by a stock car driver and a three-year-old.

****

It was a lovely day and Gwen intended on taking full advantage of it in spite of the overwhelming guilt pricking at her conscience for doing nothing on such a glorious Sunday afternoon. There were so many things she could be doing, like laundry, or cleaning closets, or telling Joel she was pregnant.

Without conscious thought, her hands settled over her still flat abdomen. There wasn't any sign of her pregnancy yet, but her body had started developing other, more subtle, changes only she recognized as what they were. She'd noticed a slightly fuller face just that morning when she brushed her teeth. And there was no way she could ignore the swelling tenderness in her breasts. The extra hormones combined with the pre-natal vitamins made her hair and nails grow like crazy, too. Subtle as these changes were so far, it wouldn't be much longer before the whole world would know. Telling Joel was definitely at the top of her list.

When she heard the back door open and shut, she found her daughter shuffling across the lawn with a mug of something clutched in her hand. Samantha had been so incredibly understanding and supportive. Her heart swelled with pride at the sight of her firstborn. It made her wonder if she would be as fortunate the second time around.

Sam placed the cup of steaming tea on the redwood table beside her mother and raised her own face to the sun. "What a pretty day."

Gwen sighed. "I feel positively wicked wasting it

like this."

"Enjoy it now," Sam told her, laughing. "Your days of doing nothing are counting down. Before you know it you'll be up to your elbows in poopy diapers and strained peas."

"Does it bother you that our lives are about to change?"

Samantha toed an abandoned softball lying in the grass and picked it up. Her hand cupped the scuffed and muddy ball; her fingers caressed the dirty seams with an instinct born of years of practice and repetition. "No, not really," she said as she took an innate side stance and lightly wind-milled the ball to the other end of the yard.

Gwen wasn't convinced. "I know these circumstances aren't the most ideal, but I'm not sorry it happened. I really want this baby."

"I know. I want this baby too. I've always wanted to be a big sister." Samantha's face twisted with indecision. "It's just that—"

"What is it, sweetie?"

"You're just so sad all the time." She squatted beside her mother's chair. "I wish there was something I could do to make you smile again."

Samantha wishing it made it so. Gwen did smile, brightly and genuinely, as she stroked her daughter's long hair. "You have to admit I'm getting better."

Sam nodded in concession. "Have you told Mr. Hubbard yet?"

"Not yet." It wasn't that she hadn't thought about it. It had been the only thing on her mind. Her problem was putting those thoughts into action. "I'll get around to it."

"I know this isn't any of my business, but don't you think you better get around to it pretty soon?"

"I know," Gwen sighed. "But he's in the middle of packing and moving right now and—"

"—then he'll be in the middle of unpacking and settling in, and then, of course, he's got his new counseling practice to think about, and then—"

"All right, young lady, message received." She swung her feet to the ground. "I'll call him right now."

Samantha sprang to her feet. "That's the spirit!"

Chapter Twenty-Seven

He heard the phone as he entered the kitchen and grabbed for it before it quit. He'd never stopped hanging his hopes on the slim chance it might be Gwen. A foolish hope, he knew, but one he couldn't stop himself from having.

He'd thought about calling her a couple of hundred times, even dialed her number once or twice but never finished the numeric sequence because he never knew quite what to say or how to begin to ask for her forgiveness.

Gwen's rejection had knocked him flat, and even weeks later he hadn't recovered. Every day he'd think about her, every night he'd pray for a miracle to bring them back together, yet every morning he faced another day without her just because he didn't know what to say to make it right again.

Expecting anyone but Gwen, he snatched the receiver off the cradle and answered with a gruff, almost angry, "Hello."

"Did I catch you at a bad time?"

"Gwen?" he breathed. A spark of hope fluttered in his chest.

"I'll call back another time."

"No, no, don't hang up."

"I know you're in the middle of moving, Joel, and I hate to bother you when you're so busy, but there's something I need to talk to you about."

She sounded so serious, he noted, so businesslike, so cool, and undetached. There wasn't the slightest hint of warmth in her tone. "What it is?"

She cleared her throat. “Do you mind if I come over to discuss it?”

Mind? Did he mind if she came over? Hell no, he didn’t mind. A thousand times no, he didn’t mind. The thought of seeing her again was intoxicating. Overwhelming. Terrifying. He had to force himself to stay composed. “No, not at all. When can I expect you?”

“Whenever it’s convenient for you.” she said in a level tone that irritated him with its indifference. “I would like to take care of this matter as soon as possible though. Are you free now?”

“I have dinner plans for later, but I’ll be here for another couple hours.”

“I can be there in fifteen minutes, if that’s okay.”

“I’ll leave the door unlocked. Just come on in.”

“Fine. I’ll see you shortly then.”

He was, to say the least, intrigued. What could she possibly need to discuss with him, he wondered.

****

Gwen turned the last corner and gripped the steering wheel just a little tighter in a symbolic reminder to keep a grip on her emotions. Her heart raced and she felt nauseous—not this time, thank goodness, for obvious reasons. Apprehension, pure and simple, was the only explanation for the queasy feeling tying her stomach into knots.

She was proud of how she’d handled their earlier phone call. It hadn’t been easy. The second she’d heard his voice she’d gone weak and woozy. Just the thought of seeing him again, to touch him… Correction, there would be no touching. From the day she’d learned she was pregnant she’d played various scenarios in her head, imagined his reaction to her news, never was there touching involved. Touching was out of the question, touching was impossible, touching would be her undoing, and how could she forget that touching was the reason she was in this condition in the first place. No, there could be absolutely no touching. She would make sure of that.

She parked on the street in front of his house. The van was pulled far enough into the side drive to allow room for her car, but that much familiarity didn't seem appropriate under the circumstances. She wasn't here for a social visit, far from it. She was about to drop a bombshell into his ordered life, one that would change both of their lives forever. The last thing she wanted was to give him any reason to think she'd reconsidered his offer, although that had been one of her favorite daydreams, at least the part about him taking her into his arms and begging her to take him back. No touching, she reminded herself as she shoved aside that particular scenario.

With the expert eye of a realtor, she admired the freshly mowed lawn, the neatly trimmed bushes, and carefully weeded flower beds as she made her way up the walk with slow, deliberate steps, but the sidewalk wasn't that long and she reached the front door much sooner then she would have liked.

She smoothed her skirt down her thighs and knocked in spite of his instructions to "*come on in*." She didn't want to catch him by surprise. The one she was about to deliver would be quite enough.

He answered slightly out of breath with a box tucked under his arm. "I thought I told you to just walk in. I left the door open."

"Habit, I guess," she answered, unable to take her eyes off him. He was appropriately dressed for the dirty, daunting task of packing in nothing more than a pair of worn, loose-fitting jeans with a frayed hole in one knee and a washed out black T-shirt that had seen better days twenty years earlier. He was dirty and smelly, bristly and barefoot, and never looked more wonderful. It was then she realized how very much she still loved him.

"Well, come in." He stood aside to let her pass.

She moved only as far as the entry and watched as he set the box on the floor near the door. A glossy photo of a vivacious, teenage Beth and another young woman that looked a lot like Maggie mugged for the camera. She could see from her vantage point that the box contained stacks of pictures and mementos—memories of a life he clung to, cherished, and refused to relinquish.

It made her sad to realize they'd never had their picture taken together, not even once, and now, of course, it was too late. There would be nothing she could take out and look at in the coming years to remind her of the passion they'd briefly shared. Then she realized that wasn't entirely true. There would always be their child. Oddly, she found comfort in that and she found herself smiling at the thought.

"Let's go in the living room," he said, taking her elbow to guide her through the maze of stacked boxes.

She jerked from his touch—*there would be no touching*—and moved into the room to take a seat in a chair nearest the door. She sat on the edge of the seat, nervous and tense, and clasped her hands in her lap to keep herself from shaking.

He sat across from her on the couch and relaxed his long frame by stretching his arms across the back and crossing his legs ankle to knee. Loose-limbed and relaxed was the only way to describe his casual demeanor. Well, she'd soon take care of that.

"So, what is it you needed to talk to me about?"

"I'm pregnant." There, that pretty much said it all—no preamble, no hemming or hawing, no clever euphemisms—just direct and right to the point.

"What did you say?" The words rushed from his lips as he sat up and stared at her. His posture wasn't relaxed any more.

Gwen let her head drop forward and felt the tension pull down her spine and radiate across her back and shoulders. He was going to make her repeat her announcement.

"I'm pregnant," she said again softly.

"Are you sure?"

"Are you asking if I'm sure I'm pregnant or if I'm sure it's yours?"

"Either way, it doesn't matter."

That response hadn't been in any of her scenarios. She hadn't covered all her bases after all. "I—I see," she stammered as she rushed into her practiced speech. "You don't have to worry. I don't intend on making any demands from you, financially or otherwise. I'll sign any papers you want to dissolve your legal responsibility in this matter. I just thought you had a right to know." She gathered her strength and stood to make a hasty exit if necessary.

"What are you talking about? I don't want to sign away my rights to this baby. If you say its mine, that's good enough for me. I'm thrilled at the prospect of being a father again. I think it's wonderful."

Her knees buckled and she dropped into the chair she'd just vacated as she stared at him is disbelief. "You do?" Again, this wasn't one of the responses she'd expected.

He kneeled in front of her and took her hand. She tried to pull away. No touching, no touching. He wouldn't let go. "Do you know what this means?"

"We didn't always practice safe sex?" she replied with a sheepish, wide-eyed glance.

He grinned at her droll yet dead-on observation. "Well, that too, I suppose. I had something else in mind, however. There's only one thing left for us to do, you know."

"What's that?"

"Get married, of course."

"No." This time she succeeded in getting her hand free. "Absolutely not."

"I don't understand. I thought marriage was what you wanted."

"It was—once. But this baby has changed everything."

"Of course it has. This child deserves to be raised by both parents."

"I won't marry you just because I'm pregnant. I can't live with that hanging over my head for the rest of my life, and you shouldn't feel obligated to marry me because of it."

"That doesn't make any sense. I want to be involved in every part of this child's life. I have every right to be."

"I want you to be a part of its life, too. I'll never interfere with that."

He sat back on his heels. She refused to meet his gaze, choosing instead to watch his knee poke further through the tear in his jeans. "What if I want more than that? What if I don't want to be a part-time father? What if I want custody?"

She struggled to control the tears that blurred her vision and forced herself to take a deep breath. "You would do that?" she choked. This was just another reaction she hadn't counted on. My God, what exactly had she expected? Nothing, obviously, within the realms of this man's reality.

"I'm raising one child on my own. There's no reason I can't raise a second one."

She sat there frozen and speechless, unable to formulate a solitary argument in her own defense. The tears rolled down her cheeks, but she forced herself to confront him face to face as she asked, "You'd take my baby away?"

He cupped her face between his hands and

swiped his thumbs beneath her eyes to wipe away her tears. "No, Gwen," he said gently. "I wouldn't do that. But I do want to be a father to this child—a full-time father—every bit as much as I am to Em. I want to be there for middle of the night feedings, and hear their cries when nightmares frighten them awake. The new house is big enough for all of us. We could be a real family, Gwen. Don't deny us or our children that."

The happy family picture he painted was tempting. He welcomed the addition of children with an enthusiasm she found difficult to ignore.

Was her love for him enough to sustain them through the rough patches that inevitably crept into every marriage at one time or another? And what would happen to them when the kids were grown and gone, when the glue of midnight feedings and frightened toddlers weren't there to hold them together? He was offering so much more than she ever hoped for. He'd told her once that something in him died with Beth. Was that part of him his ability to love again? Did she have the right to deny their child the life Joel wanted for all of them? Emme would have the mother she never had, and Samantha would finally have a father who wanted her and would be there for her.

The gaze she settled on him wasn't hopeful. "I won't marry you until after the baby is born."

"I don't understand."

"I won't have people saying I trapped you."

"That's ridiculous. I don't give a damn what people think."

"That's so easy to say when you've never felt the cut of people's cruel remarks. I made one mistake when I first moved to this town and I've never been able to live it down. You have no idea how this can affect all our lives. Your practice could suffer, your standing in this community could be damaged irreparably. I can't do that to you. I won't."

He pushed off the floor and heaved a defeated sigh. "I can see there's nothing I can say to change your mind." He rubbed his knuckles against his bristly chin then crossed his arms in a fit of frustrated displeasure.

"I'm glad you're smart enough to recognize the validity of my arguments." What she didn't tell him was how disappointed she was in how readily he'd agreed to her conditions.

"Don't think for a moment I've given up in convincing you otherwise. I'm just retreating to regroup and form a new plan of attack."

She grinned at that. "Nothing would make me happier than for you prove me wrong."

He barked a laugh and shook his head in disbelief. "Are you tossing down the gauntlet again, *Ms*. Marconi?"

"What if I am, *Dr*. Hubbard?"

"Have you forgotten how the last time you challenged me turned out?"

"Not likely," she replied as she patted her pregnant belly for emphasis. "The memory lingers on."

Chapter Twenty-Eight

Joel might not have had any luck in convincing her to marry him that afternoon, but he did manage to convince her into accompanying him to Nick and Maggie's house for dinner, but only with the condition that he not tell anyone, including Nick and Maggie, about the baby.

"Don't you think they're going to wonder why we're suddenly back together when just earlier this afternoon Nick knew we weren't?" He turned off the main road onto Cartwright Drive. They were almost at the Chapparelles door and she still hadn't convinced him not to announce her condition.

"That's my point. I don't want anyone, including your friends, thinking this baby is the only reason we're back together." She thought about what she'd just said and a disturbing thought came to her. She wondered why it hadn't crossed her mind before now. "It isn't, is it?"

He cast a quick glance at her before turning into the brick pillared entrance to the Chapparelle property. The restored sprawling Craftsman-style house loomed large and impressive at the end of the drive. "That question doesn't even deserve an answer."

"Maybe not, but I'd like one anyway." His reluctance in giving her a definitive answer didn't help to calm her suspicions.

He parked his van next to Nick's truck and cut the engine. He turned in his seat and took her hand. "The reason why you showed up on my doorstep today doesn't mean nearly as much to me as the fact that you did. From the moment you walked through the door, I knew I wanted you back in my life. This baby may not have been planned, but I consider it a blessing and something I want to share with my dearest friends. Please don't deny me that."

"I guess when you put it that way..." Gwen relented. "What other choice do I have?" It wasn't like she could hide her condition forever. In a few months the whole world would know anyway. So whether she wanted him to do this now or later didn't matter. She might as well let Joel tell whomever he pleased.

Joel didn't waste any time in sharing their blessed event. Within minutes of their arrival, after the usual round of amenities, Joel pulled her against his side with a huge grin and blurted, "We're having a baby." There was a brief moment of stunned silence before the entry hall erupted with well-wishes and congratulations.

The ear-to-ear grin plastered across Joel's handsome face convinced Gwen that his feelings about the baby were genuine and heartfelt. If only his feelings about her were equally apparent. Only time—seven months to be exact—would tell.

"I'm pregnant too!" Maggie squealed as she threw her arms around Gwen for an unexpected, though no less enthusiastic, embrace. Maggie held Gwen at arm's length and studied her tummy for signs of a baby bump that weren't quite there yet. "When are you due?"

Gwen found it odd—humorous in fact—that Joel hadn't asked her that. "Late April," Gwen answered as she kept a watchful eye on Joel. She wondered if he was mentally counting back and realizing she had in all likelihood gotten pregnant their first night together in the Lincoln. An unplanned pregnancy was one thing. But having it happen in the backseat of a car just wasn't something she wanted to think about, let alone admit to, especially when she'd assured him that a condom wasn't necessary. Her actions seemed suspicious even to her and she knew she hadn't done anything wrong. It was all the more reason why she couldn't marry him now.

"That's right around Talladega and Richmond," Nick announced. "Maggie's due closer to Lowes or Dover."

Gwen didn't have the first clue as to what Nick was babbling about. Richmond? Dover? She cast Maggie a glance that conveyed every bit of her confusion.

"Translation—late May," Maggie explained, adding, "Nick links important dates to the NASCAR racing schedule."

"Oh," Gwen murmured. "That's nice."

"It's not nice," Maggie retorted as she grabbed Gwen's hand and led her toward the kitchen. "It's weird."

Gwen cast a glance over her shoulder and watched the men gravitate toward the big screen television in the living room.

"You can't be more than a few weeks pregnant. How can you be so sure?"

Maggie grabbed a bag of romaine and other assorted vegetables from the refrigerator crisper. "I'm the most regular woman on the planet. If I'm a day late, I know I'm pregnant." She dumped her load of salad fixings onto a butcher block cutting board and reached for a knife.

"Trust her," Nick interjected from the doorway as he entered the kitchen. "After six pregnancies she's an expert." He pulled two beers from the fridge and pecked his wife on the cheek as he reached for the bottle opener. "Can I get either of you ladies anything to drink? Iced tea? Lemonade? Milk?"

"Nothing for me, thanks," Gwen said.

"You could get the big salad bowl down for me."

"Sure thing." Nick pulled a huge wooden bowl from the cabinet over the refrigerator and handed it to his wife.

"Anything else you need while I'm here." He waggled his eyebrows at her and pulled her playfully against him as he nuzzled her neck.

Unfazed by his amorous behavior, Maggie calmly stated, "Start the grill."

"Your wish is my command, oh lovely heir producer." He kissed her again and took off calling, "Hey, Joel, I just got permission from my wife to play with fire."

Gwen couldn't help smile as she watched their affectionate antics. They were truly an amazing couple. She'd settle for half as much with Joel someday. Then she was struck by something else. "I'm sorry, Maggie, I'm a little confused, "Did Nick say this was your *sixth* pregnancy?"

"Let's see," she said as she ticked off her pregnancies on her fingers. "First there was the twins, then Megan..."

"Megan?"

"She was only four months old when she died."

"I'm so sorry. How awful that must have been for you." Gwen couldn't imagine losing a child.

"It was a difficult time for all of us," said Maggie with a sad, faraway look in her eyes before she returned her attention to her present count. "And then there was Emme, Kait, Tally, and now this one. Yep, that's six."

"You were Emme's surrogate? Joel never told me who she was."

"I think he assumes everyone already knows," Maggie answered matter-of-factly as she started slicing a tomato into wedges. She stopped and glanced out the greenhouse window.

"It's good to see Joel smiling again. I don't doubt that your getting back together is the reason for it."

She gripped a crisp stalk of romaine and ran her knife through it from one end to the other until she had a neatly chopped pile. She scooped it into the bowl and reached for another bunch of the leafy, green lettuce.

Gwen braced a hip against a counter. "We're not technically back together." Gwen needed to clarify that misconception before Maggie started planning a combination wedding-slash-baby shower.

Obviously confused, Maggie stopped chopping and turned to Gwen. "You're not? I just assumed... What I mean is, I figured—"

"We'd get married?" Gwen finished the sentence Maggie obviously couldn't. "Marriage isn't an option I'm willing to entertain right now."

"Joel's the kind of man who'll want to do the right thing, and you know he won't settle for anything less than full-time involvement with this child, don't you?"

"Yes, and I'm dealing with that. I think it's more important that we focus on reconnecting as a couple right now before we take the relationship to the next level."

As much as Gwen wanted to believe Joel's sincerity, she wasn't entirely convinced he wanted her in his life as much as he wanted this baby. Maybe she was wrong in expecting him to prove himself before she committed wholly to the relationship, but she had to be sure they were both doing the right thing—for the child as well as each other. She'd been foolish and impetuous when she'd broached the subject of marriage once before. She wasn't about to make the same mistake again.

Maggie laid the knife down and faced Gwen.

"Would it help any if I told you he's been miserable ever since you split up?"

Gwen breathed a little laugh at Maggie's none-too-subtle attempt to make points with her on Joel's behalf. “It might,” she grinned as she grabbed a knife to help with dinner.

****

Gwen was a little overwhelmed. Dinner at the Chapparelles that night was a loud, rowdy affair just from the sheer number of kids and adults involved, though she doubted if it was much less toned down when it was just the immediate family. They seemed like a family who enjoyed spending time together. It was an eye-opening experience.

At first, she didn’t quite know what to make of the teasing repartee flying from one end of the butted end-to-end tables stretched down the length of the patio to the other, although she finally understood the attraction her daughter had for wanting to spend time with this family.

Sitting beside her, Joel reached for another ear of corn as he scooted closer and grinned. “Isn’t this great?” he said, reaching for the butter. “I’ll bet every meal was like this when you were a kid.”

“You’d lose that bet. My father didn’t allow chatter during meals. He said it upset his digestion. Children, in his opinion, should be seen and not heard whenever he was around. And since his opinion was the only one that mattered in our house, no one, including my mother, dared dispute him.”

Samantha looked across the table at her mother, looking truly stunned, and questioned, “Grandpa didn’t allow any talking at the table?”

She rarely mentioned her family to her daughter, mainly because there were very few pleasant memories attached to those years. She never saw any reason to talk about a childhood she’d just as soon forget, but Samantha had a right to know about her heritage whenever she asked.

“That’s right. Your grandfather was very strict man. We never spoke unless he spoke to us first.” Samantha seemed satisfied with her mother’s answer and returned to her previous conversation with Davey and his brother.

"Well, folks," Joel announced as he pushed away from the table. "I hate to eat and run, but I've got a moving van scheduled for eight o'clock tomorrow morning."

He snatched a napkin off the table and wiped butter and barbeque sauce from Emme's face and hands. "And this little one looks like she's going to need a bath before bed."

"Why don't you leave her here tonight?" Maggie suggested.

Joel never hesitated with his reply. "I can't do that, Maggie. Not tonight."

"Why not? It'll be easier for you in the morning."

"I'd like to spend my last night in the house with her there."

"I understand," Maggie answered with a tender smile. "I'll pick her up in the morning."

Gwen rose and started stacking their plates.

"Don't even think about helping clean up." Maggie relieved Gwen of the dirty dishes and placed them in front of Danny and Davey. "That's what I have teenagers for. Isn't that right, boys?"

"Yeah," they answered in unenthusiastic unison.

Samantha, however, was the first to jump to her feet.

"I call dibs on loading the dishwasher," she said as she scooped up the stack of plates and scurried up the porch steps.

"She always calls dishwasher first," Danny grumbled as he pushed away from the table.

"Guess that just means she's quicker than you," Davey teased.

"It means she's quicker than you, too, smartass," Danny rejoined.

"I know," Davey replied with a dimpled grin and a blue-eyes glint. "That's what keeps it interesting."

“I’ll see that Sam gets home, Ms. Marconi,” Davey assured Gwen as he followed Sam into the kitchen carrying an armload of condiments and the empty salad bowl.

Chapter Twenty-Nine

Gwen's no touching rule was all but forgotten. Joel drove with one hand on the wheel and the other stretched across the console holding her hand. She enjoyed this simple, familiar gesture and she wished it would last forever. What she hated was his silence, and she knew she had to break it.

"Aren't you going to ask me?"

He cast a quick glance at her before returning his attention to the road. "About what?"

"My due date. I saw your wheels turning when I told Maggie."

Under the glow of the dashboard lights, she thought she detected a grin as he stated, "The Lincoln."

"I know what it must look like, but I swear to you I was wearing a diaphragm that night." She didn't know why she felt the need to defend herself, but his believing she didn't deceive him seemed imperative.

He squeezed her hand. "You don't have to explain that night to me, sweetheart. It wouldn't be the first time birth control failed."

"Why not? I'd be suspicious if I were you."

"It never crossed my mind because if your intention was to trap me into marriage, would you be this adamant about *not* marrying me?"

"You have a point, but what if that's just a part of my devious, master plan to trap the most eligible bachelor in town."

He laughed out loud and brought her hand to his lips and kissed her knuckles. "That's a brilliant strategy, honey, but there's one tiny flaw to that master plan of yours—you don't have a devious bone in that beautiful body of yours. I do, however, think the baby should be named Lincoln in honor of the momentous occasion."

"You're kidding," she gasped.

"No, but only if it's a boy, of course."

"That's good to know. Then if it's a girl, do I get to name her? Fair is fair."

"Sure. What name have you got in mind?"

"I haven't thought about it yet," she answered. "I'm just reserving the right before you want to name a girl Serta, in honor of other places she might have been conceived."

He laughed at that as he pulled into his drive.

She climbed out of his van with every intention of heading straight for her car and home. She'd been riding an emotional roller coaster for weeks. Exhausted and ready to climb off, she wanted to plant her feet on solid ground again.

"Aren't you coming in?" Joel questioned as he lifted a limp and sleepy-eyed Emme out of her backseat booster. He shifted his daughter in his arms and smiled that disarming smile Gwen never could resist.

After a quick bath, Em was asleep before her head hit the pillow. The sight of Joel tending to his daughter, tucking her in, and pressing a kiss to her cheek with such amazing tenderness touched Gwen's heart and softened her features. He was a good father, a good man, and she'd be hard pressed to find any better. Then why, she wondered, was she so reluctant to let him into her heart and life again? When she found the answer to that question it should resolve whatever reservations she harbored.

"I should be going," said Gwen as they stepped quietly into the dimly lit hallway. The proximity of his bedroom left her feeling vulnerable, not because of what he might suggest but what her answer would be if he did. Just the thought of make-up sex left her weak-kneed and lightheaded. With her hand on the banister for support, she started slowly down the stairs. Joel followed without a word.

As she reached the front door, he grabbed her around the waist and pulled her into his arms. The kiss was deep and demanding, his lips warm and inviting, and Gwen was pliant and responsive. It was everything she remembered plus something she couldn't quite identify. Her arms wrapped around his neck as his pulled her more tightly against him. She moaned and parted her lips to the urging of his insistent tongue. And when he broke the connection with a husky, satisfied sigh, she felt real sorrow at its ending.

He pressed his forehead to hers with a satisfied grin and peered at her through his glasses. "I've wanted to do that to you all night."

"I've waited for you to do that to me all night." She pressed her palms against his chest and planted little, teasing pecks at the place where his open-collar left an exposed patch of neck and chest.

He sighed. "This is all I'm going to get tonight, isn't it?"

"I'm afraid so," she replied with a playful kiss to his chin. "You've got movers coming first thing in the morning, and my daughter is expecting me home."

"Then how about celebrating our getting back together tomorrow night?"

She laughed at his optimism. "After moving and unpacking all day I'm sure you'll be too tired to do anything but fall into bed."

"Well, at least you'll be there to fall into bed with me."

She frowned. "Excuse me?"

"I realize it'll take some time to fully merge our households, but you and Sam can pack what you need for a few days and we'll gradually move the rest of your stuff a little at a time."

"Joel, I'm not moving in with you. Not tomorrow or anytime in the near future." She did, however, move out of his arms and retreat to the living room. She sensed a disagreement developing, if not a full-blown argument, and she needed to place some serious distance between them. When she was in his arms she found it difficult to think straight. In his arms she'd be more likely to agree to anything he suggested.

"Just because you don't want to get married right away doesn't mean we can't live together in the meantime."

"You can't be serious. Have you heard a word I've said to you today?" She decided she didn't want to hear his answer and waved a hand to stop his response. "I'm sorry, but I can't do this right now, Joel. I've got to go."

She grabbed her purse from the hall table and flew out the door. The roller coaster was starting all over again.

****

"Flowers for Gwen Marconi," announced a husky voice from behind a humongous bouquet of long-stemmed roses, carnations, gladiolas, and lilies nestled in a vast array of lush greenery. The delivery man stepped into her office and set the floral arrangement on her desk as Gwen reached into her purse for a tip.

As she held out a folded five pinched between her fingers, she realized the delivery man was none other than the one man she'd been hoping to avoid. Correction—the one man she'd hoped to see but never expected. The sight of him caused her breath to catch and her heart to constrict.

She verbalized her thoughts. "I didn't expect to see you today." After the way she'd acted the previous evening, she hadn't expected to see him any time soon. Because the urge to accept his offer had been so tempting, bolting had been her only defense.

He snatched the card from where it nested in the foliage and handed it to her.

Gwen slipped it from the envelope. "It's blank," she said, flipping it back and forth with a twist of her wrist to reveal its lack of content.

"The florist didn't have a card big enough to hold everything I wanted to say." He paused and took one hesitant step toward her.

She studied him from the top of his brown brush-cut to the tip of his polished black loafers. His button-down ivory shirt was pressed and his slacks were creased, *and* he was freshly shaven. He smelled good too. Recalling the ratty tee and tattered jeans from yesterday, she questioned, "Aren't you a little overdressed for moving day?"

"For moving, perhaps..." He had the look of a puppy who'd just chewed apart his master's favorite slippers. "...but not for groveling."

Gwen suppressed a grin. "Oh," she drawled as she cupped a delicate blossom to breathe its sweet perfume. The heady scent took her by pleasant surprise. She'd never been all that fond of cut flowers, but she found this bouquet to be especially captivating. She was certain her feelings had more to do with the giver than the gift. "You're here to grovel, huh?" She couldn't imagine for what, but she was willing to play along to find out. She tucked a lock of hair behind her ears and waited for him to explain.

He rushed forward, and for a split second he appeared to contemplate dropping to his knees. He perched on the edge of her desk instead. She was glad of that. Unless there was a *really* good reason for his being there, she wasn't particularly fond of a man on his knees.

He bent over her until his face was only inches from hers and cupped her cheek. "Can you ever forgive me?"

She had to ask. "For what?" She couldn't read his expression and wondered what was different. Was it his guarded heart or hers this time?

"That dumb move I pulled last night."

She clasped her hands in her lap and stared at the chipped polish on her thumbnail. "I didn't notice anything unusual about your behavior, except for maybe you're assuming we'd immediately start playing house."

"That's what I'm talking about. My eagerness for wanting you to move in with me, to start our life together, was the very thing that drove you away last night."

"I told you once I'd never interfere with your relationship with your child. We don't need to live together for that to happen."

He sat back and stared at her, his mouth slightly agape. "Is that what you think? That I only want you with me because you're carrying my baby?"

"Would you be here now if I wasn't?"

With a deep, disturbed sigh, he pushed off her desk and strode to the other side of the cubicle before he whirled around and faced her. "Remember when I told you last night I considered this baby a blessing?" Upon her nod, he continued. "What I really meant to say is I consider this baby the answer to a prayer."

She was flabbergasted by his response, but managed to murmur, "You prayed for a baby?"

"I prayed for a miracle to bring us back together," he clarified as he closed the distance between them. He took her hand and pulled her to her feet.

"Wouldn't a phone call have been quicker than waiting for a miracle, not to mention more reliable?"

"But it's not nearly as dramatic," he said with a teasing wink as he chucked her under the chin. "You've just got to have a little faith, sweetheart."

"I'm sorry, Joel, but it's going to take more than faith, and prayers, and miracles to convince me. My father's fanaticism destroyed my belief in those things a long time ago."

"What's it going to take to convince you I need you in my life, Gwen—you."

She cast him a doubtful glance. "As I recall, it wasn't too long ago you convinced me that you weren't sure you'd ever be able to commit to another woman again. This baby is the only thing that's changed from then to now."

"You're not going to make this easy for me, are you?" He cupped her face and gazed long and hard into her eyes. Then he smiled that wonderful smile and everything inside her turned hot and liquid as her resistance dropped a couple of significant notches. He wasn't making it easy for her, either.

"I just need to be sure this is right for all of us."

"So, I ask again, what's it going to take to convince you?"

"I'm not sure, but I'll know when it happens."

He grinned at her response. "Just know that I'll be here when it does."

Chapter Thirty

Gwen was shell-shocked. In spite of her initial suspicions, she never expected this. She rolled her gaze upward to keep the tears from falling. If she started now she'd never stop. "How did this happen? How did I get cancer?"

"I concurred there was a lump in your right breast. I never said you had cancer."

"What are the chances that it's not?"

"I can't give you a definitive diagnosis until I run some tests."

"What kind of tests?"

"A mammogram and ultrasound, for starters," the doctor told her with an expression she interpreted as one he used for delivering bad news. If there had been the slightest glimmer of his usual congeniality, she would have felt better. There wasn't and she didn't.

"Aren't x-rays harmful to the baby?" She had more than herself to think about. Protecting Joel's child seemed of greater importance. In fact, it was her only concern at the moment.

"The technician will take every precaution to see that the baby is protected." He paused, as if deliberating over what he was about to say next. "You know, Gwen, if this does turn out to be malignant, you're going to be faced with some difficult decisions."

"What decisions? We cut it out or off, if necessary, and move on. If you think I'm going to get hysterical about losing a breast when my life is on the line, you don't know me very well, Aaron."

"We'll discuss your treatment options when we have a better understanding of what we're dealing with. I want these tests done today."

Her mind reeled, she barely heard the doctor's words, and she had to force herself to stay focused on what he was saying.

"Are you going to be okay to drive? Is there someone my nurse can call to pick you up?"

Gwen shook her head slowly. "There's no one." The reality of that statement smacked her with its absoluteness. There really wasn't anyone she could call. She was on good terms with the members of her staff but this was far too personal to involve any of them. She refused to burden Samantha with this unless it was necessary. And Joel? There was no way she could tell him. Like most of her adult life, she'd have to go it alone.

"I thought you said you and the baby's father were working things out, that you were planning on getting married."

"We just made it official at Christmas." She straightened the sapphire marquis on her finger. Joel had selected this ring for all the right reasons, telling her the color and clarity of the stone reminded him of her eyes when they made love. He'd let his feelings instead of traditions dictate his decision. Now dark and dim, the blue stone barely flickered under the harsh florescent lighting, as if it had lost its fiery brilliance. She wondered if that was how her eyes appeared now. She was certain they did. It seemed to be an omen. "This pretty much puts a kibosh on any future we might have had. Since we're not married yet, there's no reason for him to go through this with me."

"The way I see it, if he can't support you through something like this, he isn't worth marrying. In sickness and in health, remember?"

All her emotions rallied to Joel's defense. "I

didn't say he wouldn't see me through this. I know he would because he's that kind of man."

"He sounds like a good man to me."

"He's the best."

Aaron Jansen handed her the test orders and patted her hand as she took them. Then he shook his finger at her and peered at her over the rim of his glasses. "Then I wouldn't sell him short if I were you."

"It's more complicated than that, I'm afraid."

"Life always is," the doctor said on a serious note as he left the room.

"Ain't it the truth," Gwen muttered as she prepared herself for the challenging days ahead.

****

Once she'd changed, the receptionist ushered Gwen into an ante room. "Have a seat. Someone will be in shortly to take you for your mammogram and ultrasound."

Gwen hugged the blue-print, cotton dressing gown around her baby bump and took a seat on a hard, orange plastic chair.

She hated waiting and glanced around the small room for something, anything, to distract her from the frantic thoughts running through her head. There was nothing but posters and pamphlets touting the importance of regular breast checkups and self-examination littering the tables and covering the walls. They only reminded her that doing everything right didn't guarantee healthy breasts for life. She was a perfect example of that. The only thing it did was detect a problem sooner and hopefully in time.

Joel had said himself that Beth hadn't taken her lump seriously, that she ignored it and didn't seek treatment until it was too late. Gwen didn't understand how any woman could do that. It was all she could think of from the moment the doctor told her.

A single tear slipped down her cheek, unbidden and unwelcome. She swiped it away and cleared her throat. No more tears. She couldn't afford the luxury of feeling sorry for herself. She had to stay strong. She'd deal with this the same way she dealt with everything else—one day at a time.

A young woman who didn't look much older than Samantha poked her head around the corner. "Gwen, we're ready for you."

Gwen stood and squared her shoulders. *Here I go...* Trite but true, this really was the first day of the rest of her life.

****

Her cell phone was beeping when she reached her car. The screen said she had six voicemails and two missed called. Four of the voicemails were from the office and two were from clients. One quick call to Bette took care of all of them, as well as explaining why she wouldn't be coming back to the office for the rest of the day. Both the missed calls were from Joel. She knew he never left messages, but she also knew he expected her to call him back.

She turned off her phone and steered her car toward the outskirts of nowhere. She wanted to run away faster than her thoughts could catch her. Since that wasn't possible, she settled for an hour or maybe two of isolated anonymity. The nature preserve on the south end of the township was as far away from her life as she could get without traveling too far out of her comfort zone.

The woods were bleak and desolate at that time of year and the perfect complement for her current frame of mind. A solitary line of stately pines running along the banks of the lake colored the otherwise dreary winter landscape. When she opened her car door and placed one foot onto the frozen ground, she was promptly slapped in the face with a blast of icy wind. It sucked the breath from her chest and chilled her down to her socks. Gwen gasped in startled surprise and recoiled, slamming the car door against Mother Nature's cruel assault.

She glared at her shivering reflection in the rearview mirror and wondered what she'd hoped to accomplish by turning herself into an ice sculpture. She started the engine and cranked the heater to high in an effort to cease her teeth from chattering.

"Congratulations, Gwen," she grumbled. "You've not only probably got cancer, you've lost your frigging mind on top of everything else."

Sighing, she backed out and headed home. She reached for her phone to reconnect with the outside world and hit the speed dial.

"Gwen! Where have you been?" Joel demanded the second he picked up. God bless caller ID. "I've been trying to reach you for hours." Gwen heard Samantha in the background bombarding him with questions about her mother's whereabouts faster than he could utter them. "Do you have any idea how worried we've been?"

"My phone was turned off."

"Your doctor's appointment was hours ago and your office said you called and told them you weren't coming in for the rest of the day."

Gwen pulled into the first strip mall she spotted—not a difficult task considering how fast they were popping up in the region. "I'm shopping," she said as she parked. "I'll be home soon. Love you. Bye." She didn't give him a chance to respond before slamming her phone shut. She needed more time—just a little more time—to pull herself together.

Chapter Thirty-One

"You've been awfully quiet tonight," Joel told her as they collected the last of the dinner dishes and carried them to the sink. Even before their official engagement, they'd taken to having dinner together as a family as often as their schedules allowed. It gave the girls a chance to spend time together and it gave Gwen the opportunity to see how she'd fit into Joel's life. Some nights they gathered at her house, others they congregated at his place. Tonight they were at Joel's.

If she'd left the decision to Samantha, they'd have moved in permanently months ago. Samantha loved everything about Joel's new house, especially when she discovered it had a basement big enough to pitch in. That and the fact it was only two blocks from Davey's house was more than enough incentive to urge her mother to move immediately. She'd already started decorating her room so it would be ready whenever Gwen gave the word.

"Just tired," she sighed as she cast a glance into the adjoining family room where Em and Sam sat together on the couch watching a movie. Emme adored her big sister-to-be and although she was too young to understand the dynamics of their blending family, she took her cue from Samantha and started calling Gwen "Mom" from almost the beginning.

Her heartstrings tugged at her tear ducts when she looked at those two beautiful girls. Everything inside her was clogged with unshed tears and raw emotions and her chest literally hurt from keeping them in check. The next few days were going to be a real challenge. She kept telling herself she needed to stay strong, for all of them. If she could get through the next couple of days she could get through anything.

"How about a fire and some hot chocolate?"

She smiled and nodded at his cozy suggestion. "Umm, that sounds nice. You start the fire and I'll make the cocoa." Gwen reached for a saucepan from the pot rack hanging over the island counter. There was only one way to make hot chocolate as far as she was concerned. Instant might be okay for a quick cup in the morning, but nothing compared to making it the old fashioned way in a pot on the stove with milk and sugar and unsweetened cocoa.

"I'll do that," he said as he covered her hand and took the pot from her. He placed it on the stovetop and took her into his arms. She snuggled into his embrace and locked her arms around his waist. She felt so safe and protected there, as if nothing could harm her as long as he was there to hold her, and she pressed her cheek against his chest.

He massaged the muscles in her lower back. "Put your feet up and relax."

"You worked today too."

"But I'm not seven months pregnant." He ushered her into the living room and directed her to sit as he crouched by the hearth. Joel had become quite the expert at building the perfect fire and it saddened her to think that by the time the baby was due these cozy fires would be over for the season.

"You're too good to me." She curled into a corner of the butter-soft, camel-colored leather sectional as he tucked a fuzzy, warm afghan under her chin.

He sat down and pulled her feet into his lap. "I enjoy pampering you," he said with a grin as he pulled off her flats and massaged her arches. "It makes me happy. You want me to be happy, don't you?"

"With all my heart," she answered as she turned and stared into the fire to search for answers she couldn't give as readily. The only real conclusion she'd reached that afternoon was not to say anything to Joel or Samantha until she had a diagnosis and course of treatment decided. The coming weekend was just the beginning of her deception, she realized.

The flames danced and flickered, the logs popped and crackled, pushing her into a state of greater restlessness rather than the peace she desperately sought. Every thought revolved around Em, and Samantha, and Joel, and how her illness would affect them. She withdrew into herself and fought against the urge to fall into a sleep that would take her away from the reality of her situation if only briefly.

She inhaled deeply and tossed off the afghan. "I should head home."

"You could stay." He placed a steadying hand on her calf.

Gwen shook her head against the temptation. How easy it would be to give in and curl up next to him in that king-sized four poster bed Joel had insisted they pick out together.

"I can assure you the neighbors don't have their binoculars trained on the house to see if you go home tonight or not."

"That's not the only reason I won't stay, you know that." She swung her feet to the floor and tried to stand. Her body felt like lead and just lifting her arms was an effort. The day had taken its toll and weighed her down. Her limbs failed to cooperate.

"I don't want you driving home like this. Look at you, you're exhausted."

"I'll let Sam drive."

"An inexperienced, newly licensed driver doesn't make me feel all that much better."

"Helloooo!" Samantha called from the other

room. “I can hear you, you know.”

“Sam!” he called. “Will you come in here for a sec?”

Gwen detected a devilish glint behind his glasses. “What are you up to?” He just grinned in response and turned away.

“What’s up?” Samantha leaned her tall, leggy frame against the entry arch.

“You know where babies come from, don’t you, Sam?” He ignored Gwen’s horrified gasp.

“Yeah…” she answered hesitantly, shifting her gaze between her mother and Joel.

“So it’s safe to assume that you already know how your mother got this way, am I right?”

“Yeah…” she drawled.

“So, can you think of one reason why the two of you should have to bundle up, get in a cold car, and drive across town just to sleep in your own beds when there are perfectly good ones upstairs for the whole family?”

“Nope,” Samantha said with a casual shrug. “Not off hand I can’t. Seems like a waste of gas, if you ask me,” she added as she walked away.

He turned to Gwen. “There you have it. Samantha doesn’t care if we spend the night together before we’re married.”

“I’m not prepared to stay the night. I don’t have a nightgown or clothes for tomorrow, or even a change of underwear or toothbrush.”

“Well, actually, you do. Samantha and I took care of all that this afternoon.”

“Okay, you win,” Gwen conceded. “I know when I’m outnumbered and out maneuvered.”

He kissed her near her ear and whispered, “As long as you’re in such an agreeable mood, perhaps now would be a good time for us to discuss making this a permanent arrangement.”

“We’ll see,” she said as his lips claimed hers. He

might not be so eager once she told him about the cancer cloud hanging over her head.

****

Bedtime was another concern Gwen had considered. She'd never been particularly shy or modest around Joel. When it was just the two of them behind closed doors, she often walked around nude. Without pretense they'd settled into such a comfortable familiarity, undressing in front of each other was commonplace and more often than not the prelude to more gratifying activities.

Gwen was overwhelmed by reservations of allowing him to see her naked, let alone make love. If he touched her, caressed her breast, would he detect the lump and begin a line of questions she wasn't ready to answer? She couldn't take that chance.

That night, she undressed in the bathroom and when she exited in her nightgown and his heavy terry bathrobe she hoped it would be enough to cool any thoughts Joel had of making love. She was overcome with equal parts of guilt and sadness when a flicker of disappointment crossed his face upon her modest, almost prudish appearance. Much to his credit, he recovered quickly and smiled as she pulled back the covers and crawled into bed.

"How'd your doctor's appointment go today?" He rolled toward her and splayed his hand over her round tummy. He rubbed back and forth across the bulge with tender, soothing strokes. "Everything okay?"

She was taken aback by his question, innocent though it might be. The man was too perceptive to keep this from him for long. There were decisions she had to make, and soon. She covered his hand, effectively stilling his wandering fingers. "The baby's fine," she answered as she rolled to her side and snuggled into her pillow.

"I love you," he said as he kissed the back of her neck and snuggled more tightly against her.

She stiffened. It would all be so much simpler if he didn't.

Chapter Thirty-Two

As Joel poured himself his first cup of coffee, he heard the muffled twitter of Gwen's cell phone coming from her purse. He knew she was in the shower, and debated about answering it. He made a conscious effort to ignore the insistent sound, having learned a long time ago that a woman's purse was sacred territory and off limits to any member of the male species. The Colonel's warning still echoed in his head: Opening a woman's handbag without permission was like opening Pandora's Box, only more so and with greater repercussions. His father had always been man of cryptic phraseology.

After what seemed like an interminable length of time, the irritating noise finally stopped. He breathed a relieved sigh and congratulated himself for resisting the temptation. When it started up again, all thoughts of propriety flew out the window. He jammed his hand into the front pocket of the soft leather pouch and found the slender phone just as it stopped again. He pulled it out and glanced at the screen: A. Jansen. Aaron Jansen? *Doctor* Aaron Jansen? Why was her obstetrician calling this early on a Saturday morning?

He was probably going to catch hell for this, make that definitely, but his curiosity short-circuited his ordinarily good judgment. He pressed the voicemail option.

"Gwen, its Doctor Jansen. Call me when you get this message. It's about your test results."

****

Joel sat on the bed waiting for her when Gwen

exited the bathroom in a misty swirl of sweet-smelling steam in his bathrobe.

"Shower's all yours," she told him as she reached for a brush from the overnight bag he'd packed. She waited for his usual teasing retort about there not being enough hot water to wash his big toe. What she got was silence—uncomfortable silence.

"Hey," she said as she nudged him. "You fall asleep waiting for me to get out?"

He opened his fist.

"Is that my phone?" she questioned.

He nodded, unable to utter a syllable.

"What are you doing with it? Did I get a call?"

He pursed his lips. Even that gesture was an effort. "It went to voicemail." His voice sounded like a stranger's. "It was Doctor Jansen."

"You listened to my message?" She looked stunned by his blatant invasion of her privacy. He was stunned by his own action, but not enough to apologize.

"Yes, I did," he admitted without a shred of remorse. He rolled her phone over and over in his hand. "Is there something you want to tell me about your appointment yesterday?" His chest was heavy with dread as he corralled his roiling emotions.

"There's nothing I *want* to tell you, Joel, but I will because I can't keep this from you." She sat beside him and pressed her head against his shoulder. "I found a lump," she whispered.

He closed his eyes against those familiar words as fear turned everything inside him cold. Much to his surprise he managed to ask, "Where?" May God forgive him as he prayed for the lump to be anywhere else.

"I didn't want to say anything until I got the test results."

Her lack of a precise answer was all he needed. Deep, deep inside of him there radiated a frightening ache so raw and intense, it stole his breath away.

He held out her phone, his response exploded in a coarse, ragged breath. “Call him. Now.”

She didn’t argue. She took the cell and made the call.

Joel hung on her every word, searching for verbal clues and facial cues. He saw nothing in her expression to indicate what the doctor was telling her. She was the picture of strength and serenity in the face of adversity.

It was then he realized the reason for her distant demeanor of the previous evening, her hesitance to let him touch her when they retired. What had seemed so innocent, so ordinary, was now her means of keeping the truth from him. While she was trying to protect him, he was invading her privacy in an effort to discover the reason for her physical and emotional withdrawal. Beth had done the same thing. It made him wonder what was it about him that made the women in his life want to safeguard him from these harsh realities of life.

Gwen didn’t miss the anguish that settled over his features, drawing them into a mask of sorrow she’d seen there on numerous occasions when he spoke of his late wife. Just when she thought she’d carved her own place in his heart, she was forcing him relive his nightmare with Beth.

The doctor’s voice cut into her reverie. “What? Yes, of course, doctor. I understand. I’ll see you then. Goodbye.”

“Well? What did he say?”

She stated it as simply and directly as the doctor had. “The mammogram and ultrasound were inconclusive so he’s scheduled a surgical biopsy for Monday morning...”

The way she paused, he sensed there was more to it than just a simple biopsy. But instead of continuing, she went about gathering her clothes and headed for the dressing room.

He followed her. The scent of her freshly showered skin left a trail of pleasant memories in her wake. He wanted to capture them and keep them with him forever.

She was trying to run from him, and he couldn't let her do that. No matter how difficult this was for him, he kept reminding himself it was far worse for her. "What else did the doctor say?" He sounded just as anxious as he felt.

"What?" she said as she turned her back to him and disrobed.

It pained him to watch her hide her body from him. He wondered what she'd do if the scars of a mastectomy marred her body. He pressed a desperate kiss to the back of her neck and pulled her into his arms to let her know that nothing would ever change the way he felt about her.

"Joel, I'm trying to get dressed." She attempted to wriggle from his grasp as she reached for her bra, but he held her tightly against him, burying his lips in her softly scented hair as he ever so gently cupped her breasts. She tensed and worked harder to break from his exuberant embrace.

"Please, I need to hold you," he pleaded with a voice that cracked and broke with every word.

Overwhelmed by his behavior, Gwen didn't know how to react. He held her in an embrace that was more forceful than anything she'd ever experienced in his arms. Then she heard his quiet sobs, felt his body tremble, and it broke her heart. Her tears were for him.

She turned in his arms and cried. "I'm so sorry."

"We'll get through this, honey."

Gwen wriggled out of his embrace as she tugged off her ring and dropped it into his palm. "I can't ask you to do that. No man should be expected to go through something like this twice in a lifetime."

"No woman should have to go through this at all, let alone without the support of her family."

"Then I guess it's lucky for you we're not an official family yet."

"I don't need a minister or a judge to make us a family, Gwen. As far as I'm concerned we've been one for months. Commitment and love is what creates that bond, not permission from the state. I'm committed to seeing you through this because I love you." He held up the ring. "Don't ever think that giving this back changes anything."

"But what if I die from this?"

"What if you don't?" he countered. "Are we supposed to put our lives on hold because of this? If there's one thing I learned from Beth's illness is life doesn't come with guarantees. We take the time we're given and be grateful for every minute of it."

"I realize that, but this is—" Any further argument was stifled by two large, insistent fingers pressed against her lips.

"Before you finish, let me ask you this... Would you still want to marry me if you knew I'd drop dead from a heart attack next month?"

"Of course I would," she answered without hesitation. "I'd want to spend every minute..." She faltered. "...with... you," she finished as she locked gazes with him.

A wealth of understanding passed between them.

"Then what makes you think I'd react any differently?" He slipped the ring onto her finger where it belonged. "My love for you has no boundaries or conditions." He pressed his forehead to hers and locked his arms around her. "Married or not, sweetheart, I'm committed to you for a lifetime—for however long that might be. So you'd better get used to it."

She gazed at him with love and wonder

glistening in her eyes. “I finally know what to name this child if it’s a girl.”

“What’s that?”

“Faith.”

Epilogue

The town's annual Moving Toward a Cure day dawned sunny and mild. It was the kind of perfect day runners and walkers alike hoped for but rarely experienced. The vivid blue sky had just enough of a cloud cover and there was a gentle breeze to cool the participants and keep them comfortable.

With Emme at his side, Joel maneuvered the stroller to a place near the finish line before the first runners came into view. He glanced at the sleeping infant and smiled. Faith was the spitting image of her mother. Her wispy blonde hair fluttered across her head and when she opened her eyes and looked at him, he saw the same deep, startling blue as Gwen's. She was chubby, rosy-cheeked, bright-eyed and perfect in every way, showing no adverse effects of her six week early birth. Joel had considered her premature arrival a blessing in disguise since it had allowed Gwen to start her chemo treatments that much sooner.

Nick and Maggie soon joined him curbside. Their newest addition—another girl named Savannah born two months to the day after Faith—lay nestled against her father's chest in a red quilted baby sling. Tally and Kait sat side-by-side in a double-wide stroller with a front end shaped like the nose of a race car. Joel grinned every time he saw the custom-made conveyance. Nick was nothing if not predictable.

Maggie placed a gentle hand on his forearm. "Are you ready for this?"

"As ready as I'll ever be."

The spectators broke into a frenzied round of encouragement as the lead runners rounded the corner. The sudden burst of noise startled both babies and soon they wailed in discontented, two-part harmony. As Nick comforted Savannah, Joel lifted Faith into his arms and snuggled the infant against his chest until her crying switched to coos and gurgles as she lifted her head and looked around.

Joel scanned the cluster of runners coming into view. Although he knew she wouldn't be there, he searched for her nevertheless. He did, however, discover Samantha among the early finishers flanked by Davey and Danny Chapparelle which prompted Joel to add his husky baritone to the supporting throngs. Faith never flinched at the sound of her father's voice as he turned her in his arms. "Look, Faith, here comes your big sister."

Then the most amazing thing happened. As each and every runner approached the finish line, they stopped before crossing it and started forming a single line on both sides of the street. As more arrived, they did the same until they stood two and three deep in places.

Murmured speculations rippled through the crowd at the same instant Joel realized what was happening. The community was showing their undivided support for one special runner in the event. His vision blurred and he quickly removed his glasses and wiped the tears away. After all, how often is a man given the opportunity to witness a second miracle in his life?

More and more runners filled the street until there was only a single, narrow lane leading straight to the pink tape stretched across the finish line.

Randy Meyer, in all his official capacity, cleared a path for Joel and his daughters to move into position on the other side of the tape to officially greet and congratulate the winner. Joel's heart swelled with pride as the last, lonely runner came into view. He locked his gaze on his beautiful wife struggling to finish.

With her head down, her fists pumped to hold her unsteady pace. Her stride was short and stilted and her gait was faulty and awkward, but her determination never wavered. The bright scarf wrapped around her hairless head was damp with sweat and her breathing was labored, but when she heard the roar of the crowd, she found the strength to square her shoulders and face the end of a long personal struggle. Everything she'd ever hoped for, battled so hard to live for, waited for her there—her husband and her children. Her faith had been restored tenfold.

Beneath a snapping banner announcing the *Gwen Hubbard Living Memorial Moving Toward a Cure Benefit*, Gwen stumbled across the finish line and into her husband's waiting arms.

A word about the author...

Michelle was a 2006 finalist in RWA's Golden Heart contest with her contemporary romance, **Damn the Man.** It was published a year later with The Wild Rose Press and received 5 Angels and a Recommended Read from Fallen Angels Reviews.

She lives in Northwest Indiana with her husband, Marv.

You can reach her at michellewitvliet@sbcglobal.net

www.ingramcontent.com/pod-product-compliance
Lightning Source LLC
Chambersburg PA
CBHW070843250626
47159CB00003B/914